THE

SMALL

THINGS

THAT END

THE WORLD

THE

SMALL

THINGS

THAT END

THE WORLD

JEANETTE LYNES

Coteau Books

Edited by Janice Zawerbny
Book designed by Tania Craan
Typeset by Susan Buck
Printed and bound in Canada

Library and Archives Canada Cataloguing in Publication

Lynes, Jeanette, author
    The small things that end the world / Jeanette Lynes.

Issued in print and electronic formats.
ISBN 978-1-55050-933-5 (softcover). – ISBN 978-1-55050-934-2 (PDF)
ISBN 978-1-55050-935-9 (HTML). – ISBN 978-1-55050-936-6 (Kindle)

    I. Title.

PS8573.Y6S63 2018   C813'.54   C2017-907479-2
                                              C2017-907480-6

2517 Victoria Avenue
Regina, Saskatchewan
Canada S4P 0T2
www.coteaubooks.com

Available in Canada from:
Publishers Group Canada
2440 Viking Way
Richmond, British Columbia
Canada V6V 1N2

10 9 8 7 6 5 4 3 2 1

Coteau Books gratefully acknowledges the financial support of its publishing program by: the Saskatchewan Arts Board, The Canada Council for the Arts, the Government of Saskatchewan through Creative Saskatchewan, the City of Regina. We further acknowledge the [financial] support of the Government of Canada. Nous reconnaissons l'appui [financier] du gouvernement du Canada.

For my students

"Explorer, you tell yourself this is not what you came for."

– Gwendolyn MacEwen

LITANY

The small things that end the world: a windblown fuzz fleck snags a song spinning on vinyl; a goldfish gives up the ghost; an airborne mumps virus that might land *here*, lands *there*; a silver coin, tossed with a wink; a button; a single cry croaked from a homely baby's throat – *Mama!*

Why, oh *why* didn't I have a fresh white blouse? For some reason, I imagined a babysitter would wear a white blouse. But when the call came, I only had time to rake a brush through my hair, jam in a poodle barrette, and change into my least-dirty turtleneck and slacks. I pinched my soft inner arm into a rose, into *real*, that it really was *my* turn at last.

I wouldn't have heard the phone *at all* if the mote, the tiny fuzz ball from a pilled sweater, or seed-pod fluff or something, hadn't sailed in through the window I'd cracked open ever so slightly to ease my bedroom's stuffiness. It drifted, as if choosing a landing spot, then landed dab-smack on my new spinning vinyl record. Snagged in the stylus. The Chordettes' "Mr. Sandman" furred and slurred. The dream those divine singers asked Mr. Sandman to bring them ground down to *Bang me a drum*.

To pluck the fluff away I'd lifted the stylus, and in that songless second the telephone clanged in the kitchen. I hot-footed it there. If my mother and I lived in a house instead of a flat, I wouldn't have made it to the phone on time. But I only had to dash a short stretch to answer the phone. A satin voice summoned Sadie Wilder.

1

"That's she. I mean, me," I burbled.

The caller was Shirley Bannister. *The* Shirley Bannister. I already knew all about her, from my friend Wanda Keeler, the Bannister's official babysitter. Oh, I'd heard about Shirley, pretty wife, baker of pineapple upside-down cakes, her dashing husband, Forest, who fetched Wanda and drove her home in his Austin-Healey and tossed an extra coin her way at the end of each night – raising her babysitting fortune to $4.00 – and winked, "Later Gator." Wanda never once fumbled the coin. She rode the gravy train. To me it seemed brash for a married man to wink at her like that, and him so much older, but she must have found it harmless enough, and she got paid. How Wanda loved to lavish the litany of dreamy items she bought with her babysitting fortune before my eyes, sashaying in her poodle skirt, darling sweater sets, snazzy saddle shoes. Wanda called 1954 a *ring-a-ding year to be a girl, the living end!* Easy for *her* to say, I thought, with her steady job, her pretty things. Maybe she meant Marilyn Bell, the swim champion. No, she meant herself. I'd known Wanda long enough to bet on it.

Drop the quarter, Wanda, just once. When Forest flicks the coin in your direction, fumble it into a dark, unreachable spot in that flying chariot. It was fall, after all, perfect season for a fallen leaf, a blundered coin. Let it be palmed, for once, by another girl – *me*, a dowdier life form.

My mother had promised I could babysit when I turned fourteen. I turned fourteen, slipped my hand-printed flyers – *Reliable Girl for Hire: Available to Babysit* – under windshield wipers in parking lots, pin-stabbed them to grocery store bulletin boards. Seemed you had to know the right people. Wanda Keeler's mother played bridge with Shirley Bannister's set. My mother pinked seams at Don Vale Textiles. She had no time for games.

2

Yet now Shirley Bannister's voice silked through the receiver quaking in my hand. She was awful sorry for the short notice. She'd gotten my number from Mrs. Keeler. Wanda had caught the mumps and couldn't babysit for them; they were in a pickle. They had the De Havilland dinner and dance. If I could help out they'd make it worth my while: $4.50.

I *had* noted Wanda's empty seat at school earlier that day. Now I pictured her swollen face, like a stricken chipmunk sickened by bad acorns. No gravy train for *her* tonight.

Heyzoose Marimba! I reasoned if I really shone I could squeeze Wanda Keeler out of a job and it would be *me* raking in almost $15.00 a month, *me* cruising in an Austin-Healey. And that didn't include Forest's tossed coins. *Duck soup.* No more second-hand peeks into Wanda's big fat gazing ball. She'd lorded her babysitting wealth over me long enough. Whoever commanded the Universe Express was letting *me* ride, for once – was giving *me* a crack at the good life. Too bad my friend had to fall ill for this to happen, but the world was chipmunk-eat-chipmunk, a sad fact.

To gallivant into my future, I only had to open the window and allow it in, and it had taken the shape of a tiny fuzz ball.

I told Mrs. Bannister I'd be punch-pleased to help out.

Static fizzed the line. Her silk voice returned. "You've never babysat before, have you Sadie?"

Wanda's mother might have left out that detail. "Uh-uh."

A worried sigh buffeted my ear. Rain ponged the kitchen window as wind backhanded a branch against the pane, making me strain to hear Mrs. Bannister. Normally, she was saying, she didn't hire inexperienced babysitters, but given how last-minute this whole thing was, how important it was for her husband – who was lined up for a promotion – to attend the De Havilland dinner and dance, how based on Mrs. Keeler's report of me as a "good, well-behaved girl, if a touch shabby in grooming and appearance," they'd take a gamble on me, green as I was. Mrs. Keeler had added I was of "Jewish persuasion," but Mrs. Bannister and her husband held no prejudice, she said, and it would be good for their children to meet a person "of my persuasion."

Shabby? That was the moment I wished for a white blouse, proof I *wasn't* shabby. What Mrs. Bannister said next sounded so queer I bit my lip to stamp my laughter: I hadn't been sharing Coca-Cola with Wanda Keeler, had I, or getting in her germ zone, like, heavens, kissing her, had I? Mrs. Bannister knew girls sometimes played pretend games. She needed a mumps epidemic in her house like a rip in her nylon stocking.

I assured her no Colas had been shared, no kisses. I felt fit as a fiddle. Shirley said her husband would fetch me at five-thirty.

Her pencil scritched down my address.

Her silk-voice declared me an absolute lifesaver.

I'd barely hung up the receiver, when my mother phoned on her break at Don Vale Textiles. She'd be working late. Again. Big contract. She said she'd much rather be home. Malton Weather Station had issued a wind and rain warning. *Oy vey.* My father's old phrase brought him back more vividly than the photograph in our foyer. I'd memorized what my mother had penned on its reverse side. *Family Picnic, Kew. Robert. Baby Sadie. Me. We ignored the 'Gentiles Only' sign. We love the beach.*

I'd just gotten out the words, "I'm sorry you have to work late, Ma," before she had to get back to pinking.

I scrawled her a note: *Gone babysitting!*

How surprised she'd be!

Then I bopped into my bedroom to throw myself together as best I could. On my small desk, my homework was piled high; I'd tackle it in the morning.

Tonight, *life* beckoned. Universe, you've tapped me at last. Thank you.

While I swatted at my hair – which was unrulier in damp weather – I tried to recall what Wanda Keeler had told me about the Bannister kids. Oddly, she rarely mentioned them. When I'd asked, clouds scudded across her pink face; she'd have pie in the sky if not for those *little firebrands*. The giant baby, Faith, was *a stink missile sent straight from Russia*, who could only be left to seethe and howl in her crib until she wore herself out. Whiny Bobby, a first grader, who jabbed his toy pistol into Wanda's thigh, *bang-bang*, scaring her half-dead. And always wanting more.

Of small boys, I knew nothing. "More what?"

My friend's eyes rolled back like numbers on an old-fashioned cash register. "More treats. More Mr. Potato Head games. More Dennis the Menace. More play dough. More everything." The boy, at least, could be bribed with cookies to climb into his little bed. "Those kids are spoiled silly and I can't tell you how often I'd like to smack both their precious bottoms crimson, Sadie. Babysitting for the Bannisters would be the cream gig if not for that pair of flies in the syrup. But the job pays a fortune, which makes it worth those two annoyances."

Wanda had been swishing about in her new poodle skirt the day of her 'flies in the syrup' speech. I'd begun to worry that I might be a bit *stunned*; week after week, I'd let my friend *torture* me with her new threads after school at her house. The way she lorded her litany of profit over me razzed my berries, turning me the brightest emerald shade of envy. But always I trundled back for more, I did, just to hear those swishing skirts, and to finger those soft knits. She made me *drunk* with her peep shows. Drunk on the Bannisters' *whole beautiful life*. Such a stylish, gallivanting couple, out dancing or fine dining with their boating friends at least one night a week, even now, with the school year under way. My mother and I didn't know anyone like them. Wanda Keeler told me about their house – 67 Humber Green Drive – "It's utterly grand. The prettiest home on the block. Right out of some glossy magazine." There was pineapple upside-down cake in the sparkling seafoam green kitchen and Wanda could stuff away as much as she wanted. And, of all things, they had a *dumb waiter!* I didn't tell Wanda she shouldn't talk so harsh about the servant. I chomped back my opinion, since I was a guest in her house, a lowly spectator, I was, of her peep shows.

Lately I'd been letting Wanda Keeler win the spelling bee at school because if she lost – and Wanda could *not* lose with grace – she didn't invite me over to her house. Earlier that week she'd blundered. *Moat.* As in: *ditch filled with water around a castle, village, or fort.* My friend thought *mote*, as in tiny speck, even though the word had been explained pretty clearly to *my* ears. I'd had to out-blunder her blunder, either that or trot home alone. Even the nights my mother returned from work at a decent hour, she made for glum company. And school was all dire film reels – *Beware of Communists! Drugs make you a raving maniac. One day the sun will burn out.*

I checked my watch. The Austin-Healey was due any minute. I stashed extra feminine protection in my purse, and glanced out the kitchen window. The trees doled their leaves, punted about by gusts, down to the soaked earth, in the steady, determined rain. Just another October night for *some* people, but not me!

"Later Gator!" I trilled into our empty flat. I tented my head with my pea coat, my makeshift umbrella. Then I sprinted towards the idling Austin-Healey, a sleek vector purring and shimmering in an aura of raindrops.

My friend was right. Forest Bannister was one cool daddy in his tweed overcoat and driving gloves. He had an English accent. Whenever Wanda had spoken of Forest, her mouth gushed into Niagara Falls. "What a dreamboat! He could be Montgomery Clift's twin." My friend just *vaporized* when he charioted her around; now it was *me* vaporizing. I felt shabbier than ever. My damp, worn pea coat across my knees in the Austin-Healey, its interior all soft rawhide and silver gizmos and resolute dials.

Forest thwacked his chariot into gear like he expected nothing less from it than to rocket us straight to Jupiter. He drove fast and didn't seem worried about speeding tickets. Given the fortune the Bannisters paid their babysitter, and given they had a servant – a dumb waiter – I guessed he could afford any fine the cops threw at him.

Beneath the sky's grey soup, the Healey gobbled Lawrence Avenue. *Sh-boom, sh-boom*, the wipers sang, as my stomach flopped like it did when riding the rollercoaster at the Exhibition. Wanda and I had, once. The Keelers' Nash Rambler was a wheelbarrow compared to this magic-on-wheels.

Against the darkening bruise of sky, Forest Bannister's headlights were bright, burrowing concepts. Flying along in high style like that flooded me with possibility. That's where I lived now: in possibility. Like the poem by Emily Dickinson we read in literature class. Poor Emily, never rode in an Austin-Healey.

Veils of rain whipped the beautiful car. I stroked the leather seat delicately as if it were some thoroughbred racehorse. I half-expected the seat to nicker back at me. It was warm inside the chariot. I'd had no time to apply *Stoppette* under my arms. I worried about my smell. I was on the ride of my life with the coolest daddy. I only hoped his aftershave, a walnut tang, masked my damp parts.

Forest didn't speak for a long time. He'd been riveted to navigating the wet streets. "So, you're the Wilder girl," he said at last, gearing down. We slowed enough that I could see shops aglow with their crates of apples, peaches and pears out front, tarps thrown over them, buckling and slapped by fruit-hating weather. At first, I thought Forest Bannister meant wilder than Wanda Keeler. That would be a cinch. She was a Sunday school teacher. A Goody-Two-Shoes. The speed at which we travelled really strung me, it did. He must have meant my name. Wilder. I fought to ignore the monthly jabs in my pelvis and sucked in my stomach to look shapelier in my turtleneck.

"You're prettier than the Keeler girl," Forest added, "Matter of fact you're the prettiest babysitter we've ever had."

I had to reel myself back into orbit. *Sadie, return to Planet Babysitter this minute. This is employment.* Forest then remarked what a lifesaver I was. First, I thought candy, lifesavers. After a few more wiper *sh-booms*, I twigged.

"No sweat, Mr. Bannister. I hardly do anything at night except maybe go to Wanda Keeler's house or watch *Howdy Doody*."

Dense Bunny, I scolded myself silently, *for reminding them of their real babysitter. Keep Wanda's ghost out of this Healey!*

Forest barrelled onwards, leaving me in the conversational dust. "You'll love the house," he said, like he was a real-estate agent and I was a home-hunter instead of a pinch-hitter sitter. Seemed he liked pretend games. His voice surged forth: how he and his wife came from England, both only children, took the trans-Atlantic plunge, how the Humber flowed right behind their house, *prime riverfront property*.

"You tell me, Wilder girl, how many people can claim to live right on the banks of a river?"

"Not very many, Sir?"

Forest Bannister amped up his talk many revolutions per second: how they'd modernized the house for full pleasure and convenience, including a dumbwaiter! Then he dropped some builders' lingo on me about the house, called it balloon-framed. "We had the original downstairs redone," he vaunted. "Knocked out the walls – gutted it like a giant pickerel, opened it right up." Then he described the "stately maple" in the back yard, tree-house potential up the *wa-zoo* once Bobby and Faith were old enough to climb; they'd explore the Humber's shore for arrowheads, too, some history for the kids.

Silently I wondered if history was that easy. But he seemed like the kind of man who could make a concept hold water just by talking about it. Forest then extolled the virtues of their neighbourhood: swell for raising a family, everything within reach. Two golf and country clubs, Lambton and Weston. Heck, the riverbank practically spewed golf courses. Humber Heights School was nearby. The racetrack, fairgrounds, a stone's toss away.

"We've got it all here – made in the shade," he trumpeted, releasing some switch that greened a dial as he turned off Lawrence onto a side street. A good life, theirs, on the riverbank, though they could do without the Hospital for Consumptives so nearby. But every silver lining had its cloud, didn't it?

I couldn't imagine clouds right now, even though the sky was clotted with them. I was inside the perfect dream. I might dress shabby but I was enthusiastic, reliable. All I had to do was be the perfect babysitter, the *absolute lifesaver* Shirley Bannister said I was, and I wouldn't be shabby much longer. Her husband had a soft spot for me already, I knew from his pretty remark. I just needed to impress his wife.

Forest went on about his Healey, which he'd had shipped

special from England.

"How do you fit them all in here? The family, I mean, Mr. Bannister?"

He spanked the car along the liquid street, maneuvering easily around a fallen branch. The headlights had their own piercing intellect. Maybe English light was smarter.

Forest told me Shirley used the Saratoga for running the kids around, groceries, her Wednesday girls' bridge club, though he had to admit she heartily enjoyed a spin in his Healey. The Saratoga was a junk heap, he added, but once his promotion at De Havilland came through, they'd upgrade.

His spin remark heated my cheeks. He turned onto Riverstone Road. Everything around there had river names. A few short jabs along yet another street. "Almost home," Mr. Bannister pivoted his face for an instant to wink at me.

After several more spurts of speed along another street, we shot across a swing bridge. A final thrust up a driveway on an incline, then he braked behind a blue Chrysler Saratoga in the driveway of 67 Humber Green Drive. I had arrived at the fabled world of Wanda Keeler's babysitting spoils, all of which, if I did a topnotch job, could be mine.

Duck soup.

The house rose, exalted, before me. It was white, with green shutters above the sloping lawn. Lights blazed within. Rain and a dim milky sky only threw the home's *hominess* into greater relief. A stately maple towered darkly behind it, its branches brushing the roof. Wanda had told me about the short path behind the house that led to the river's reedy banks. I wouldn't be going back there tonight, and I was glad of that, not being a water person. Last summer, with the Keelers at Sauble Beach, I'd hunkered under the umbrella while Wanda, who'd had diving lessons, cavorted like a dolphin in the blue sparkle.

I trailed Forest up the stone steps to the front door's wreath, graced with orange berries and a merry yellow bow. Shirley Bannister flung open the wreathed portal and stood, backlit, classy, in a maroon lace cocktail dress. With a trim waist and billowing skirt, she looked so much like Grace Kelly I couldn't help but gawk.

Wanda's stories sadly missed the mark with the wife. My friend hadn't done this feminine vision justice in any way, shape, or form.

As the rain pelted down, Mrs. Bannister waved us inside with quick little 'hurry, hurry' gestures. I planted my feet at last within the open-concept main floor, hearing strains of soft music mingled with dog-barks. There must have been an entry hall once but clearly it, too, had been gutted like a pickerel.

Taking my pea coat, Mrs. Bannister, smiling brightly, told me not to fret about my sneakers. The carpet was slated for cleaning in a few days. She scanned my rumpled slacks and turtleneck; I worried that her eyes, for the briefest instant, grew critical, but her manners were so flawless I decided I dreamt trouble where there wasn't any; a hair later she beamed at me again. I wondered where the dumb waiter was, why hadn't he answered the door? Maybe he had the night off? I decided the firebrands must already be asleep, though it was only a little after six o'clock. *Huzzah*, piece of cake, easiest money in the world.

A smallish tousled dog the shade of caramel candies whirled in circles near Mrs. Bannister's feet. "Okay, Shuster, yes, yes, okay, boy," she cajoled the circles into half-circles, as the barking waned and the dog, wagging, sniffed my damp sneakers. I could hear the music better now. Perry Como. I took in the place gradually, spying, on a small table, a hand-painted note folded like a greeting card. *Welcome Babysitter Sadie! October*

15, 1954. A few of the same decorative sprigs of berries wreathing the front door were taped to the note's corners. I wondered if Wanda Keeler had received a similar note. If she had, she hadn't mentioned it. Maybe it was something special, an omen of my rising star. I remarked on the note to the Grace Kelly ringer.

"We like to make our babysitters feel welcome," she smiled. "Especially those of other – persuasions."

Angel that she was, I wished she'd drop the 'persuasion' stuff. My mother and I hadn't observed any official religion since my father's illness took him from us when I was six. It was like we lost faith. We didn't keep a kosher kitchen. I wasn't even sure how I felt about God.

Mr. Bannister declared himself bound for the wet bar downstairs. On his master's heels the dog skirred along. How different, husband and wife. Forest's commando driving style keyed me up. Shirley was all warmth and cream. I could have listened to her lollipop voice all night.

I'd often wondered if Wanda Keeler had plumped up her stories of 67 Humber Green Drive to fuel my envy. But other than downplaying the wife's splendour, my friend's account of the swish house where she babysat was spot-on. It was queer to be outside looking in for so long, and then, suddenly, *inside*. My sneakers reveled in the plush carpet. I noticed the house's "clean lines." *Chatelaine* always praised "clean lines." The open concept flowed. Two steps cascaded down into the sunken living room, which had a sexpot feel, with its black pile carpet, gold sunburst wall clock, red Naugahyde sectional sofa, and sleek black lamps with ceramic cougars crouched at their bases. A regular passion pit. The lower, open area contained several vertical beams fuzzed with broadloom; they extended to the ceiling like arms bearing an offering. Supports, I guessed. The section of wall above the hi-fi console was papered in black and gold shapes like from a geometry kit. Only one thing didn't jive with the open concept: a curtained cart on wheels, for serving drinks, maybe?

"You have a truly beautiful house, Mrs. Bannister."

Shirley smiled sweetly. She spied me looking at the book on the coffee table. Dr. Spock's *Baby and Child Care*. "Oh, that's our bible," declared the pretty mother. "Everything you need to know is in those pages." From a smart case tucked in a pocket in her lace dress, she retrieved a lighter and sparked a cigarette. She wanted to show me the kitchen; after that we'd meet the children.

So, they weren't asleep. The silver lining clouded. Into the kitchen, I followed Mrs. Bannister. She showed me the dumb-waiter, which wasn't a bald man bearing a tray, but a little box that lifted and lowered through the house for convenience, a flying cabinet of sorts. I marvelled at the seafoam green appliances, which were every bit as brilliant as Wanda Keeler had painted them with her words. Everything gleamed.

"Sadie?" Shirley Bannister tweaked my elbow in the gentlest way. "Are you all right? Are you with me?" Smoke garlanded her face.

"Sorry. Sure. I am."

This vision in a lace cocktail dress flashed me a quizzical glance. Then, "Oh, *fiddlesticks!*"

I worried I'd done something wrong already. She hurried over to the Formica table and seized a goldfish bowl, which had a little castle in it, and water, slightly cloudy with a few strings of fish turd. Everything but fish. Out she plucked the castle, before draining the water down the sink, her high heels clacking with purpose across the tiled floor. Then she stowed the empty bowl in a high cupboard.

"Davy Crockett is dead," she said, her voice riddled with distress.

I could only look at her, blankly.

"Bobby's goldfish died this afternoon," she explained. "If that boy spots the empty bowl he'll get all tied in knots again. I was here, in the kitchen, baking squares. I looked over at the fish and" – her lovely claret lip trembled – "I swear, Sadie, it raised its dorsal fin in the way of a salute, rolled once, gopped, and floated to the surface. I'd never witnessed any living creature die before, Sadie." Her lip quivered harder.

I imagined the fish floating inert as a wedge of mandarin orange. "I'm sorry, Mrs. Bannister."

She sniffed. "Bobby is inconsolable. I didn't want to go into it over the phone earlier, Sadie, but it may take a bit of extra work to cheer him. He'll be confused that his regular babysitter, Wanda, isn't here. But don't worry, we'll make it worth your while."

I told Shirley Bannister I knew a few magic tricks, and tap-danced, so that by the night's end Bobby would feel so chipper he wouldn't remember the day's loss. (For crying out loud I couldn't dance a single tap, but in that magic house with its flying cabinet, what skill couldn't be conjured?)

Mrs. Bannister resumed her kitchen tour – such divine seafoam appliances, I thought – until, suddenly, *Bang! Bang!* A little boy wearing a Davy Crockett raccoon hat burst into the kitchen, shooting toy pistols into the air, *Bang! Bang!* He scared the jeepers out of me. Seeing me, he stopped, breathless, and stared all doleful. He had to be the older firebrand.

"Bobby, stop shooting guns and say hello to Sadie Wilder, the babysitter," Shirley Bannister ordered her son.

The boy lowered his pistols. "Hell-woe, Sadie Wilder the maybe-sitter. Mommy, can I watch telly-wish-on?"

(Too cute. I figured the little monkey could talk normal if he felt like it. He was trying to charm his mother and I could see by her face, it was working.)

"Yes, for a while." Shirley turned to me. "Maybe some telly will take his mind off Davy Crockett. The poor kid's so down about his goldfish."

He didn't look down to me, but what did I know about kids?

Bobby galloped – guns, holsters, and all – out of the room just as his cool daddy swanked in with two drinks. "Rye and water, just how you like it, Shirl – straight from the wet bar." Forest passed one glass to his wife, advising she "chug a lug," because time ticked onward. Shirley took the glass in her exquisite fingers, her nails painted a lovely coral to offset her maroon lace cocktail dress. Her hair was stacked and looped, and though she lamented she'd had no time to Toni-wave it, she looked as polished as a beauty queen.

From the sunken living room, the television clamoured, a laugh track. Wanda Keeler once told me those weren't real people laughing, only machines. I hadn't wanted to believe her, that seemed like a nonsense burger to me, but now I saw what she meant. The screeches of mirth were too extreme and frequent to be normal humans. They sounded like maniacs.

We convened in the spacious kitchen with its gleaming floor tiles. A brief, odd cocktail party except no cocktail for me. The husband and wife didn't seem that concerned about being late for their dinner, but glamorous people like the Bannisters, gallivanters, must know the drill.

Forest chortled. "My wife says Wayne and Shuster are too coarse for a six-year old boy, what do you think, Sadie?"

"I don't know," I answered honestly.

Forest swanned his glass sideways, a startling gesture for such a manly man. "I told her, 'don't be silly, Shirl, the jokes are way over the kid's head'."

His wife grimaced indulgently (still managing to look stunning)

and excused herself to do her "finishing touches." She told me
Forest would pick up where she left off, and light-footed it out
of the kitchen.

Dousing me with directions, about snacks, bed times, diaper
changes, some things his wife already went over, Mr. Bannister
showed me a cookie jar. "Bobby's rations – two before bed."
He found this very droll. I figured I'd better stay serious. He
pointed out the jars of baby food for Faith. Lots of puréed
squash. Then *my* rations, stored in a new Tupperware container, note taped to it, *Babysitter Squares*. A letdown it wasn't
pineapple upside-down cake, but what could I do?

Forest strode around the kitchen distractedly, glancing at his
watch, pointing out this and that. Why I'd need the toaster I
didn't know, just kept nodding *uh-huh*. Rain splatted the window with the cherry-print curtains. Bobby's shrieks of glee
reached us from the living room along with the spasms of
canned laughter, regular as some kooky heartbeat, on *The
Wayne and Shuster Show*. I heard a crazed outburst that
sounded like *"Toga! Toga!"*

Shirley Bannister whisked into the kitchen, a freshly lit cigarette between those divine coral fingernails. Loading down
her other arm was a large being: part-baby, part-toddler. A
jumbo baby.

"Have you ever changed a diaper, Sadie?"

I shook my head. She bid me follow. I trailed in the wake of
her smoke and perfume. The being smelled putrid. I scrunched
my nose, trying not to breathe. If I hoped to be a contender for
Wanda Keeler's job I must remain unflappable. Shirley Bannister breezed ahead of me into the open concept where the machine still meted out roars and guffaws. Bobby was sprawled
out on the floor, until his mother ordered him to turn off the
telly, hurry upstairs, bathe, brush his teeth, and change into his

pajamas. The boy obeyed with a moping posture and stomped up the steps, gun holster flapping desolately against his small thighbones, the tousled dog at his heels.

Mr. Bannister chugged back downstairs, to the wet bar, I guessed.

The sunken living room felt very quiet after the pulses of mirth, only the sound of muffled wind and drumming rain. Shirley Bannister slanted her cigarette in a ceramic ashtray with a goose about to fly. They owned such stylish things. She led me over to the strange cart on wheels with its curtained lower section. For the first time, I noticed its padded surface. Onto it she lowered the huge baby. "And here's our Faith. Fifteen whole months old, our little Plum."

For the first time, I got a good look at the being. Despite the smell, I managed a poker face. She rattled me; I'd no clue what to do with babies, especially giant ones. I bent my mouth into a smile, supposing they felt reassured by such gestures.

The 'Plum' made a face at me, an ugly, scrunched, confused scowl on the brink, I was sure, of erupting into ear-splitting wails. She didn't look like a Faith to me, more like a Gretchen or Hilda or some cranky space alien. Several babies lived in our apartment building, and many were pushed around in prams out at Golden Mile Plaza; *any* of them looked better than this creature with her crib-hair and blotchy complexion. There was something wrong with her one eye. Warped. Off-kilter. The full force of Wanda Keeler's declaration hit me now, along with a new wave of diaper stench, about babysitting being the dream job except for the firebrands.

Shirley Bannister bent, removing equipment from the lower part of the table, its curtain shoved aside. She told me to stand tightly against the table to block the baby from rolling onto the floor. That meant getting closer to that wretched smell. I willed my nose to not wrinkle. Beating her fists into the air and squirming, the baby shifted from side to side on the table and a sound like *ech ech ech* spurted from her mouth. She rocked harder from one side to the other like a flipped-over beetle trying to right itself. She terrified me.

"Hello Little Plum," I ventured.

That did it. Faith exploded into panicked screams and bawled with unbelievable fury, even louder than the earlier television.

Shirley, her hands full of power and cotton and pins, rose and stroked the baby's crimson forehead. "There, *there*, Sweet Pea," the mother crooned. The baby wailed. Over the din, Shirley explained that the baby "made strange," that this was perfectly normal, she'd grow out of it. Geez Louise why couldn't she grow out of it *tonight*?

Her racket finally subsided. Trembling, I wondered if the money really *was* good enough, if my throat *wasn't* a bit swollen or sore. But I felt fine. Aside from monthly cramps. I bucked myself up by picturing the saddle shoes I'd buy. Just a matter of getting through a few hours.

Mrs. Bannister unbuttoned the baby's pink sleeper. Her husband came back upstairs and hallooed over to us. He'd ring the Old Mill restaurant to hold their dinner reservation and his wife called that one crackerjack of an idea.

"I'm sorry I made her cry," I told Shirley Bannister.

"Don't be silly, Sadie, she's just not used to you. Give her a little time."

The face with its askew eye skunked me from the changing table and though the bawling rage had stopped, the *ech ech* whimpers continued, along with the huffs and puffs of wind sucker-punching the house.

"Observe," Shirley Bannister advised. So, there I was, in diaper school. She set the clean, folded diaper, cotton wipes, pins and baby powder near the Plum's robust, kicking feet. Then grabbed the baby's ankles and lifted her chubby legs high enough to lay a clean diaper under her bottom. The baby still wore her fouled diaper, which puzzled me but the mother's movements were so flowing and assured, my doubts dwindled. The mother had often performed this trick. The squirming and kicking lulled, the baby's expression shifted to a dull stare, one eye drifting blankly towards the ceiling light fixture, or Mars. The mother chattered praise to me, how 'Little Faith' would take her first steps any day, how her Plum had started saying a few words, quite precocious, according to the child-rearing books. I had to take her word for it; I'd only heard screaming and *ech ech ech*.

Forest Bannister's suave telephone patter reached us from the kitchen between rain needles against the house that sounded like angry rice hurled at a cursed wedding.

His wife unpinned the soiled diaper, releasing the full icky force of its contents, the outcome of all that puréed squash. Shirley cooed. "Oh, you *little smelly Nelly*." Then bunched the bad diaper in her hand, holding in the smell. She slid it down into a pail behind the curtain. Then she asked me to pass her a clean wipe, and I did, marvelling at how she cleaned the baby's cleft with a few deft strokes. She released her daughter's ankles. Faith kicked her legs and gurgled like a happy fountain. The purplish blotches on her face paled to a less bilious shade, but she was still homely, a face like hers wouldn't appear on a baby-food-jar label any time soon.

"Always wipe front to back," Mrs. Bannister instructed. "I almost forgot, Sadie. It helps if you sing. Try it."

I thought of the vinyl record on my Cobra-Matic, the fluff snagged on the stylus that delivered me to this dreamy home. Striving to mimic The Chordettes' honeyed strains, I sang

"Mr. Sandman."

"Lovely, Faith likes that," the mother said, sprinkling powder on her child's nether parts. The baby seemed indifferent to me, but at least she wasn't crying. Then Shirley pinned on the clean diaper, careful not to jab any tender flesh. She took another clean wipe and swabbed her own hands and her daughter's, those tiny perfect fingers the baby's best feature.

"All done," Shirley beamed, buttoning the sleeper and scooping up the baby, holding her high like some offering. "Nothing to it. Now we'll take Faith upstairs to her crib and with any luck she'll settle down and you should only have to change her once tonight."

Queasily, I trailed them upstairs, stunned by how much *work* it all was, astonished at the Bannisters' ability to gallivant so often, filled with wonderment at where they found the steam. The house's second floor was predictable enough, carbon copy of Wanda Keeler's home, a hallway sprouting rooms. The Bannisters had thrown their renovating energy into the downstairs. Easy to know which door was the bathroom, gushing water behind the closed door, Bobby's bath.

Shirley Bannister led me through the second door on the right to the nursery. A lamp with a ceramic lamb for a base beamed soft and muted, across a room so small, the crib occupied a quarter of it. Wall shelves held stuffed bears, a Tiny-tears doll. Bronzed baby bootie. A dormer window's curtains starred kittens. A furry unicorn shared a rocking chair with a single book. Mrs. Bannister saw me eyeing its cover. "Dr. Spock, upstairs copy," she remarked. The mother lowered her baby into the crib over which dangled a dancing seal mobile. The seals swayed lightly and the Plum gurgled and pointed to them. I was still afraid of the giant baby, how *alive* it was, who knew what it might do next?

In the corner, there was a dresser, on its varnished top, a tin carousel. The sweetest thing in the room and the prettiest toy I'd ever seen. Must have cost plenty. Shirley spied me admiring it and wound it into motion. The tiny horses on their red and white twist poles began to rise and lower, the carousel's wispy song like an ice-cream cart's tinkles along a summer street. Mrs. Bannister said the carousel sent the Plum right to sleep and sure enough when I glanced over, through the crib's slats, the baby's eyelids drooped, nearly closed. Maybe she'd sleep the whole time. Maybe this *would* be a piece of pineapple upside-down cake after all.

"Shirley!" Forest summoned from downstairs.

Mrs. Bannister formed a *shhh* signal with her coral fingernail against her lips as we tiptoed out of the nursery. She pointed out Bobby's room and advised he should be in bed by nine at the latest. As I followed her swishing lace skirt she added I should check on Faith every half hour or, if she broke out crying, carry her downstairs and change her diaper. My brain dog-paddled with instructions, the thought of picking up the jumbo baby brought new jitters.

At the bottom of the steps Forest met us. He wore his fine tweed overcoat and his driving gloves again and held open his wife's coat in a debonair way. And *what* a coat – elegant, rose-taupe in the latest silhouette style with a draped back, oval collar. Like one in Morgan's Department Store window. Shirley looked darling, drifting into the coat, like a girl in a romantic play, crooning, "Why thank you, kind Sir." I could see playacting meant a lot to married people. Playing dress-up. The coat pantomime stirred something in me and silently I vowed to be the best babysitter they'd ever had, light-years better than chipmunk-cheeks Wanda Keeler.

"I thought we'd take the Healey tonight," Forest told his

wife. She beamed at him, then me. I decided she was just one of those naturally cheerful human beings. Her husband said he'd left some phone numbers for me, and a few more other notes on the kitchen counter.

"Have a boss time, Mr. and Mrs. Bannister, and don't worry about anything. I'm earthbound as they come – I'll take good care of Bobby and Faith, I promise."

(*Earthbound* was me showing I knew the latest lingo. What couple wants a babysitter who's out of date?)

My *own* eyes witnessed the Bannisters' storybook life, their fine coats as they smiled in tandem, acting out their romantic play. The husband took his wife's arm in that gallant pantomime way, like he escorted her to the last great ball on earth.

"Later, Gator," Forest turned to me, and winked, leading his dreamy wife out into the sodden night.

Except for wind walloping the windows, the house was very quiet without the father and mother and their married-people pageants. I walked gingerly through the downstairs. Must not break anything, must make good impression. I felt like an explorer in the world's most elegant pavilion, this was what I came for, to be amidst all this *beauty*. There was no going back. No more second-hand peering into Wanda Keeler's big fat gazing ball. Around the kitchen I tiptoed, loving the seafoam green appliances all over again. On the counter, a note Mr. Bannister must have written while his wife demonstrated how to change the big, smelly baby.

Babysitter Information Sheet
Restaurant Telephone number Cherry 1-4766

De Havilland Dance Telephone Grover 3-2100

Other Notes
Bobby has asthma, we forgot to mention. Do not panic.
He has coughing fits, cough syrup in bathroom medicine cabinet,
give him two spoonfuls, coughing should stop.
If fit seems severe telephone us at one of the numbers above.
Baby may fuss and cry when nothing is wrong, Shirley tells me, baby
does this to get attention – leave her alone in crib for approx. 10 minutes,
she will likely go back to sleep – you will soon learn difference between
this and real crying. (For more information read section on crying in Dr.
Spock's book – on coffee table.)
Help yourself to squares in Tupperware. (Bobby will try to wheedle
these; don't allow him.)
Do not let in the Fuller Brush Man under any circumstances.
Good luck. F.B.

I studied the note, such a manly script. Odd they wouldn't have left the hospital emergency number, even odder to forget mentioning asthma. Maybe dressing in their lovely clothes distracted them. Wanda Keeler hadn't mentioned Bobby's asthma, either. But she spoke little of the firebrands. I left the note on the counter. The wife's note, with the pretty berries, its aura of success, was so much nicer.

The stately maple behind the house creaked and sighed in the night.

It began to feel like a very long time before I'd get paid. The asthma part of Forest's note sent a shudder of dismay through me. The bit about real crying or crying for attention and being able to tell the difference sank my spirits. Why were there different types of crying? I pondered the thought of a Fuller Brush Man calling on such a rainy night. I fixed my thoughts on the saddle shoes I'd soon sport. The tossed coin I'd catch at the end of this.

Bang, Bang, Bang! The little boy. Bobby. Such a racket. His toy pistol poking the soft flesh of my thigh unthreaded my nerves.

"*Bang bang!* You're *dead*, Sade-ee Wilder!" With his silent footfall he'd popped, toting his gun, out of nowhere.

I whirled around to face him. He wore flannel pajamas with *Roy Rogers* printed all over them, a holster buckled around his tiny waist, that furry raccoon hat, a striped tail dangling down the back.

"*Bang,*" he re-fired, blowing imaginary smoke off the pistol's tip. "Gotta make sure you're dead."

"Jeepers, you scared me, Bobby. And I'm *not* dead. I'm here to babysit you and you have to do what I say." Wanda once told me, when it came to the firebrands you had to seize the upper hand right out of the box. "Don't sneak up on me like that again, Bobby." I strove for a firm but gentle tone, like the mothers at the Golden Mile addressing their children – except those moms, at their wits' ends, scolding harshly, which only fueled their offspring's cries.

His freckled face sulked. His pistol jerked towards the big jar on the counter. "Cookie."

"I'll give you a cookie if you promise not to sneak up on me again, but only one, and don't poke your gun at me like that either, okay?" I must have struck the right chord; the boy's face shifted to a sorry puppy look.

"Kay."

I glanced at the wall clock. Still one hundred and twenty minutes until this kid's appointed bedtime. As Bobby took bites of cookie he moved about the kitchen in exaggeratedly long strides as if stepping over imaginary puddles. The tail of his Crockett hat swagged from side to side as he navigated his terrain. I hoped his queer stomping about would help him forget his dead fish.

He stopped. Jabbed his finger towards the Tupperware container marked *Babysitter Squares*. "Want wanna *those*."

(Bobby will try to wheedle these; don't allow him.)

"Hey, can you read, Bobby?"

He eyed me warily, unsure of the right answer. Clearly didn't trust me, reckoned I was out to trick him. And I was.

"I can read my *Dennis the Menace* book," was his cautious reply.

I showed him the part on the *Babysitter Information Sheet* about the squares. He sounded out the words under his breath before meeting my eyes. *"Widdel?"*

"Wheedle, Bobby. That means beg. You can beg all you want but those squares are mine."

Beneath the Crockett hat, his eyes pooled. Rain drubbed the window. The drubbing subsided for a minute, replaced by a clicking sound. Shuster the terrier crossed the floor tiles to his empty bowl, wagging his tail. Ignoring the dog, Bobby bounced to the far end of the kitchen to the table. He stared at the spot where the goldfish bowl had been and asked me where Davy went.

Jeepers, I should have given the little boy a square. He began to breathe shallowly between short, gulping cries. Alarm clenched me. Asthma attack?

"Davy went to fish heaven, he swam right up there." I lamely pointed to the ceiling.

"I know *that*," the boy sniped. "Mommy told me about fish heaven. But she said Davy was just resting up there. So, we gotta keep the bowl here for when he swims" – a choked, squeezed cry – "*back*."

Was it always such a *conundrum* with kids? Quite a mouthful for such a small monkey. I dreaded an asthma attack. Who'd look after the big sour baby in the crib upstairs if I had to take Bobby, in a taxicab, to a hospital? Or would I call an ambulance or the De Havilland number or just what *would* I do?

There seemed no choice but humour the kid. I reached into the cupboard where the fishbowl was stowed, and placed it on the Formica table. "There. Now Davy can swim home."

"Put some water in it," Bobby sniffed.

I sighed my way over to the sink bearing the bowl and half-filled it with water. I set it back on the table and turned to the little boy. "There. Happy?"

"Castle. Put his castle back."

I plucked the tiny ceramic castle off the draining board and lowered it into the water. "Everything's hunky dory now, Bobby, just like before, okay? Davy can swim back home whenever he likes, it's all here waiting for him."

He shrugged gloomily. I began to twig that children were easily distracted. "Say, Bobby, let's feed Shuster, and then why don't you show me your bedroom?"

The boy bounced his shoulders into a hopeful shrug. "Sure!"

I foraged around, found the kibble and dumped some into the terrier's bowl. Bobby had already scooted towards the stairs. Grabbing my purse from the open concept, my soaked feminine protection dire, I followed the bobbing raccoon tail upstairs, relieved that the nursery's only sound was no sound. All well in Smelly Diaper Land. Ducking into the bathroom, I was finally able to pin a fresh pad to my sanitary belt. What a nuisance on the night of my first real job! A night demanding perfection. I thought of the large baby, the stink bomb, Faith. How she scared me. So glowering, so red. Her leaking body. My leaking body.

Shirley Bannister's words returned to me: "You're an *absolute lifesaver*." I bucked myself up. When I sashayed, fresher, into Bobby's bedroom, he was chipper as anything, terrier at his side. Rain lashed his windowpane as he chattered away, showing me his train set (making spewing, farting sounds as he *choo-choo*'ed the caboose around the track until it soon crashed), his *Slinky*, his rocking horse, his propeller beanie, his spacemen made of *Silly Putty*, his Mr. Potato Head, his tin robot, his crayon drawings of green Martians and giant purple insects with the faces of his parents. His boxed games: Tiddlywinks, Chinese Checkers, Cootie, and others. Comic books. His Roy Rogers jeans and jacket. The kid sure had snappy threads and I said, "Jeepers, that's *some*thing, Bobby," after each flourish of rancher shirts and the rest of it.

The kid smiled, now, as if he liked me, and I dared to feel smug. He was a cinch to win over; I'd get through the night, and maybe even come out of it liking *him*. My hunch, all I had to do was send Bobby to sleep in a contented state and not let the baby roll off that changing table or explode, crying, and I'd be hired here again. I hadn't forgotten how Forest winked at me. Or his wife's special welcome note. Wanda Keeler would be furious, but what can you do when you live in a mumps zoo?

A hefty possibility that I wouldn't be wearing my dowdy clothes much longer.

Bobby tugged at my pilling sweater sleeve. "You know what, Sadie? You're way pwitty-er than my other babysitter. And you got bigger melons!"

My cheeks warmed. I was surprised a six-year-old would notice such things. (And his parents worried about Wayne and Shuster!) Praise like this, even from a kid wearing Roy Rogers pajamas, batted my joy ball right out of the park. The only fly in my ointment was the wind. It no longer sounded like *just* wind, but a King Kong of nasty air, or a giant reptile writhing, bashing its lizard-tail about in the night. The dog noticed it too, twitching his hairy eyebrows towards the window, before letting go a low, rumbling growl. For the first time, it seemed, Bobby heard the reptile, too, his eyes wide, anxious.

"Listen, Bobby, let's go back downstairs and watch television."

He brightened. I told him knock-knock jokes as we soft-shoed our way downstairs, my goal being to distract him from the stately maple's sawing and creaking louder now, pained groans like some evil lumberjack was tearing it apart, limb by limb. Between the branch-moans, a mercy, the nursery still silent.

We reached the sunken living room.

"Knock, knock, Bobby!"

The wind bucked hard against the house.

"Who's there, Sadie?"

"*Beets*, Bobby!"

"Beets *who*, Sadie?"

At the punchline I tickled his spine. *"Beets me!"*

The kid giggled in his Roy Rogers pajamas, asked to watch telly-wish-on. He was just plain *cute*. I clicked the General Electric Deluxe to life. Our Pet, Juliette warbled her heart out. Bobby called me prettier, even, than "the singing telly-wish-on lady." Again, my cheeks warmed. Employment suited me, I grew better-looking with each passing moment, I felt sure of it. Geez Louise, I'd *glow* once I wore new saddle shoes and took over Wanda's gravy-train job. Even my *own mother* wouldn't recognize me!

I wondered if I should let it slip to Forest and Shirley that Wanda Keeler would like to smack their children's bottoms crimson and had told me so often. I didn't know if Dr. Spock advised spanking. Either way, I'd win Wanda's job fair and square, through sheer talent. No need for dirty pool. I was above that.

As the wind battered the house, I beefed up the television's volume to drown out the ugly weather. Shuster coiled himself into a small circle beside Bobby. No rule against pets on furniture on the *Babysitter Information Sheet* so I allowed the dog to stay. I was so pleased that every living thing in the house seemed content. No crying upstairs. Bobby edged closer to me and before Juliette warbled another song the boy rested fully against me. I'd tamed the firebrands and it hadn't been so awfully hard. I had a natural knack for this work. My mind paint-brushed the scene: *Babysitter, Boy, Terrier Relaxing in Living Room.*

I was an absolute lifesaver.

To my joy, the clock over the hi-fi console had leapt ahead a whole hour. The wind was still giving me serious jitters, though. I ramped Juliette higher. I paced the open concept – feeling like I'd landed on the moon – and thought how much nicer it was than anyone had imagined, except for the weather. I flipped through Dr. Spock's *Baby and Child Care* on the coffee table, curious about the famous doctor's advice on the subject of noisy weather. Seeing no index entry for noisy weather I opened a page randomly:

> Sitters are a boon to parents and can help a child to develop independence. You and your child should know your sitter well. Let's assume for this discussion that it's a woman, though there is no reason why it should not be a man. For night sitting with a baby who doesn't waken, it may only be necessary for her to be sensible and dependable. But for babies who waken and for children above the age of five months who might waken, it's important for the sitter to be a person they know and like. It is frightening to most children to waken and find a stranger.

Criminy, this hardly fit my situation. The big, homely Plum didn't like me, all she'd done was scowl and scream. I worried the television's blare would wake her, but it helped drown out the wind and the stately maple's sawing noises. If that baby awoke I'd know it. She'd make sure of that. From my trips to the shopping plaza and rides in the new subway, I knew babies were born with an ambulance tucked inside their lungs. Faith had ambulance lungs, I already knew that; even with Juliette and the King Kong wind, I'd hear her if she cried.

I shivered. To take my mind off the wind I opened Dr. Spock's book once again, turning to the section on crying. *What does it mean?* I read: *there is a lot of fretting and crying that can't be explained.*

Gobs of help, Doctor. Again, I recalled Wanda Keeler's temptation to spank the Bannister kids' bottoms red. What say you, Dr. Spock?

> There are several reasons to avoid physical punishment, I feel. It teaches children that the larger, stronger person has the power to get his way...Some spanked children feel quite justified in beating up on smaller ones. The American tradition of spanking may be one cause of the fact that there is much more violence in our country than any other comparable nation.

Useless as a soggy cracker. This was Canada. Was there a *Canadian* tradition of spanking? And I wondered, if it came down to it, whether the big, ugly baby couldn't give her undersized brother a run in the fisticuffs ring.

I set aside Dr. Spock, and thumbed through the Bannisters' record collection. Harry Belafonte. Doris Day (yawn). Artie Shaw (double yawn). Eartha Kitt (better). They owned some real gone stuff: The Crew Cuts, The Chords, and *Huzzah*, The Chordettes. Those dreamy ladies sent me an inspiration. Already I fretted over what to do when television clicked off-air for the night and we'd hear the wind worse. Bobby would get scared and if he didn't go upstairs to bed and the Bannisters landed home and found their son sleeping on the sofa I might not get hired back. Music would rescue my turtleneck! After television would come records. The Chordettes would set heaven to rights, their harmonies a lullaby for the house. I'd play another record, then another. Songs to save the night. I'd eat my squares and have a little party for myself. Celebrate my ingenuity and the babysitting fortune that seemed more and more headed my way.

The tables are about to turn, Wanda Keeler.

The music plan steadied my nerves. I left Bobby to television. In the kitchen, I ate a rainbow square, its tiny marshmallows foamy on my tongue. I opened the seafoam refrigerator, poked around inside. Not only did the Bannisters dress like royalty, they *dined* royally. Waldorf salad. Glazed ham. Asparagus. Cheese croquettes. Leftovers stored in the prettiest Tupperware tubs. Chop Suey from a restaurant. Hurriedly, I helped myself. Never did I get Chinese food. Two cheese croquettes. I forgot myself for a minute. What the Bannisters might think when they discovered that their babysitter pilfered food, didn't occur to me until after the delicious edibles galloped down my throat. I'd say Bobby wanted a snack.

I closed the fridge door, brushed the croquette crumbs off my sweater, and sauntered with the most casual steps I could muster, back into the sunken living room. More animals joined the wind-zoo. Off, on, a lamp's glow shuddered. Juliette warbled back, bless her. On the sofa, Bobby dozed; I'd leave him there for the time being, then ferry him up to bed. The room's air felt iron-heavy. I recalled Wanda Keeler's stories of the upstairs, the wonders of the large, walk-in closet. She'd even mentioned a *merry widow!* I'd never seen one, and longed to witness just *how* merry.

A dim bulb behind a wall sconce lit my tiptoes up the steps. Its milky ray snapped off for an instant, then returned. The terrier tagged after me, wriggling his hindquarters as he scaled the stairs. Maybe he hoped more dog kibble was stored upstairs. What a hopeful breed, terriers. Maybe he just wanted to be with someone not asleep. I preferred him to stay with Bobby so I pointed towards the sunken living room, in low, encouraging tones, "Go back, Shuster, lie down." But the ball of fur stuck to me like a burdock. Well, he was company. And awful sweet, like Dorothy's Toto.

Silence from the nursery. Good Plum.

Wind antlered the house as the dog shadowed me into the master bedroom. Wanda had gabbled so much about the closet she hadn't said much about the *room itself*. I groped the wall for a light switch. Discovered it. Turned it on. One bed. That didn't surprise me. The Bannisters were dancers. What surprised me was how modern the open concept downstairs, yet this bed, so very *old world* – four-poster kind with a canopy, ruffles everywhere, skirting the bed's base, like some pioneer ball gown. When it came to their sleeping chamber, the Bannisters were ruffle-minded.

The rest of the bedroom was cookie-cutter. Dresser, rocking chair, nightstands, lamps. I opened the closet door. Jeepers the Bannisters' closet was the size of my whole bedroom! Neat as a pin. The only things out of place were two business cards that must have fallen on the floor while husband and wife dressed for their night out. One card was for a Dale Carnegie Public Speaking course. The other card said, *20th Century Dance Studio*. His and her sides of the closet emerged like two dynasties with a longstanding treaty. A full-length mirror occupied a neutral zone in the middle. His dynasty smelled faintly of aftershave. Her side wafted perfume. The smells mingled into the air, ringing with cocktails and Bossa Nova dances and rides in breathtaking cars. The Bannisters' closet vibrated with good times. Happy ghosts of charmed nights. I heard the clink of crystal champagne flutes. This was the life I wanted for myself, how could I not explore?

The terrier snuffled along the tidy rows of Forest's brushed-suede bucks, golf shoes, chukka boots, and lounging slippers. What topped all the finery on his side was a rack slung with ties. Monogrammed. *F.B.* Many bore designs, a jumping fish, a pair of flying mallard ducks. Soft maroons and russets and slates, designs in emerald and teal blue. Neckwear worthy of an art gallery.

Shirley owned darling pumps with and without ankle straps, calfskin sandals with Spanish heels and flat slippers with rhine-stones. I stroked the calfskin. It reminded me of the soft leather seats in the Austin-Healey. If cattle had to sacrifice their lives, sandals or car upholstery was a classier end than ground chuck. Despite my fondness for hot hamburger loaf.

My reverent fingers worked their way higher, aching with appreciation. I fingered the soft, folded slacks, the sweater sets in tangerine, aqua, and cream on upper shelves. An alligator shoulder bag, a saddle leather satchel (more cattle), and, the icing on the cake, a covered-wagon-style purse with western stitching and (I peeked inside) a matching little mirror and com-pact. The top shelf also housed hats in velvet and straw. Stiff-ened taffeta with upswept brims and veils and helmet-style hats with buttons and ribbon trim. I didn't try them on; they looked so peaceful there in their hat places. I envied all the shopping trips Shirley Bannister must have taken, buying these hats and all her other exquisite things. Pennyworth's, Morgan's, T. Eaton Company. She was above Chainway – that was clearer to me than the freckles on her son's face.

Shirley was dotty for skirts. Gored skirts, hobbled skirts, little numbers with kick pleats for dancing, likely. Hoop skirts with boleros. Pencil skirts, several vagabond skirts.

Skirts were the closet's heartland. Until the dresses. Wanda Keeler had under-told this section of the closet. My fingers raced over buttery cocktail frocks, silk sheaths, dotted shirtwaists, waffle piqué dresses, frothy tulles, lustrous sateens. I buried my face in Shirley Bannister's divine dresses, inhaled their folds and pleats while the good-time ghosts tripped the light fantastic.

The only downside was, the dresses made me sad about my mother. Before pinking seams wore her down, she loved dresses. Marked history with them. She could recall what she'd worn on every landmark occasion. How the third button from the top of her blue voile dress hung by a thread during her first date with Robert Wilder, August 16, 1933, at the baseball game in Willowvale Park, where she'd watched the man who became my father catch fly balls handily until some bleacher-sitter's curdled shout, "Nice catch, Jew boy!" Then more mean names were hurled until an ugly brawl spilled onto the wooden spectator benches where Rose, my mother, sat nervously until Robert pulled her to safety, away from the fists and the terrible names hurled and how, in that moment of his rescue, her button fell off and Robert returned the next day to the ball diamond to search for it and miraculously, amid the tire irons in the torn and trampled grass and the smashed eyeglasses and debris, found it, and the finding of it captured the heart of my mother Rose McCann, with the certainty that the handsome outfielder, Robert Wilder, was the one for her. My mother told me when he appeared at her door with the button, she *knew*. That's how much meaning a button can carry. After my father's death, she packed that dress in mothballs.

I'd almost overlooked the most bewitching dress of all. It was rayon satin, periwinkle blue, with a deep V neckline done in soft folds, and a full skirt nipped in at the waist and clinched with a rhinestone buckle. The sleeves were simple and short. Very Bette Davis in *All About Eve*. I peeled off my turtleneck and pulled the periwinkle dress over my slacks while the wind gave the house a stiff kick, audible even from inside the closet. The bedroom window hated the kick. If glass could gasp, that was the sound. To distract myself from the scare, I swiveled before the full-length mirror as the dress's taffeta underskirt settled over my hips, an elegant rustle that comforted me. I reached back and zipped up the dress. The rhinestone buckle enhanced my eyes. The nipped-in bodice removed inches from my waist. Shirley Bannister was taller than me so the dress was a bit long, but even worn with my sneakers, oh, I dwelt in possibility. Imagined I was a married lady acting in a romantic skit. If the city crumbled, King Kong would snatch me up first. Fay Wray had nothing on me!

A shining future strobed before my new, pretty eyes. One small thing was missing, so close was I to perfection. I scurried into the bedroom and snatched a gold locket I'd seen on the nightstand. I hooked it around my neck. *Heyzoose Marimba*, the finishing touch.

The happiest dream of myself, I spun, adoring the dress' regal swish, my young, promising curves. The merry widow, wherever it was, held no interest, now. A whole brigade of the merriest widows couldn't trump me in the periwinkle dress.

More strobes. The closet light blacked out, the bedroom, too. Shuster's barks from the sunken living room boxed my ears; he'd trotted back downstairs while I preened. The strobing hadn't been my bright future, but the house's power supply.

Darkness swamped me. Bobby's nasal cry reached me. "Scared!"

I tied my turtleneck by its arms around my waist.

I felt my way downstairs best I could. The power had gone bust through the whole house. I settled onto the sofa beside the little boy, the kid needed comfort. "It's only the wind, Bobby. Its force killed the lights. It's okay."

His hand inched over into mine. "Dark," he wheezed.

The air was wet-mop heavy. Bad air, devil air like this couldn't help asthma.

I placed my face close to his. "Say, listen, Bobby, do your Mommy and Daddy keep a flashlight somewhere?" (I didn't suppose he'd know but I'd read in *Chatelaine* that children could be surprisingly observant so worth a try. It was too dark for him to notice me wearing his mother's dress, or he *didn't* notice, thankfully.)

A tear hop-scotching down the boy's cheek glinted through the darkness. His head shook slowly. "Dunno, Sadie."

Nearby on the sofa I felt his Davy Crockett hat. I reached over and seized it by the tail. "Put this on, Bobby, it'll keep you safe while I find us some light, all right?"

He obeyed. Someone rattled the front door's latch, hard, ramming clicks, not like a neighbour or Fuller Brush Man. The terrier resumed his barking. How I wished the Bannisters had left candles and matches. I needed those more than babysitter squares now. The door-rattles persisted. Bobby cowered under his hat, the small dark shape of him, and whimpered. "Boggy-m?" (Bogey-man?)

Bumping into the coffee table, I shuffled over to the picture window and parted the drapes. The streetlights were out, but squinting into the night I detected a candle's flame in a window across the street. Because the houses on Humber Green Drive were set back from the street on gently inclined front lawns, the flame was distant, tiny. I saw no other lights anywhere. Had everyone gone dancing except for the candle house? Should I run over there? What would I say? What would Wanda Keeler do? I thought about ringing her for advice but didn't want her, or her mother for that matter, to know I was in a pickle. I thought about my own mother, working late. Were the lights out at Don Vale Textiles, too? Once more I considered sprinting across to the lit house and asking to borrow a candle, or flashlight. The tiny flame called to me. But I couldn't answer its call. I couldn't leave the children alone.

At least the large baby slept like a winter orchard.

The winds went ogre, heaving nasty chain-link rains. Who'd been rattling the front door? Would a Fuller Brush Man venture out on a night like this? Squinting through the darkness again I saw gushing rain, gallons and gallons, turning Humber Green Drive into a river. Water carried its own evil light. The street-river gave me a cow, and if Shirley Bannister's Saratoga hadn't been parked at the top of the driveway, on its rise, it might lift and sail down into the bigger flow's mad, moving glint. Across the street, a parked car held its place, but the current tumbled near the tires' tops. The car wouldn't stay parked for long. A whopping tree branch, splintered, a letter-V over its hood.

I shuddered. Chilled, I rubbed my upper arms rapidly as if they were sticks I tried to spark into fire. "No Bogey-Man," I called over to Bobby sniffling on the sofa. "Now you sit tight, okay?"

Mouse squeak. "Kay."

The living room was inky hulking shapes. I groped my way through the lighter spaces between them and found myself in the kitchen, where my fingers brailled through drawers in search of flashlights, candles, matches. The Bannisters smoked, they must have matches. Everyone's kitchen, ours too, contained a drawer jumbled with matches and flashlights, old bills, receipts, ticket stubs. But the Bannisters' kitchen was so spic and span my groping located no such drawer.

Bulls charged the house. Bobby cried "hooey up." I yelled back, "Sure, sure, just getting a light." Knocked myself out, rifling through drawers. Finally, I reached some sort of broom closet – a tall, vertical cupboard. Objects hung on hooks inside its door and *Heyzoose Marimba*, looped over a hook, on a little strap, my happy hand discovered a flashlight.

"Good news, Bobby-O!" I trilled, clicking on the light, but he couldn't have heard me because something crashed hard underneath us, then I heard shattering glass.

There was someone down there – below us. I heard the dog tear over to the basement door and go berserk yipping and I wished he'd stop. The racket had to be scaring the little boy. It didn't soothe *my* nerves, either.

I beamed my way into the living room, to Bobby's confused teary gulps. As my eyes adjusted to the darkness slightly, I made out his small, quailing shape on the sofa. Where were Wayne and Shuster when you needed them?

I shone the light at Bobby's teary face. He squinted. I apologized, and lowered my beam. His shaking made me feel lousy.

"Some – down – there," he croaked, finger wood-peckering the carpet.

I was about to say I'd check into it when the telephone rang in the kitchen. Hard on its shrill heels a loud baby-squall from upstairs. I could tell it was real crying, not 'get-attention' bawling. Good grief, I was getting the squeeze from three stories at once. Basement and baby had to wait. The note advised let her cry for ten minutes. The phone wouldn't wait. Maybe it was the Bannisters checking on me. Whoever called was persistent for it rang and rang.

Beaming my way ahead, I snatched the receiver off its cradle in the dark kitchen.

The line sizzled with static. "Shirley?"

"No, they're out. I'm the babysitter." I had to shout through the poor connection.

The woman's words were waterlogged rasps. I only caught, through the rippling scratch – "neighbour," "Etobicoke Creek," "the Humber" – what was this? Geography class? Her next scrap of speech fuzzed but I heard "the swing bridge is out," then, "has someone phoned and told you to leave the house?"

"I don't think so." Guilt punched my heart. What if I'd missed a telephone call while trespassing in my employers' closet, preening in the periwinkle dress?

"Can't hear you," the woman's syllables seethed with frustration.

Leave the house. Swing bridge. What did she mean? What did it have to do with me?

After that, my mind tried to stitch the patches of sound into meaning. Something about: *flood. If anyone phoned and told me I should get out, I shouldn't listen. I should sit tight right where* [unhearable] *inside the house.*

Why would I leave? The Bannisters paid me to stay *in* their house, mind their children. I'd promised them. Even if I *could* drive, I didn't know where Shirley kept her Saratoga key, and where would I go? I wondered if the call might be some kind of prank, but it wasn't Halloween for a couple of weeks.

Stronger static stung my ears. The woman still strained to tell me something but hearing was hopeless and I moved the receiver away from my ear to listen to the house. I should have listened better before this. I heard the wailing from upstairs. Criminy, I'd likely have to change that baby's stenchy diaper. The sofa overflowed with Bobby's sobs and Shuster's *ruff-ruffs* sounded near the basement door. I heard crashing down there. Everything was happening at once. My plate was too full for telephone talk. The woman's voice faded out.

The line went dead.

I hung up the useless receiver. Streams of baby screams, from her ambulance-siren lungs. I feared the big sour Plum might choke or explode into a thousand pieces and I'd have to quickly paste her back together again before her parents returned. I had no clue where the family stored their glue. Could all the king's horses, all the king's men, and one scared girl whose dream job was turning nightmare, raindrop by raindrop, put that baby back together again?

Regroup, Sadie Wilder, I told myself. *Or never will you catch the silver coin. Never will you trump Wanda. It'll be second-hand television for the rest of your life.* I still wore Shirley Bannister's periwinkle dress while the wind continued to harrow the house. Gazing into the mirror's silver eye, I'd forgotten children, diapers, time itself. Why, oh why hadn't I paid better attention to my *job?* What if this very moment the Bannisters parked the Healey in their driveway? Maybe they were so worried about the stormy night, and their greenhorn babysitter, they'd chosen to skip the dance. I wondered if they'd still pay me the full amount if they cut their night shorter? Maybe they'd phoned and I hadn't heard the ring from upstairs. If Shirley caught me wearing her dress that would spell the end of babysitting and any jobs after that, for who'd hire a brazen little snoop?

A piercing crash from downstairs (human?) –

Short, concerned ruffs (canine) –

I unzipped Shirley's dress, scrambled out of it and stuffed it inside the dumbwaiter. I'd hang it back in the closet later. Right now, I had to face whoever, whatever, prowled the basement. I peeled my turtleneck back on. I still wore the locket. There was no time to fiddle with its delicate chain so I stuffed it down inside the neck of my sweater. I needed to move faster. *Please don't let the Bannisters come home until I sort this out.* The baby had been crying now for ten minutes, but she'd have to wait. Down. One step. At a time. Below me, I heard glass exploding. The wind-wolves snarled *bad bad* at me, for wearing the mother's dress. Shuster revved his agitated *rarfs* but hovered on a higher step while I descended. The dark I couldn't fix; the dog I ordered quiet. He didn't listen, instead he sprouted new, ferocious-guard-dog fur.

I flung my beam around; the noise from downstairs had drowned out Bobby's footsteps. He now crouched beside the dog on the step above, offered his toy pistol. "You want shoot, Sadie?"

The kid looked so deadly earnest, a fierce, sudden love for him flooded me despite the darkness and the sounds of breaking glass below and the baby's lungs blowing themselves to smithereens upstairs.

"You use it to keep everyone safe up here, okay?"

He nodded, serious as a tiny judge. "Kay."

I noticed he was wearing rubber boots, now. His pajama pants tucked into them. He must have put them on while I toured his parents' closet upstairs. Whatever spun the kid's vinyl. I beamed my way slowly down, stair by stair, frightened by the thought of a burglar, maybe even a murderer, down there, with only a flashlight to clobber him, a flashlight I couldn't afford to lose. What did Wanda Keeler tell me about the Bannisters' basement? Only that it had a wet bar and some kind of bomb shelter, in case of Russians. I wished I'd grabbed a rolling pin while rampaging through the kitchen drawers for a light.

The wind bullied and brawled, but even with its demon noise and the baby's wails and the terrier's barks, I heard a strange gurgling at the bottom of the stairs. I began to think what lurked below wasn't Russian.

I stopped just above the bottom step and razzed my beam around. "Stand back, you jerk!" I shouted to the intruder.

No jerk answered.

I bounced my beam about. Its tunnelled light revealed a wet bar at the basement's more fixed-up end, and at the other, rougher end there was a furnace, wringer washing machine, drying rack, snow shovels, rakes and skates looped by their laces over a hook. I saw a cinder block hut about the size of a bathroom, its wooden door padlocked. The bomb shelter. It gave me the willies.

Hard weather whomped the house's foundation, vibrating through my sneakers' soles. Above me the children's cries worsened. Descending the final stair, I spun my light along the floor where several inches of water burbled and swirled, glass shards pitching about, tiny points of jagged light like smashed stars, and the hurly-burly of more water pouring in from somewhere. I swizzled my beam higher. Water jetted in through a broken window, an inky waterfall. That explained the crash, the glass shattering. Pushed inward by the water's force, the window's frame dangled askew. A steady surge of water splashed in through it, down the wall.

The problem wasn't human. It couldn't be spoken to or sung to or bartered with or beaned with a rolling pin. The voice of the woman on the telephone returned to me. *Flood.* She'd used that word. Like in the Bible. Sent to punish schemers like me who plotted to steal their friend's job, vain girls who snooped in their employers' closet. No ark in this cellar, only a padlocked cinderblock hut that did no good since, as I probed my light across the eddying pond beneath, the water was rising. And fast. The wet bar was growing wetter, and shorter. Soon a garden gnome could order a highball.

Where was all the water was coming from?

The most wretched thought walloped me, spurred by Forest Bannister's earlier remark, that the Humber River flowed right behind their house. *Prime riverfront property.* Nausea surged through me. Bobby had been right, there was someone in the house.

The *river* was in the house.

The river had risen partway up the furnace. I swept the light's beam along its churning roil. The washing machine was partly submerged. Snow shovels, now loosened, tossed in the swell. The rakes followed suit. Dolefully, I eyed the fallout shelter. The Bannisters would have been smarter building a life raft.

I knew there was no point sloshing through the water and trying, somehow, to block the window. Never have I had fix-it skills. Not handy. Anyway, there was no way to replace the shattered pane. The river was stronger, and would only batter-ram its way through. A hunch pinged my ribs – there was nothing water couldn't penetrate. It could bend and roll and crush. Like wind, it could make itself into any shape, any size. An even nastier wind swarmed the house, like a thousand attacking wasps were boring through the foundation. Wasp Air Force. There was nothing I could do about the basement, so I inched my way back upstairs. A line from the school play, *The Tempest*, jabbed my mind. *Now would I give a thousand furlongs of sea for an acre of barren ground.* In the play a magician makes everything right in the end. My magician was – *where?* My own voice reached me – *Sadie Wilder why do you lollygag with Shakespeare?* The rising water had strangely hypnotized me. I snapped my fingers in front of my own face.

I returned to the sunken living room once more, where Bobby had also retreated, and flashed my beam in the little boy's tearful face. He asked who I'd been talking to just now, who was down in the basement. I told him nobody. I was talking to myself. The terrier bulleted out of the darkness, all alarmed *ow-ow-ow* noises, which upset Bobby even more. I hushed the dog crossly. I decided to call the De Havilland dance number left for me on the kitchen counter until I remembered the phone line had fizzled.

That's when the situation fully struck me: I was alone. Couldn't Wanda Keeler have caught mumps any *other* day? How was I supposed to make a good impression with all this mess?

My ducks weren't in a row, criminy, no. They were being buffeted about on a river with no edges. The monster baby upstairs had stopped screaming at last. Maybe she blew herself up. Maybe she was *dead*. If that was the case, then not only would I not get paid, I'd be charged with murder. Bobby and I heard objects from the basement bumping into each other, floating clanks and bangs. The sound of the river's rush cascading into the house through the basement window was unmistakable. Terror lit the little boy's face, his finger pointed jerkily to the floor. "Water?"

I nodded miserably.

"Big weak, Sadie?"

"Yeah, big leak, Bobby."

"What we do, Sadie?"

"I don't know," I confessed.

Mistake. I shouldn't have agreed the leak was big. Bobby's choking sobs splintered my heart. "I want Mommy," he cried. "Want Daddy."

"You'll be fine," I said, distractedly. "You're wearing rubber boots."

The boy was right. That's just what needed to happen. The parents needed to return. I was in over my head, the deep end. I would have traded all my earnings now for a way out of this nightmare. Surely the Austin-Healey would purr up the driveway any minute. I told Bobby something to this effect. But the woman on the phone said the swing bridge was out. How could Forest and Shirley drive back here? Maybe a magic chariot like the Healey could, maybe it had pontoons folded underneath. Maybe if I hadn't closet-snooped I could have done something about the broken basement window before the flood had hit fully. But how do you keep a river out when it wants in?

I cracked open Dr. Spock, the last page. I fixed my flashlight beam on "Emergencies." Animal Bites. Burns. Choking. Convulsions. Head injuries. Poisoning. "When to Call the Doctor." Calling assumed the telephone line wasn't dead. There was no entry for "River in House." I tossed the book onto the coffee table.

The baby was alive. She hadn't exploded. Her renewed howls ricocheted through the sunken living room. Bobby tugged on my slacks. "Faith mad."

"Yes, Faith is very mad. Let's go upstairs and make her happy again."

I couldn't fix disaster below, so I headed for higher ground. The nursery. The big ugly baby's den. *Universe, why oh why can't you help out a girl on her first job?*

Taking Bobby's hand, I beamed our way upstairs, the terrier at our heels. The foul diaper smell clobbered us. I'd have to lug the smelly Plum down to the changing table, and somehow clean her up in the dark. Shirley showed me diaper changing, but not in the dark with a river in the house. I'd do my best. *Ducks in a row*, I whispered. The Bannisters might arrive home to a flooded basement but at least they'd smell a fresh baby.

"Pee-*ew*." Bobby pinched his nose with the hand not clamped by mine. "Smelly Faith."

He was on the stick with that one. If they wanted to keep away the Russians they should station smelly babies along the Canadian border. A wrong thought for an aspiring babysitter.

I stuffed the thought inside my turtleneck with the locket.

We entered the nursery. The baby, writhing in her own filth, sent me into a flap. What if her parents arrived before I could change her diaper? I swung my light around the nursery and saw what had upset the baby so badly. A blown tree branch crashed against her window, splintering the pane from corner to corner. Rivulets of rainwater forced a continuous stream through the large crack, into the small, rank chamber.

I crept, fearful, over to the crib. The baby's face was a scrunched, mouldy pink rag. Her eyes were swollen slits from her screaming. If she wasn't so homely, so *toxic*, I'd have pitied her. She couldn't help her bodily functions any more than I could, but that didn't ease my nose. Seeing the light and me, she gulped air and flailed her arms. Through the crib's slats Bobby watched his sister helplessly, like she was a prisoner in a cell he'd no key to open.

A *very* severe crash came from the master bedroom, *so* strong Faith's crib lolloped sideways. The terrier volleyed out barks. I told Bobby, "Stay with your sister, be brave for her. I'll be back in a jiffy." I needed the flashlight to investigate the noise; he'd only be in the dark for a minute.

Lighting my way along the hallway to the master bedroom I didn't dare dwell on how high the water in the basement must have risen by now. Evil jaws were chewing the house apart. River jaws.

A glassy *clunk*. Downstairs. Vase? Now a vase broken on my watch. What next?

I surveyed the master bedroom. A window had blown in, rain drubbed the ruffled bed. Another thing I couldn't fix. Bobby shrieked, a new alarm. "Wiffer! Wiffer in the house!" Did he mean 'weather' or 'river?' Both were true.

Hurrying back to the nursery I flicked my light where water

stained the wallpaper kittens; my beam revealed a large rip, lightning-bolt shaped, across the ceiling. Next a *zang pi-choo* sound, like a mean lion tamer's whip, from the roof – sparks sprayed in through the cracked window, across the nursery. Bobby and Faith bawled.

Now I was *really* cross with the Bannisters. How could they be out dancing the night away while their house was being eaten alive? Wouldn't they have the sense to come home early? Darn them and their Austin-Healey and their highballs. I fought back furious tears. Darn those lost hours I let Wanda Keeler swan about and strand me under the spell of her litany of beautiful profit. And darn *me* for thinking I could steal her crown of official babysitter.

I lifted the big, smelly baby out of her crib. It was awkward to do while holding the flashlight. Faith was large-boned, a dead weight. A stink. My own smell hardly daisies, either. I needed a fresh sanitary pad badly. The river in the basement bumped and crashed things about. Bobby heard it too. I could tell by his eyes – pained moons. The river roared louder, closer to the sunken living room, to us, as we descended the dark stairway.

Bobby held the flashlight for me as I fumbled to undo the baby's terrycloth sleeper on the change table. My fingers trembled and I jabbed the homely lump with a safety pin. She shrieked the bluest murder, then kicked and almost rolled off the table. I cleaned her up the best I could. At least she'd be wearing a fresh diaper when her parents returned. Because that's what parents did, wasn't it? They returned.

The dog snuffled in an agitated way around the bottom of the changing table. As if something was hidden there that could fix all this. Bobby whimpered and grasped my slacks. To cheer him along I sang a hit from Wanda Keeler's vinyl stack, what words I could recall, that *Sh-Boom* song.

Boom! A boom not in the song. The basement door blasted open all by itself. Water charged towards us. Into the living room the river sundered its ungodly gush, tumbling in like a giant liquid acrobat. Bobby bawled. I choked back tears. Water eddied at our feet hard and fast. The flood swallowed the television console's legs. Then the sofa's legs. *Higher ground, Sadie.* Again, I wrangled the baby, a chore, while grasping the flashlight. I seized Bobby's hand and heard him wheeze. Criminy, that's all we needed now, an asthma attack. He blubbered something, "Ooze-stir?" I couldn't make him out, the devils outside whipped more *zang-pi-choo*s, hydro lines, it sounded like. The fast river slobbered over our ankles. Cold, brown murk. Death water. We pushed against it, towards the staircase.

"What are you saying?" I squalled down at the tearful boy, tugging his hand.

"Shuster!"

I'd forgotten the dog. I released Bobby's fingers long enough to sweep my light beam around and call the terrier's name and to my relief, he paddled out from behind the submerging television, towards us. Bobby snatched him up. The drenched mutt quaked in his arms. Clutching the heavy baby and hauling the little boy with his soaked, furry burden, we slogged through the living room's rising water, which was surely heaving its deathly hose across the kitchen tiles, too, ruining the seafoam appliances.

Halfway up the steps I turned and cast a backwards glance, bobbing my light across the sunken living room. The surging tide had knocked over the vinyl records. Eartha Kitt's tropical eyes flashed soggily back at me. Belafonte floated. Day-oh. Hank Snow drowned with Bill Haley and his Comets. The coffee table shimmied, dislodged by the current. I couldn't look any longer. So much musical sorrow. The ruined vinyl records skewered ridges through my heart.

The house's highest point, I reasoned, must be the attic. But it was the sort of attic with no steps to it, only a square hole with a wooden lid, in the upstairs hallway. I'd noted this on my way to the master bedroom earlier. A ladder was needed and the ladder swilled about in the basement. Next to the attic, the highest ground was the Bannisters' bed. We scrambled up onto it, under the ruffled canopy. I lowered the baby onto the quilt. The bed's canopy a brief frilly hut. Another window had blown in while I changed the baby; rain sliced across the bedroom. Beside his sister, Bobby shivered in his pajamas. Shuster slid from the boy's arms and parked himself, on high alert, near us on his wet, scruffy haunches.

Over to the bashed window I squish-squished in my soaked sneakers. I squinted outside. The street in full darkness, no candle-glow.

Something really terrible was happening.

I squinted harder into the night. A very low grade of vision was possible. A dark river teemed where Humber Green Drive had been. It flooded the Bannisters' driveway, up and over the lawn's smooth bulge, probably to the front door's pretty wreath, though I couldn't see straight down. Soon the water would ring the doorbell. *Hello, did you order a river?* Only a boat could bring the Bannisters back home. Black shapes of toppled trees twisted in the river-street and then, right below my stupefied eyes the current lifted Shirley's Chrysler Saratoga, turned it sideways and sucked it into the bigger flood. Along it floated like a barge for a short distance then pranged into a hydro pole. The collision only paused it, before it bounced off the pole, lifted by water, and continued down tempest road.

I hoisted myself onto the quilt under the ruffled canopy, beside the baby and boy, and tried to think what to do. I pictured my *Babysitter for Hire* flyers clamped under windshield wipers, tacked to hydro poles. They'd be soaked rags. I *hadn't* advertised myself as a mermaid or lifeguard. I couldn't swim.

I could hear furniture thudding against other furniture downstairs. The water no doubt rising. I recalled the lady's words on the phone, *sit tight, inside the house.* But what *was* the house?

Bobby huddled against me; I laced my arm around him. I drew the baby closer to us, as she made fretful squawks. The terrier looked like a wet mop with eyes. I struggled to sort some facts.

The river was in the house.

We were in the house.

The lady on the phone said stay but what did she know? What facts did she have at *her* disposal?

We were in the river in the house.

In the house without a paddle.

A thousand furlongs of sea.

No dry land.

Where was Marilyn Bell when you needed her?

Where was my mother? Stranded in a dark factory with her pinking shears, waiting for the light to return? If she'd made it home, found my note, she'd be worried to pieces. Maybe her phone line was dead. Maybe the same dark river ripped through our apartment. As for the Bannisters, they didn't have a driveway now, only a river. They'd need to call their boating friends, but who knew if telephones remained in the world?

A monster smashed through the roof, right above us, the sound of sickening gashes like explosions, splintering ceiling joists. The bed clattered about, sudden, violent jolts rubber-balling us along the mattress, sending the baby and little boy into screams. The ruffled canopy smothered us. I ripped away at our ruined tent, found its edge and yanked it aside, so we could breathe. I glinted my light around, its beam clotted with dust and plaster. The stately maple behind the house had crashed down through the roof and across the bed, rocketing rubble and hunks of roofing throughout the room.

The maple missed us by mere inches. A dark, ragged hole gaped above us now. Wind and rain hammered down. My eyes were clogged with wet leaves, I palmed away the blinding maple leaf forevers. Flailed some more at the wet, heavy canopy, where the barks sounded. The dog bellied out, alive. A hellish hammock, now, the bed listed badly, knocked to one knee. Bobby's Crockett hat was askew, its tail fur wet and matted as he sobbed gasping sobs.

"Deep breaths, Bobby. Take big breaths." I had to shout this over the wind, the rain, the baby's wails. My shouting only upset the little boy more. A branch blew in through the hole in the roof, turning the baby into a bawling heap covered in leaves. I pulled her closer.

My own breaths were jagged work. I tried again to think. I wished I'd been more religious, I'd have prayed. The fallen maple marooned us in a grave of wet ruffles. There was no nice magic Daddy Prospero to put everything back like before and tell us we imagined the whole thing so he could teach us a lesson.

"All right, I learned my lesson, it was wrong to scheme against Wanda Keeler, stricken with mumps, wrong to snoop in this family's closet!" I cried my sins up into the hideous rains. I should have paid attention all night instead of trying on the mother's divine dress, drowned, likely, in the dumbwaiter, where I'd stuffed it.

I was the worst babysitter in the world.

The world was the worst world in the world.

Even with her swollen throat Wanda Keeler was the luckiest duck in this worst world. *Darn her and her litany of profit.*

Shirley's locket I still wore might be the only object in this house I could save. There was no story for this situation; it was *past* a situation, it was *the end*.

The harder I strained to think my way off the broken bed, out of the river ripped loose, the more confused I grew. *Make a plan, don't just cower, soaked, with these kids, Sadie.* I staggered to the room's treeless side and seized a blanket still somewhat dry, under the tipped-over rocking chair. I smoothed the blanket over the baby, and tucked it around Bobby's shoulders. His teeth chittered, poor kid.

Cold rain glued my hair down and turned my turtleneck into a sopping noose. I heard a few squawks from the baby. The bedroom's full-length mirror still clung to the wall, crooked. I shone my flashlight onto its silver and beheld there a wreck of a girl.

The river had pummeled its force into the bedroom. Somewhere, I heard a distant cry, a faraway siren, then shouts in the storm.

"Help us!" I bellowed. I'd heard the shouters; maybe they'd hear me. Nausea clenched my gut. "Someone, anyone, hear me. Mr. Sandman, hear me. Dumbwaiter, hear me and I'll never call you dumb again. Universe, hear me. Even a Communist, hear me." A litany of 'hear me's' spiraled from my mouth through choking sobs.

Why oh why didn't anyone hear me? I tried one last time. "God? You *could* hear me if you wanted to, with your God-ears. Please let these kids be all right even though I think you're a real Class 'A' *Stinker!*"

No more time to call God names.

Just when I thought it couldn't get any worse a fatal surge of wind kneed the house hard right in its stomach; one wall went *oomph*, then buckled inwards, tossing us off the mattress, into the water. Plaster vomited all over us.

The only higher place left was the roof. Out into the hurricane night. The terrier wheezed. Criminy, an asthmatic dog, too? Bobby wheezed, "wet, wet." Faith cried. She smelled bad again. How long did flashlight batteries last? We'd need light to claw our way out, along the fallen tree trunk, onto the roof. A backup beam would be a good plan. Maybe the Bannisters kept a flashlight in the bedroom. My mother did, in case of burglars. Casting my ray across the wreckage, I noted nightstands bumped sideways but intact. I'd check the drawers. I began to muscle myself off the mattress' mushy slope, then a monster cracked my head. I felt a searing pain.

Everything went black.

A form of rest, at least, syrup-thick. A slow, dark gurgle. Death. I. Guessed.

<hr />

I woke to a child's urgent cries: "Sadie, wake up! *Please! Wake up!*"

Searching for more light, I'd struck my head so hard on the fallen tree trunk it knocked me out. I fell face-first into the water, the very water waging battle on us awoke my determined lungs. Along with the little boy's fingers yanking on my hair, to raise my face above the water. On my knees, I sputtered and coughed and spewed wretched brown soup. *Water, I won't be your fish.* I'd been searching for something, but what? One shred of luck, the flashlight had flown from my hand and didn't land in the water, but on a semi-dry spot on the bed, a beaming ringlet. *Ech ech ech* went the baby, and smelled worse than before the tree fell. The evil wind had kicked parts of the house out from under us; I swore the house wept, great hooping sobs. The dog. I didn't know what had happened to him. My fingers dabbed my hurting head's gash.

I swung the flashlight's beam upwards through the branches and wet leaves, to the hole in the roof.

"Listen, Bobby," I hollered to be heard through the storm. "We've got to climb up onto the roof and you have to help me, can you be a big boy and help?" Water dripped off his hat's raccoon tail. Where was Davy Crockett when you needed him?

Teary, Bobby nodded a slow, dubious nod. He pointed to my forehead. "Buh-wod."

Blood, he must have meant. I told him I was all right, though my skull felt like it had been skewered by a giant fork.

I needed a method for ferrying the little boy and the big baby. I needed my hands to climb the maple's trunk and haul us upwards onto the roof. Then I remembered the closet. There was a heavy cotton bag, thick, like canvas, looped over the hook on the door. A laundry sack.

I groped my way over branches and jerked open the closet door. I scanned my beam across all the beautiful clothes still on their racks and shelves. The bag had a wide sturdy strap made of the same heavy cloth and an outer pocket.

The carrier called for a sharp object. Fancy pins on the hats in the closet wouldn't work, they were too delicate. I stepped out of what would soon be a clothing cemetery and back into the bedroom. There was a letter opener on the nightstand. I used it to slash two holes in the bottom of the cloth bag. Leg holes.

Over my shoulder, I slung the strap of the crude baby-carrier, bent to the sodden mattress, careful not to knock myself out this time, and with great difficulty scooped the baby, stuffed her – *peee-ew!* – into the cloth contraption. I pushed her legs down through the holes, and how she howled! She was heavy, I could only hope the carrier's sturdy weave would support her. She was one squalling millstone on my shoulders. I dumped the contents of a dresser drawer into the water and dragged the drawer to the tree trunk. Inverted, the drawer served as a step to launch us onto the trunk. I squinched my eyes up through the hole in the roof, into the tempest, where we were headed. It was there, or drown in the house. The tree that nearly killed us formed our ladder to the roof. But what if the water destroyed what remained of the roof? I couldn't even think about that.

"'Okay, Bobby,' I hollered steady as I could. "I've got Faith and I'm going to climb this trunk and tow you, too, and I'm not letting you go, all right?"

The little boy's eyes flickered through the dark. His breaths were laboured. "You're going to save us, *arn-choo*, Sadie?"

"Sure, but *now*, Bobby, come on!"

Then his jolting, hysterical cries, "No go out ooster!"

After a desperate second, I saw he meant the dog. Fires of heck what *next*?

Hearing his name, the terrier sloshed his short legs through the floodwater.

The floor convulsed beneath us. I'd seen a smaller, similar canvas-like bag in the closet. Was there time to go back? Was a dog worth it? I sent hard eyes to the wet terrier, jiggling like a pudding in an earthquake. His beseeching look and the panicked face of the little boy grasping his dog's matted neck left me no choice. I wouldn't abandon the helpless mutt to the Big Puppy-Hater to destroy. *Damn mutt!* I spat into the black hole above us, rain coursing into my open mouth. Why was the lady on the phone so daft? She'd said stay in the house, and look what came to pass. No one knew anything, not even Dr. Spock.

Still 'damn'ing, I scrambled back to the closet, seized the smaller bag and shoved Shuster, very wet, inside it. The bag whimpered, a living dishtowel, but the terrier didn't try to struggle out.

I lobbed words at Bobby. "If you want that damned dog you'll have to carry him, and he'll be heavier than you think."

Before the boy could peep an answer, I hung the bag with the terrier in it across his small shoulders. We were running out of time.

One side of the house hobbled and lurched, reeling us crazily. I gained enough footing on the tree trunk to begin climbing with my sack of stink, grasping Bobby's hand tightly. I'd stashed the flashlight inside the sack's outer pocket. I needed both hands to scale the tree trunk. "Grab the waistband of my slacks and don't let go," I ordered Bobby. I kept the light burning. I couldn't bear to be without it. Through the cloth, a small lantern appeared. Maybe someone would see it and rescue us. I worried the flashlight battery would go kaput before then. I shifted the baby-carrier so it rested on my spine, more like a backpack, though if she squirmed too much, the bag would twist around and hinder our climb.

I inched us up the rough bark, slowly, inch by painful inch. The pressure of Bobby's hands on my waistband wrenched my sanitary belt out of place. I felt warm stickiness. Near my eye a branch poked, another pierced my cheek. I groaned, lugging my bagful higher up the trunk. My hot tears, melded with cold rain, pasted my bangs to my bloody forehead. Tree bark scraped my palms. They weighed me down mightily, my burdens. The dog must have shifted his weight in the sack, making it noose-like, because Bobby gagged, the wet bundle of his pet chuffing his breath. Either that or he was dying from an asthma attack. Helpless to comfort him, I couldn't let go of the tree. I could only keep dragging him, us, upwards.

Our clothes and the heavy cloth bags soaked in so much water, the whole grim endeavour sapped my strength. I hauled my sins, too. Envy. Vanity. I bared my teeth and screeched, like an animal bleeding in the jaws of a trap.

Some branches at last, rungs for my feet. I reached around to my back, to the pocket in the baby-sack, and grabbed the flashlight. I needed to find where the roof began. There was nowhere to put the flashlight, and still crawl upwards, except my mouth, so I made my mouth a pocket of light. We'd climbed along the broken tree through what was once the attic crawl space, to the open gash in the roof.

One more grinding, teeth-clenched screech from me and I thrust my burdens out into the storm's fangs. If the house didn't sink under us, pitching us into the monstrous new lake where we'd drown, the winds would knock us senseless.

Even through the storm's roar, human cries battered my ears. Names called. Pleas for help. We'd reached the end of the world. And I only got to be fourteen.

To the roof's peak I clawed us. The baby wailed in her foul, soaked carrier. There were rasping sobs from Bobby. He wanted his mama. I wanted mine, too. Could hardly grasp hold of the peak in the gale's force. Water roiled all around us. I caught its dark, moving glint. I'd invented a baby carrier. Now I needed to invent a boat. How? Nothing was solid. Not even my slacks. Bobby's clinging tore off the side button, the zipper opened, and they stretched, sagging, downwards. My sanitary pad was soaked, I bled into the storm. The big, stinky bag a boulder around my neck.

Bobby fell quiet, yet clung to me still. I struggled for one reassuring word I could say to him, but it sapped all my energy to hold onto the roof's peak. The flashlight stuffed in my mouth kept me from offering any comfort; it made me gag as I swung its beam back and forth, hoping someone would notice my distress signal. I heard a horrible gurgling, loud, human, not far away. Suddenly I realized what the sound meant and it made me weep, and weeping jerked the flashlight loose and hurtled it down into the churning void.

The Bannisters didn't come. There was no magician, no Mr. Sandman, and sure as that flood, no God.

Bobby wouldn't be able to hang on much longer. I sensed his strength waning and now, when I *could* speak some words of comfort to him, my mouth being free of light, I had no soothing news and that was the worst feeling in the world. I should have knotted him around my waist, somehow, with one of his father's ties, the one with the leaping sturgeon.

It was so very cold. We were so very drenched where we clung to the roof, like half-dead bats, buffeted through the longest night. I wept up there where the good world had been. Where they'd had it all, made in the shade.

I couldn't tell how long we'd clung to the crooked roof peak of what had been the prettiest house on the street. There *was* no street.

The sky at last lightened to curdled milk. Distant sirens droned. Rain still drubbed us but with withered intent. My body's flow trickled, sticky, down my legs. I'd turned liquid with the rest of the world. How Bobby held on still I couldn't fathom. The bag of Faith was silent. For all I knew the hard rains had beaten her to death. Struck senseless against the tree trunk, my forehead throbbed.

The dog wriggled back to life and sent out alarmed barks. He understood the world had ended and now he must do something about this wretched state of affairs. Out of the smaller canvas bag he squirmed and onto the ragged hunk of roof. He looked about, his hairy terrier brows twitching, his barks hoarse, pitiful yodels.

We hovered not far, ten feet, maybe, above a sea of debris. It wasn't *so* light that a lantern's glow below might not push its way towards us. I heard a voice inside the beam, "Hallo? Can you hear me? *Hallo?*" The voice must have heard the dog. My vocal chords were shredded raw from calling for help through the night, and crying. But I mustered my aching throat to croak with all the puny strength left in me. "*Up here. We need help.*"

The light halted right below us. A boat flittered there, too, like a rowboat for fishing. Its sailor razzled a lantern in my tearful face. "For the love of Pete, it's a girl! Hold steady up there."

Setting aside his lantern, the sailor moved about purposefully in the boat. He uncoiled a rope with something tied to the end of it, then tossed the rope to us. The terrier barked louder. It took me a minute to grasp the sailor's concept – he'd thrown us a cord of hope. The cord jounced through the wind, still robust, the thing at the end of the cord bit into the roof right below us. It was some sort of grappling hook. The sailor had tethered himself to us. He pulled on the rope in fits and starts, towing himself closer to our ruined peak.

While he yanked his way closer, my sorrowing eyes surveyed, through grey drizzle, what remained. The houses of Humber Green Drive had accordioned into the vast mud lake. Brown water burbled, coursing over the ghostly shapes of smashed trees, half-submerged automobiles, picnic tables, blades of picket fence, chesterfields. Pianos. Golf clubs stranded in branches. Chunks of wall, pictures still clinging to them. Barbeques. This evil lake nothing like the clear blue one at Muskoka where Wanda Keeler and I roasted marshmallows and traded secrets about boys we liked at school. This lake wasn't for marshmallows or boy secrets. This sea of sorrow was nauseating sewage, rotten grass, its current deadly.

Grave water.

Suddenly there was yipping, and the terrier bounded to the edge of the peak. The slope was steep and I feared the little dog might plunge into the putrid flood but he dug his long toenails into the angle and balanced there. Bobby and Faith seemed deep in a coma, or worse. Maybe I'd killed them when I'd only striven to be the best babysitter. I'd promised their parents I'd take care of them.

The boat wobbled almost directly under us. The sailor close enough I saw he was more boy than man. He wore some kind of close-fitting black cap, like a milk-store mugger. His eyes were kind.

I hollered at the boy. "I've got two kids with me!"

"Huh? Kids? Where?"

"One's in the bag around my shoulder. Her brother is clinging to my slacks, behind me. He's – pulled them almost off me." Even in this barely-alive state I was ashamed. No boy had seen me with my pants partway down, not to mention the blood. Worst-timed monthly ever. Even the moon didn't cycle on my side.

"Tell the little boy to let go," the sailor shouted. "He'll roll down the roof. I'll catch him."

The roof's slope formed a chute of sorts, a foot or so of open water between it and the boat. That gap scared me. What if the sailor didn't catch Bobby and he fell into the swirling lake of mud? It was a miracle he'd hung on this long, and hadn't died from an asthma attack.

"Bobby," I wailed. "Did you hear? Let go of my waistband. You'll be all right Can you do that?"

He drooped there like a dishrag but had to be breathing or he'd have let go ages ago.

"Hurry!" the voice urged from the boat below. "I don't got all day!"

With no response from Bobby, I corkscrewed myself around and wrenched his small fingers one by one, free of me. It was like they were welded to my waistband. I uncurled the final finger.

"Here he comes," I called.

The little boy *bump-bumped* down the roof's slope, heartbreaking thuds. I watched him clunk and roll in what seemed slow motion. He'd been attached to me for so long, my lightness without him unsettled me. But the baby remained a bulging burden foul of smell.

The sailor reached out and hauled Bobby into the boat. The poor little boy crumbled into a heap. Shuster, yes, that was the dog's name, barked his way down the chute, shunting his tail on seeing Bobby roll, lost his footing and plunged into the muddy swell. Despite the terrier's struggle to paddle towards us, the current pulled him farther from rescue. The dog's predicament made Bobby frantic, but there was no time for comfort. The roof peak lurched, almost throwing us into the water, too. Over siren dirges from all directions, the sailor beckoned.

"You're next, Miss. Turn yourself into a spindle and push yourself away from the roof when you hit its lowest edge, mind the gap."

Faith in her baby-bag, soundless for so long, I'd begun to fear the worst, maybe she'd been smothered. But she chose this moment to kick and squall. I bawled to our rescuer, "How'll I roll with *her* on my back? I'll squash her!"

The sailor bristled. "You got a better idea?"

I became a spindle, a rough, makeshift sort. The baby screeched and hunchbacked me as I struggled to propel my spooling, blood-soaked body downwards in a way likely to do least baby-harm. I felt a wet surge against my back. She peed on our descent. I surely hurt her on my final push because she sent out a torturous shriek and I shrieked along with her. On the final bit of roof my slacks snagged on something sharp and ripped wide open. My shame was complete. But a final surge of strength propelled us over the gap far enough for the sailor to grab my upper arms and drag me, with Faith, into the boat, his frame slender but his arms strong.

With all of us in the boat except the tragic terrier, the vessel wallowed low, the muddy water quite near its rim.

"You're pretty torn up," our rescuer said. "And what happened to your forehead?"

I started to bawl. Not waiting for an answer, he pulled the baby out of the homemade carrier and passed her, squalling, to me. How many of her bones broken, who knew? She kept crying, upsetting her brother even more.

It was fully light. A panting sound closed in on us. Somehow, the dog, pumping his short legs, paddled towards us.

"Shuster!" I was crazily glad, despite my shameful state. Bobby's sobs turned to joyful gulps as the sailor snagged the terrier and lifted him into our little ark. The dog shook himself, showering us with mud. Wagging lustily, licking Bobby's face. The baby stopped screeching so maybe I hadn't crushed her bones.

We were all in the boat.

But the boat remained hooked to the ruined roof. And the water's swell, still higher. Taking a handkerchief from his jeans pocket, the sailor dabbed at my bloody forehead. I'd be left with a disfiguring scar, likely. During his first aid, I noted he wore his denim jeans rolled at the bottom like Marlon Brando in *The Wild One*. Our rescuer had a lean, arresting look, like Brando's when he walked into the café. His kind eyes I'd first seen, stayed kind. I couldn't tell anything about his hair because of the mugger's hat.

"I'm Cullen," the sailor said. "Quick."

At first I thought he was giving an order until it struck me Quick must be his last name. I was dizzy. Ashamed. I laid the soaked baby-sack over my disastrous nether parts. Quick swabbed my bloody face again. His glove-fingers had been lopped off. "That your baby?"

"Oh gosh, no."

He jerked his thumb towards Bobby. "This one?"

I shook my head.

"Good thing. You're just a baby yourself. Then what's your tale, nightingale?"

This wasn't story time. "I'm the babysitter. Hey, aren't you worried we're still hooked to the house? What if it drags us under? It almost killed me and these kids already."

"Yeah, I'm worried, Babysitter." He got moving again, grunting with exertion, his hands grabbing the rope, hand over hand, until he released the hook and freed us to float away from the roof.

Suddenly, though, a demon wind slammed a muddy tidal wave over the boat, dousing us, and snatching Bobby into its maw. Before we could blink the mud from our eyes the little boy had been ripped, choking, away from us, the puffed back of his pajamas a balloon from a nightmare. We shouted at him to hang on, but to *what*? He grew smaller and smaller, his cries fainter. Soon he was just a speck in the flood's roiling muck.

The dog jumped in after Bobby and spun through the current, a receding dot. Bobby and the dog were gone so fast.

Absolute lifesaver. I heard this in Shirley Bannister's telephone voice.

"I'm *no* lifesaver – I'm an – *absolute failure!*" These words I wailed to the sailor.

He didn't answer. His small boat had taken on gallons of wretched silty tidal wave. Tossing a bucket to me, the sailor commanded, "Bail! Bail as fast as you can." He dipped and dumped. I dipped and dumped too, and we rose a bit higher in the water.

Through my tears, I didn't see the baby in the boat. Didn't smell her.

"Mister – Quick – the *baby!*"

He was thinking the same, groping over the boat's edge, clawing the murk with his hands. Desperate, empty claws until my eyes followed the sound, burbled shrieks, to a curve of floating chocolate with fists.

"*There!*"

The baby was barely near enough the boat to reach. The sailor leaned so far over its edge, what if *he* tumbled into the flood, too, leaving me alone in a boat at the end of the world? He must have had the same thought, for he grabbed my hand, to turn us into a sort of chain. I gripped the side of the boat with my other hand, that hand alone keeping us out of the flood.

The sailor lifted the blubbering mud-baby into the boat and shoved her into my arms. She was so heavy I didn't know how she hadn't sunk like a stone. She was completely caked with mud, even the open hole of her mouth, gasping, wailing, mud. Mud with lungs. Now two smaller slits, her eyes, one canting crazily to one side of the boat. "*Boo!*" she cried, clutching my arm so hard it hurt. "A *boo!*"

We saw where her crazed eye locked. One rubber boot. Bobby's. At the bottom of the boat.

A camper floated on its side not far away. Several people clustered on its highest part, shouting at us. Cullen hollered over to them, trying to explain the lost little boy. They only tipped their hands upwards in 'we can't hear you' gestures. They receded down the dark, moving lake.

Slimed with mud and blood, clutching Faith, I slumped in the boat. I wiped mud off the baby; her skin had turned blue. She was that cold. All I kept saying was, "Sadie the failure. Promise-breaker!" The sailor gave my shoulders a brief squeeze and said it wasn't my fault. He told me I was in shock, and wasn't thinking straight. He told me, "It's a *natural disaster*, kid." But nothing made it better. Casting my eyes across Heartbreak Lake I wondered how far it extended. Was all of Toronto under water? Where were the Bannisters? How wretched they'd feel about Bobby. How badly I'd failed them. Where was my mother? She'd be beyond frantic. I stared at the muddy bundle in my arms. Bawling for attention. Crying for all the right reasons. Hunger. Cold. She wanted *her* mother. And me so wrung out, my brain in shards, I couldn't recall her name.

Faith. Yes, that was it. Faith. Such an optimistic name her parents had chosen.

What I'd heard on radio news, after other, faraway catastrophes, was there were places people could go, relief stations. Surely the Bannisters were waiting at one of these. What would happen when they heard about Bobby? They might have me cuffed, arrested, hauled to jail. One of those hellish prisons we'd learned about at school. I'd wear the same outfit with a number on my back every day for the rest of my life. Not a hint of any of this on Forest's instruction sheet left on the counter in the kitchen, and now forever gone. I needed to hand over their baby. I told Cullen Quick to take her to a relief station. Along with a message: *Forgive me. I did the best I could.*

"I don't need to tell you it's bedlam out there," he said. "We'll take her to my place, get her cleaned up first. You, too. Until things settle down. You both need rest more than anything."

"We need a doctor," I argued.

"It's not like we can phone one. Listen, I know first aid," Cullen said. "I can tell if anything's broken. I'll patch you two up."

I was too exhausted to argue. All my fight sunk with the house. I felt as dead as Bobby's rubber boot in the boat. The sailor rowed like a varsity athlete, shunting us around debris, to the shore of that mud sea. Shore? More like marshy verge. A long, rickety dock, almost submerged in the flood, led to wooden steps, then up higher, to a faded building on a hill. We'd have to slog through floodwater swamp, who knew how deep, to reach it. I thought of Bobby. I couldn't lose the baby, too.

The only warmth left in me were tears tacking over my cheekbones. "No, no more water, please. I can't go through that swamp. This baby can't."

"You're not alone this time, kid. I've got you. Her, too. You can't stay in this boat."

So violent, my shaking, as we pushed through the reeds and floodwater to our knees, I could hardly keep hold of the silt-slimed baby. Cullen held my arm to steady me, and hauled the boat by a long rope with his other arm. He was strong. He tied the boat to the dock. Dragged me, the baby slumped heavily in my arms, to the ramshackle building's back stairway. Then he led us into a large, rough room with a barn feel. He lowered me down onto a cot, the baby spooned in beside me.

"My digs aren't fancy," Cullen said. "But it's home."

Then he got busy. He gently prodded the baby and declared no bones broken. He tore his own shirts into strips to make pads for me and diapers for Faith. "Lady rags. Baby rags." He gave me an odd, long shirt to wear, a nightshirt, I guessed. All that mattered, it was dry. He heated water on his hot plate for a sponge bath for us. He was gentle with the baby. He turned his back to give me privacy while I cleaned myself. Then Cullen heated broth on a hot plate for me and found milk in his icebox for the baby. He blanketed us when we laid back down on the cot. As I tumbled, exhausted, closer to sleep, scratchy voices reached me – his, others. Snatches of him describing Bobby.

When I awoke at last, Cullen was feeding the big baby something that looked like custard.

"Who were you talking to a while ago?" I asked my rescuer. "And how? It didn't sound like a telephone, besides those died."

"Ham radio," he answered. "Chums of mine. They're out doing rescue work. Pulling people from the flood. I was out helping, too."

The baby seemed calm enough. Cullen must have cleaned the cut on my head while I slept. I touched my fingers there lightly and felt a bandage.

His place had a wood stove with a crackling fire.

"How long did I sleep?" I asked, fogged.

"Eight hours, almost. But you must have been awake in spurts long enough to care for that mite" – his thumb jerked towards the baby – "she seems peaceful enough. I shouldn't have let you sleep, though, you could've fell into a coma from your banged head, but you were so wrung out, it would've been cruel to keep you from sleep."

He asked me my name. *Absolute Failure.*

He asked me what day it was. *The day after the world ended.*

He told me I wasn't funny. He was trying to tell if I had brain damage.

I said he was right, it *wasn't* funny.

The baby had slept soundly. The baby was alive. Then I remembered Cullen had left cold porridge for her and diaper rags.

I'd awakened when she cried, changed her, fed her, rocked her. Slept in the gaps of her needs.

Cullen couldn't sit still for long. He handed Faith over to me while he scrambled eggs. He no longer wore his milk-store mugger's hat. His hair was brown, crew cut. Groggily I gazed around his large room. A leak in the ceiling drip-dripped into a chamber pot. Several large paper pin-up girls smiled down from the plywood walls. A crude counter extended from one end of the place to the other, cluttered with jars and beakers like in science class, Bunsen burners. Faint, charred smells reached me. Dried plants dangled from the rafters, long-stemmed, bundled.

Stirring eggs, he saw me study the raftered bundles. "Poppies," he said, like this was nothing out of the ordinary.

He peppered the eggs. "Hey, you got a last name, kid?"

"Wilder." I don't know why it mattered. I was a zero, a nothing. I'd failed on a grand scale. I was still so tired. I lowered Faith onto the cot, then maneuvered myself to my feet. Balancing was tricky, my body felt like it was still in the boat. It felt like nothing under me would ever be solid again.

Cullen set two plates out on a rough wood table. He poured boiled water from the kettle on the hot plate into two tin cups. He beckoned me to the table. Distant voices rumbled. More ham chums, I guessed. Ham and eggs.

My mind's eye saw Bobby, snatched by the evil current. Suddenly I wasn't hungry. I could only cry there at the table.

"I don't want to go to jail," I sobbed.

He said I should really eat my eggs. "It's not your fault, kid. Can't you grasp that fact?"

I shook my head. My promise had been to keep Bobby safe. That was a fact. I thought about how he'd first burst into the room, all freckles and toy pistols flaring and though that frazzled me, beneath the frazzle I'd loved him right away. That was another fact.

Cullen arranged some queer cigarette. "Not your fault, kid," he repeated, flaming it. Inhaling hard. *"Act – of – God."*

His cigarette smelled like a plant dredged from the flood, then dried. The smoke was setting off my stomach. To wave its wafts away I raised my hand, an abrupt, jerking motion that toppled the plate of eggs to the floor. "You're *wrong*, Sailor. It can't be an act of God. *There is no God!* Only failed babysitters."

The baby began to cry. My stormy voice had upset her.

Cullen held his cigarette out to me in offer. "Try some? Might make you feel steadier."

"Is that *drugs?*" I asked. "Drugs make people *dangerous and insane*. We learned that in school, they showed us a film."

He laughed for a full minute. His eyes comedic through the smoke. "You believe everything they tell you in school, kid? Swallow it, hook line and sinker, doo-ya? If they're such geniuses at your school, or *anywhere* in this city, for that matter, why didn't they know the hurricane was headed this way?"

I had no answers. "Are you a communist, too?"

Cullen Quick didn't deny this. A communist who used drugs, yet he'd saved us, nursed us, fed us, and all I'd done in return was call him names and topple the scrambled eggs.

He pulled in more smoke as I stared at the floor. "That's the last of the eggs, kid. You want them now, you'll have to eat them off the planks. And there's not a root vegetable anywhere. Hurricane tore them right out of the earth, even up at Holland Marsh. My ham radio associates told me."

A long moment passed. Cullen stubbed his cigarette, then turned the hot plate burner on again to boil more water. He sat back down at the table, across from me.

"I'm not dangerous *or* insane, Babysitter," he said.

"Don't call me that. My name is Sadie. *Sadie.*"

"Swell you remember it. With your head cracked open like that."

The baby erupted into wails. Cullen fed her some warm milk and after a few minutes, she settled.

Silently, I prayed to what stars might remain that she wouldn't remember any of this.

Cullen Quick left for more rescue work, so many were still lost. He promised he'd try to find out about the Bannisters. And my mother. Rose Wilder, I told him. Last known whereabouts, Don Vale Textiles. He'd tossed me a package of lifesaver candy. "That's all the food I got left, sorry."

Much later, time still a grainy shuttered strand of film, Cullen tramped back, flicked a cigarette from his shirt pocket, and lit it. Regular smoke. I sat up in the cot.

"Those Bannister people drowned in the Humber River. The city posted lists. Trapped in their car, likely." He swooshed his smoky hand through the air, towards Faith. "That mite's an orphan now."

I felt sure there was more. There *was*. "Lots still missing. But, kid –"

"Cullen?"

"A hydro pole crashed down on that factory where your mother works. Worked. Sparked an electrical fire. Her and one other lady died. They found your mother's scissors, shears, whatever, all charred. Sadie, I'm sorry. I wish it weren't me, telling you."

"Wait," I said. "How do you know this?"

"Like I told you, they got lists," Cullen said. "In the relief stations. The part about the fire, one of my associates told me, no reason to tell me something like that, kid, if it weren't true."

Fire. Water. Burnt in a flood? Why didn't the water extinguish the flames? The world had stopped making sense long ago. Yesterday.

Cullen's report pressed me deep into the earth. I cried for hours. Then slept again. The same heavy syrup sleep as when the Bannisters' stately maple punched out my lights. Just one more thing they didn't tell us in school, how grief exhausted a person to the bones.

I didn't think I'd ever crawl out of the earth again, after Cullen's report.

When I awoke, the rubbery bit of egg I picked off the floor had gone very cold. I didn't see Cullen. Or smell his smoke. He must have been out rescuing more people, or finding food. Beside me on the cot, the baby stirred. Wiggled, restless. I set her down on the floor for something different. She had no toys. I thought of her carousel, its miniature horses on their twist poles. She used to have such pretty toys. Now she had a plank floor. She bumbled about on her bottom then suddenly pushed herself higher. She stood up on her chubby legs. Wobbled. Took one step, then another – I cheered her on – then another. Three little reeling steps, but *steps!* Faith stayed on her feet and walked right *to* me! I clasped her waist; her steps were the last bright things in the world.

Sudden tears splashed down from me onto Faith's head. Her mother hadn't seen her baby's first steps. That same baby looked up at me, stamping her feet in a comical way, like she'd found the best toy, her own legs. Like she wanted to run back home.

I wiped her head dry with my sleeve and looked at her with her funny eye. She waved at me, gurgling, a balled-up Kleenex, fisted in her hand. I pulled her closer. Her face sparked a smile.

"*Mama!*"

"No, Plum. I'm not your Mama."

Her face crumpled, shadowed – my words had done this to her. Suddenly I was swamped with pity. None of this had been her fault. Nor could she help it that her brother had been the cute one. A new fact throbbed through my weary limbs; some permanent glue fastened her to me. Neither of us had a mother. Was I still her babysitter? When did I stop being her babysitter? Did I *ever*?

I'd promised to take care of her. I'd voiced those words, but I might as well have etched them in stone; a blade blown by wind, slicing through air, carved our names onto each other, looping the 'a's and 'i's. *Sadie. Faith.* Lodged within each other's vowels, we were. Our names, melded, stitched together from the world's remaining rags. Spoken at the same time, our names should have sounded something like 'safe'.

I had to keep her safe. She was all I had left. I was the only person who'd seen her first steps. She'd walked right to me. Who would she walk with now, if not me? She might be all that could keep me above the earth. And who else did I have now? These thoughts hurt my head. It would have been so easy to have Cullen just take her away to a relief station. But I couldn't. She was lodged inside my story, and I inside hers. We were, I imagined, like two soldiers who'd been through a war together.

Again, her broad smile, crooked eyes, and cheerful shriek rent my heart. "Boo, Mama! A *boo!*"

I thought she must have meant her lost brother's boot, in the boat.

She'd done it, my face burst into a flood for every last lost boot out there in the world. For Bobby.

Then Faith, whose vowels would be looped, always, through mine, reached out and, with the Kleenex balled in her hand, took urgent swipes at my tears. She dabbed them dry.

"No wa-wa, Mama," she said.

No water.
Our thoughts threaded through the same needle.

Cullen Quick asked if there was anywhere we could go. He couldn't keep us. There was no more food, among other things. After my complete failure as a babysitter, I couldn't face the Keelers. Anyway, maybe they were dead, too. Wanda and her beautiful litany of profit. I spun my thoughts hard to avoid the fact; there was only one place to go. I didn't want to travel to the lonely farm up north, my grandmother's. Della-Mae McCann. She'd cut off contact with my mother for marrying my father, 'one of *that* ilk'. My grandmother didn't know I lived and breathed. She didn't know my father was a prince of a man. Then his sickness, she'd never know him. People shouldn't be so mean about other people. We all float down the same river. No, the vowels of my name would never mingle with the farm-grandmother's, but we needed dry land. Faith needed food. And no matter what Della-Mae thought about my father, whether or not the cold shelf of her heart's larder held even a single mason jar of mercy, she needed to hear what had happened to her daughter, Rose. To us.

I told Cullen, "maybe we should phone my grandmother first, try getting her number from Information, let her know we're coming?"

He shrugged. "Got no phone, only my ham radio. And lots of phone booths blew away in the hurricane, remember? Do you know where she lives?"

My mother used to recite this jingle, when I was small. *Beware the Witch of Tipping Creek, Concession 3, by the old elm tree. Long dirt laneway. Stay away from Della-Mae.* I hated this glum ditty, it brought shivers.

Now it was a map.

The world's last remaining map.

⟡———⟡

Cullen had an associate with a van. He'd drive us to 'the boon-docks' for $5.00 – gas, vehicle wear and tear. "They barely got *roads* up there," he'd kvetched to Cullen.

"I don't have $5.00," I lamented.

Cullen would pay, in return for a favour from me. He pressed a small package into my hand. "They're seeds," he said. "Plant them in May. In a sunny spot. Behind the barn, maybe. Keep your mouth shut about them, no blabbing to the hillbil-lies. In summer, I'll blow up there, harvest them, and see how you and that baby are holding up."

No doubt he saw my eyes spout, water globes.

"I'll go with you now, Sadie, to this farm; then I'll know where to find you."

The driver of the panel van was surly, his smell like the onions rotting everywhere in ruined gardens; we smelled the decay through the van's open window.

For a long time, we beetled north. Canted west, then north again, west, then north. A lurching, rick-rack road. Bobby's puffed Roy Rogers pajamas tossing in the horrible flood-swell, away from me, made a wretched picture in my mind as the miles passed. I thought about my own mother. Slow tears dripped from me; the bumpy road bounced them down onto the baby's sleeping head. Cullen had given me his only towel, to wrap around Faith.

Finally, we stopped at a crossroad, gas station. I thought the sign said Marsville, but my eyes smarted, blurred, from crying.

The driver stayed surly. I asked if I could dash inside to use the bathroom.

"Make it snappy," he groused.

"Hey, go easy on the girl. She's been through the wringer and then some," I heard Cullen tell his associate.

Fires of heck, what a blessing Cullen rode with us. I handed the baby over to him. As I scurried through the cluttered gas station – luckily the bathroom key hung on a hook easy to spot – all I heard through the station's diner section, was, *Hazel. That Hazel.* Was she missing, too?

We drove through keener hunger. The front seat fogged with smoke. After about another hour, the van jounced along Concession 3. The old elm tree. Long dirt laneway. Hand-lettered mailbox: *D-M McCann.*

"This is it," I said.

We stopped. I gathered Faith. Cullen Quick helped us out of the van, said, "make sure you got them seeds, kid."

I told him I did.

"C'mon, Quick. Stop writing a book. Let's drop your little girlfriend off and get back to the city," the van driver hollered out to us.

Cullen gave my shoulders a quick squeeze and patted Faith on her head. This was meant to comfort her, but she started to whimper.

I started to whimper.

"Good luck, Sadie," Cullen said, as he folded himself back into the van.

"I'm sorry I called you dangerous and insane," I called out to him. "You're not." I couldn't tell if he heard.

The van's tires sprayed gravel as it burned southbound rubber. Its passenger door flung open and an object hurtled through the air. I ducked so it didn't bean my head. Soon the van was a plume of dust in the distance. The air was cooler in the north. I'd no jacket. The baby, at least, had her towel.

I looked down at the hurtled object. A boot. Bobby's. I couldn't abandon it to road dust, it was all I had of him. I shoved the sad little rubber sole under the towel, against the baby. I slogged forward on my ruined feet that would never dance in saddle shoes, down the long dirt laneway, into tomorrow.

THE MARL HARROWER

(Almost Twenty Years Later)

The small things that end the world: fungi; maraschino cherries; a locket; a wig-hat; little sparkly disks with tassels; spirit gum; a bit of spangled string; darkening mood ring; spruce seedlings; blackflies; brief girls; a Frisbee dusty on the sill, idle as an abandoned dinner plate.

My mother has always associated me with a bad smell; at least, that's how it often seemed. When I entered a room, her habit was to behold me like I'd brought an *odour* with me. Her nose went all rabbity, quick, wiggling sniffs.

"*What?*" I'd ask about her bad-smell look. "*What?*"

"Oh, Faith. I was just thinking of when you were a baby."

"*Groovy*. Do you remember anything *nice* about that time?"

"Of *course*. I saw the *first steps* you took, *right there*, I was. And good grief, you're *nineteen* already."

Then she went closed clam. Gads, my mother was hard to propel forward in a conversation. She was more the looping-back type. Or clam. Even Malibu Barbie, with her dramatic eye-liner, and plastic toes poking into my ribs to signal agreement, communicated better. I used school writing assignments as an echo chamber, a way to talk. They were the *only* good thing about All Disciples Secondary School. I wrote: *Most days the air hung like a heavy soup in that place of vapours and mists, marl and swamp and silt. Stone-pocked pastures wedged between tracts of brambled waste. The doors of our outbuildings whined, swaying on their rusty hinges on the stillest day, no one in sight. That's why Malibu Barbie's pretty hours passed inside her special pocket sewn to my jacket's lining. For comfort. The Marl Harrower was never far away.*

The English teacher said our homework had been to write about home, not a ghost story. She'd buttonholed me after class, on my way out the door. And, she wanted to know, what, *exactly*, was a Marl Harrower?

"It's *this thing, this lurking force*; it lives in low, swampy places on our land. This *whole county*, I think. It comes out at night. Brings nightmares. Crams my mouth with clay and mud, and pulls me down into its darkness where I can't breathe. It harrows me."

She asked if things were steady at home.

She kept using that word, *home*.

"Steady as ever," I'd replied.

Steady? My mother and I were about as steady as two souls pushing a cart loaded with sodden clay over a swing-bridge built from popsicle sticks. At one end of the bridge, the farm, the chickens. At the other end, *life*. We were stranded with our burden in the middle; the bridge sagged, who knew how long the popsicle sticks would hold? Below us, a deep canyon filled with sludge and sinking sand. I'd seen that place in my nightmares many times.

I'd lift my hand from the cart handle long enough to point to the shore called *life*. "I think we should go *that* way," I'd call out to my mother. Pallor-stricken, weary from struggling with the cart, she'd yell back, "Oh no, Faith, we need to push the cart the *other* way." She meant the farm. We'd never agree. Just remain where we were, stuck on that flimsy bridge. And sure enough, I'd hear the splintering sounds from the popsicle sticks, then feel myself falling, my mouth crammed with mud to mute my screams. Then someone would be shaking me while I gasped and flailed. My mother. "Faith, you've had another one of your nightmares. It's alright. You're *back*. You're *alive*."

But it *wasn't* alright. Most days the air hung like a heavy soup in that place of vapours and mists. It *wasn't* a ghost story; it was our lives, my mother's, mine, and Malibu Barbie in her safety pocket like a soft kangaroo pouch I'd made to carry her close.

I'd once asked my mother what she thought brought on my nightmares.

She'd looked pained. "There was a terrible rainstorm when you were a baby. It left these pools of muddy water all over the yard. You fell into one face-first, I hauled you out. Good thing I was right there. You've been spooked by water ever since. And you're lucky to be alive, a person can drown in an inch of lousy water, they can."

We were planting potatoes one day. I stood to straighten my back and spoke to my mother's bent form. "Have *you* ever felt like there's a dark force, lurking, waiting to wipe you out?"

She didn't turn, just jabbed her potato piece into the soft earth. Her voice reached me muffled. "I did, Faith. And I was right. Now let's plant these potatoes."

I longed to know *where*, *exactly*, she'd felt it. When. But she planted fiercely, which told me she was knotted tighter than macramé when it came to that topic.

For the past year, my mouth had been sending this prayer upwards into the barn dust: "Please God, let me funky-chicken-dance out of here and into *life*! Otherwise I'll be sentenced to these mournful fields, riddled with pangs, to the egg shed and funeral announcements on Tipping Creek Radio. "*CKCR Tipping Your Day!*" People *lived* for that death roll call – it made them feel blessed to slog over the stubble – and, bonus, the radio program was basically a list of free meals, since every funeral was followed by food.

The only fun anyone seemed to have around this county was crafts. People were always making things out of popsicle sticks. Lampshades. Small cabins that sheltered free ballpoint pens from the farm insurance company.

Macramé was the purest art, each hitch, each knot, had to be firm and exact, or the whole project unraveled. I liked to think the macramé hangings I fashioned would hold if dragged through a landslide. The one thing I was good at was knots; the other was marathons.

My mother didn't do crafts. I wish she did, maybe crafts would, somehow, have evened out her quirks. Her bad-smell look, around me, was only one quirk. Another was her habit, suddenly, during chicken chores, of scanning me with urgent eyes – "Faith, you're lucky to be *alive!*" Or we'd be in Tipping Creek Grocery and she'd turn to me in the detergent aisle and say, "Faith, you're *alive!*" *Man*, that was embarrassing, sometimes kids from my school were in the store, or their parents, hearing this. Still, it was hard to be cross with my mother. In those moments, she seemed spun from only her spoken words, as if formed from air, like she could easily vanish in a puff of feather dust.

But if I was so lucky to be alive there on the farm, why did I keep a small suitcase packed with a change of clothes for me, and one for Malibu Barbie, under my bed?

Last week, my mother caught me saying my funky-chicken prayer. I hadn't heard her footfall in the egg shed. Her hurt look tore straight down to her hands and yellow yolk-goo splatted over her rigid wrists. She hardly ever lost an egg, every broken shell shrunk our cheque from the poultry company. People think chickens eject shiny white eggs in neat rows all ready for the breakfast menu. Wrong. It's a dirty business, the way eggs enter our world, rolling into scruff and mites and manure. Human eyes inspect each shell, buff away the barn scruff. I told my mother some day giant machines would wash eggs, our hands wouldn't be needed, and she just laughed, which was groovy because she didn't laugh easily if a Frisbee wasn't involved.

Hearing my prayer to dance out of there, my mother looked – no other word for it – *wounded*. She seized another egg, the dirtiest one in the basket, and swiped at it roughly with her brush. Miraculously, its shell held. "And what's *so very awful* about being here with me, Faith, *what?* We do *nice* things, like Frisbee. And the garden."

It was true. We had our good moments. And when my mother leaped high above the grass to catch the Frisbee her hair, short as the brush we used to scrub pots, shot straight up, turned into cartoon hair, and I wished I'd bought a camera with my share of last year's morel profits instead of platform sandals; I was already too tall. A camera would have snapped her Frisbee bliss. Grooviest of all, in mid-leap she'd laugh and chime out sounds like bells, like *a-lang-a-ding-a-ding*! She never struck happy, bohemian notes like that any other time.

"Let me get to the *straight edge* of this, then, Faith. All you've ever wanted was to *get away* from me? *That's* your prayer? Not world peace, anything like that?"

'No, no! It's *not you*, it's this place, it's –"

But it was pointless, trying to explain. My mother would never understand how these forlorn swampy wastes ruled us, how they had it in for *me* in particular, watching, waiting for the right moment to push me into a living grave where I couldn't see my way out or breathe for *the sheer sorrow of it all*, and – this force – would one night win if I didn't leave, and soon. My mother could tell me how lucky I was to be alive until the clouds fell, but it wouldn't banish the bad feeling this place had always given me. She'd inherited the farm from my great-grandmother, Della-Mae, who'd meant her to feel that these thorny fields were some blessed, shining gift.

One woman's gift is another woman's curse, I told Malibu Barbie. Her plastic toes poked into my ribs; she dug my concept.

<hr />

By early May, my mother had been fretting that I wouldn't scratch through the year and receive my high school diploma. English was ace, but other teachers sent her notes of concern. *I'd* been fretting, too. My fate rested on Environmental Science. They were *high* on it. It was *the very cutting edge* of their *progressive curriculum.* Man, I just *couldn't do it.* I couldn't trudge down into the boggy hell behind All Disciples and collect my sludgy little sample of swamp water with microscopic beasties paddling around in there, then observe those same beasties pulsing in their little glass quagmires that grew scummier each day. I tried. Once. I needed that course to pass. I teetered in my platform sandals to the swamp's edge, trying not to imagine what might lurk down in that gross, stagnant murk that smelled like rancid egg salad, and was likely run-off from The Lake of Marl near All Disciples Secondary School.

Only in Tipping Creek County would they build a school near a stinking lake, the perfect habitat for The Marl Harrower.

As I lowered my sample beaker, that very Harrower grasped me by the throat. I gasped, choking, for air, like a heart attack even though nineteen is too young for an attacked heart, and this voice inside me screamed *Faith, run!* I raced back up the hill and into the Environmental Science room, my empty beaker quaking in my hands. I told the teacher something spooked me, tried to *get me*, down there. He only scowled and said, "this isn't *drama class*, Faith, do better tomorrow."

But I couldn't go back. Such a foul, boggy place, teeming with microscopic monsters. For the other kids, Environmental Science was a joke; they weren't collecting samples, they were smoking, goofing off, and I'd heard worse, that a girl got swarmed by greasers down in the marsh behind the school. The teacher just sent us off on our own to collect cups of rancid water.

I didn't even want a goldfish. My brief friend Katie, an All Disciples girl whose family moved away suddenly, gave me one for my birthday last year. I had to return it. I wouldn't be able to change its water, those thready turds would become their own swamp and the swamp would wake The Harrower. I managed to carry the goldfish home to the farm in its squishy bag for one night, so I wouldn't hurt my friend's feelings. Then I told my mother it would die.

"All things die, Faith," she said. "Goldfish top the list, they do."

That wasn't helpful.

Our final English project was a speech about someone we admire. Our idol. Our "beacon in the dark." Most girls chose their mothers. For the boys, hockey stars or guitar players or astronauts or their fathers. One kid ranted about how we're meant to have a single idol, God, who'll fly into a jealous fury and flatten our crops if we worship anyone else. Typical All Disciples, a sermon lurking in the swale.

Hairy eyeballs burrowed into me when I presented my idol, Betty Kennedy from *Front Page Challenge*: classy, smart, unflappable, her probes so elegant, her aura so serene. Betty Kennedy chased down the truth. And she had glamorous hair. Dark, like mine. My mother's lid was washed-out like undercooked corn bread. Except for bangs she kept long to cover a scar on her forehead, she was shorn like a summer sheep, ever since her heart got battered at Woodstock, the Festival of Love. She'd caught Cullen Quick shagging some hippie chick between Janis Joplin and Sly and the Family Stone. Somehow, in the crowds swirling like mud flies, she'd gotten separated from him. She'd been parched and needed his water flask, then saw his sandals, the chick's sandals, in a shoe-orgy nearby. She banished Cullen from our farm after that and ravaged her hair with the sewing scissors. I left the hair part out of my speech, the Festival of Love, too.

I missed Cullen. I liked how he mowed the lawn, with that slow, cambered attention, his zagging switchbacks, smoke twisting from his mouth's grim set, his long hair tied back. I liked how tending the plants my mother let him grow behind our barn lit his face. And *he* never thought it was any big federal case that I talked to Malibu Barbie and she talked to me. Everyone needed a friend.

No one mowed the grass after Cullen. Our lawn became Dandelion Island. It looked like a jet-plane loaded with canaries had crash-landed, bringing an air of disaster to the farm. If Great Grandmother Della-Mae still lived, she'd have gone ape in her apron over that scraggy mess. Tipping Creek County prided itself on well-kept gardens and lawns.

My Betty Kennedy talk wasn't the only time the other kids lobbed bloodsucker looks or chucked mean words my way. They sharpened their word-knives inside the school bus rumbling us over dirt roads to and from our farms.

One kid above all, Otis Greebing, mullet-boy: "Hey, Faith, your mom chop her pigtails yet? How come she's so young?"

The bus was an orange crate of misery on wheels. Mullet-head sparked other kids. "Your mother take a roll in the hay when she was *twelve*, Faith? What's wrong with *you*? Late bloomer?"

"Who's your daddy, Faith? He a juvie, too?"

One day, in the parking lot behind All Disciples, Malibu Barbie tumbled out of her special pocket in my jacket. I'd bent to scoop what I thought was a two-dollar bill on the concrete, but it was only a crumpled shard of brown paper bag. A few boys, that Greebing hornet at the helm, strutted over. "What? Grade thirteen and still playing with *dolls*, Faith? You should have walked in your *mama's* shoes, you'd have a *real doll* to play with by now!" Then Otis did something terrible; before I could scoop Malibu Barbie back into her travelling pocket, he grabbed her and with one violent twist, like he wrung a chicken's neck, snapped the doll's throat and tossed her, in two pieces, back onto the concrete. He laughed and strutted away.

I duct taped Malibu Barbie's head back onto her body when I got home that night. She'd wear the neck brace for the rest of her life. What cruelty, part of the venom that seeped, like a poison gas, from the fields of Tipping Creek County, a morose world where no one forgot anything from one generation to the next. They formed one picture of you, like a frozen TV dinner, and you'd never be anyone else. You'd never be any other flavour, they'd never change the channel. My mother, I'd heard from other kids at school, who'd heard it from the town gossips, was forever the fourteen-year-old girl lugging a baby down the long dirt laneway to Della-Mae McCann's house. Likely *to this day* Tipping Creekers nod their knowing heads and say, "That's what happens when you go to Toronto. You don't come back empty-handed. You return with your arms full of shame, like the Wilder girl back in '54. Draw a lesson from *that*, girls."

That shame was *me*. Heavy in arms. Della-Mae made sure I knew that every day. Woe was her! Woe was my mother! Woe was me! The only good that came of it, she liked to say, was the extra help from my mother on the farm.

I worked to jump start sorrow the day, ten years ago, when Della-Mae collapsed in the dandelions she'd hated; woe had wound itself, like a giant yarn ball, so tight around her woeful heart, it blocked the blood that pumped the woe through her woeful veins.

I'd always liked reading out loud, my own voice resonating back to me. My only audience, often, Malibu Barbie. But as soon as I read my "Betty Kennedy, Angel of Calm" paper to my mother, I saw that it was a mistake. My hunch: it made her blue I hadn't chosen *her* as my idol. When I came to the part, "Betty Kennedy's serenity is a tonic, albeit temporary, for my nightmares," my mother cringed, needed no reminder; she'd heard my night-screams for years. I tucked the paper back in my satchel.

Front Page Challenge gave my mother bad nerves. She didn't like the unknown person, the mystery guest, hiding behind the screen. I don't know what I'd *thought*, sharing my paper with her. I guess sometimes you just want to be heard on your own turf, kick at the words you already imagine inked on your report card beside Environmental Science: *Faith exhibits loner behaviour. Does not participate in field experiments. It isn't possible to award a passing grade.*

Maybe I thought the words I'd written could save me a little.

Bad Nerves? If *any*thing gave a person bad nerves, it was chickens! They lived by the laws of suspicion and mass panic. As soon as we entered their pen to feed them or collect eggs, just as we'd done *every* day, they'd flap crazily into the air, sending up one big storm cloud of feathers and dust and petrified squawks as sour as the concert band at All Disciples.

Even though those dumb birds had seen us every day of their lives, they mistook us for foxes. They never remembered. They never figured out we were on their side. Their brouhaha was contagious; I never got used to it. Their mass panic startled me every time.

I'd wanted to read "Betty Kennedy, Angel of Calm," to my mother to show her I was good at something besides macramé plant hangers and woven string belts and chokers. She'd warned me that macramé projects were a fine hobby, but a girl shouldn't hope to build a career on string. She'd also said it wasn't normal for *Front Page Challenge* to be a teenager's favourite show (she kept forgetting I was pushing twenty).

"Faith!" She'd holler through the screen door: "why don't you turn off that program, come out into the sunshine, and throw the Frisbee with me!" Or, her mittened thuds on the frosted frame: "Faith, grab a snow shovel and pitch in out here!" Or late winter: "Faith, let's spigot some maples for syrup." Or spring, through the open kitchen window: "Faith, come help me plant potatoes and peas!" Or autumn: "Faith, shut off the tube and do your homework, or give me a hand in the egg shed!" Or any time it wasn't cold: "Faith, you're *alive*, let's just sit on the porch in the fading light."

Faith, Faith, Faith! I *will* say, though, and as I told Malibu Barbie, I loved throwing Frisbee with my mother. In those bubbles of bright, sailing discs, woe and shame vaporized. Then, and during our annual morel hunt – a day more special, for us, than Christmas. For my mother, the money from our morel sales at Tipping Creek Farmers' Market paid bills or bought new tires for her Studebaker. Though two years ago she surprised me – went hog-wild! – splurged on the Princess 300 typewriter. That puzzled me. My mother was never the typing type. I could see why she'd been tempted, though, the instant she lifted that baby out of its box, *such* a pretty coral, with Bakelite keys. Everything about it called for something to be *said*, for words to be tamped down. Maybe the typewriter would unclam her. It brought hope; maybe she planned to take some correspondence courses, finish high school. I asked her why she bought it.

Peck. Peck. Peck-peck. Wham-o [carriage return].

"No courses Faith! Just going to type, I am."

I'd pressed her. "Why *not* courses? Don't you ever want *more than this?*" I'd glanced outside, to the canary-crash-landing lawn. "This Dandelion Island? This life of chicken panic and barely scraping along?"

My heart chugged hard. I'd longed to ask this for years. Somehow felt like the moment, while she was all industrious there at her typewriter.

She backed her fingers away from the keyboard. Her face a hobbled alphabet I struggled to read – resigned, fierce, mournful, splintered hope, all of those – a marled face.

"Oh, I *got* more. One night long ago. I got what I wished for. *Had it all* for a few bright hours, I did. But then my bed was made, and I've been lying in it ever since. But I got *you*, too, and a four-star fact it is, Faith, you're *alive – sideways eye and all.*"

More of *that*. Then after another *wham-o* carriage return, she told me typing might be a more useful skill for a kid like me, than macramé.

She kept forgetting I wasn't a child; her memory would shrink to chicken-size if she wasn't careful. I lived on the cusp. Next birthday, I'd blow out twenty candles.

May's midriff. My mother had been typing. Then she'd gone to collect the eggs. I'd begged off, claiming homework. Maybe she'd typed a letter to my Environmental Science teacher? He'd sent another note of concern, about my marks, no doubt. My mother had left her paper clamped in the typewriter. I wondered what she'd told the teacher about me. It couldn't have been that private, since she left the letter right out in the open. I ferried my peanut butter sandwich – none for Malibu Barbie, she'd need to fit into her zebra swimsuit, soon – over to the typewriter on the dining room table. I folded back my mother's sheet and read:

Faith is alive
Faith is alive
Faith is alive
Fait is live
Faith is alive
Faith ix/ alive
Faith is a live
Faith is live
Faith is % alive

More of the same, down the page. The peanut butter gummed, mud-like, in my mouth. I didn't see how my mother's letter, if that's what *this* was supposed to be, would help my marks at school one bit.

According to the laws of Environmental Science, some things can be known by gazing into a microscope. Those weren't *my* laws. Most things I knew bolted suddenly from some other dimension, clocked me hard, like a spasm of weather, the biggest, sharpest, iciest pellet of hail in the storm, sharpened to a scissor point, piercing my head. And I'd *know*. Not long ago, a hailstone of knowing skewered my skull. What it *was*: my mother's beef against *Front Page Challenge*. I'd been tying the last knot on a macramé plant hanger for her birthday in the attic – a space I'd cleared, my own planet for crafts. I felt artistic up there. I dug doing crafts in high places, the confettis of light the attic's window sprinkled onto the planked floor. Suddenly, tying the final knot, knowledge struck. I felt smart, like Betty Kennedy. My mother's wrangle with *Front Page Challenge* boiled down to this bitter syrup: that program stood for the capital-B Big World, a world of current affairs, beyond the egg shed and the rutted roads and the pangs of Tipping Creek County. More than once I broached it with my mother, my plan to leave after high school.

She'd sighed into tomorrow. "Oh, Faith. Why do you have to *go* anywhere? You don't have to worry about that yet, you don't."

But I *did*.

The capital-B Big World also entered our farmhouse in the silk-smooth pages of *Chatelaine*, a subscription I'd bought with my allowance from helping in the egg shed.

After supper, I'd pour us glasses of Wink, hoping to read to my mother from *Chatelaine*. "This sounds interesting, Ma. 'Toronto: Could You Live There?'"

"I don't want to hear about that place of lost dreams, Faith."

"*Here's* something, then! 'How to Understand Your Teenage Daughter.'" I'd shot hopeful eyes over to her by the stove. I was almost too old for that story, but I wanted her to listen.

"As if *Chatelaine* knows. As if *anyone* does. Faith, put that magazine away."

Another feature. "Let's hear about 'What Happens to Girls

Who Leave Home'?"

My mother rattled the ice cubes in her glass like they were small, disobedient bones. "You're wasting your breath on *that* one, Faith. I already *know* what happens, I do. Those girls end up on chicken farms."

I pitched again: "'A Visit to Canada's Communes'?"

"No cults, Faith. Why do they print such things? It'll give young girls bad notions, it will."

"'The Single Mother Subculture'?"

"Heavens, Faith. Why do you think I'd want to hear about *that?*"

She had a point.

She didn't even want to hear about Margaret Trudeau.

Chatelaine never wrote about Tipping Creek County, why would they? So far from Toronto, what story could be gleaned from our area's gloomy cedars, dying elms, and rumpled pastures pocked with stones? Its swales and forlorn air that even the trim, perfect lawns couldn't turn into a Hallmark card.

The only thing my mother liked in *Chatelaine* was the pineapple upside-down cake recipe; even then she called ten maraschino cherries a brazen amount. We baked the cake together last year, on my eighteenth birthday. "Oh, let's *live!*" I'd coaxed. "You keep telling me I'm alive, now prove *you* are!"

We scarfed the whole cake, and I think every cherry she swallowed broke her heart a little more, with its unreasonable sweetness, than the cherry before.

⌒⎯⎯⎯⌒

Even Betty Kennedy, Angel of Calm, couldn't stop my nightmares. I'd breathe better for a bit after *Front Page Challenge*, but the hideous swirling muck that enveloped me was never far away, clotting my air passage so I had to scream even louder, or try, for I wouldn't last much longer.

I could only hope leaving this place would be leaving the Harrower behind. It didn't want to travel, I felt. It wanted to remain in its familiar darkness. Even it had a concept of home.

⸻

One night a year I slept the most divine sleep, when a beautiful peace radiated through me, through my bedroom, onto the face of Betty Kennedy, whose picture I'd torn from *Chatelaine* and taped to my wall. The Harrower couldn't shove me under the murky sludge *that* night because of something stronger than it: the hope of harvest, the bliss first light would herald, when my mother and I set out with our wicker creels on the Annual Morel Hunt.

I rose from my un-harrowed slumber, so light in my bones, so *alive*. Spring serenaded my ears – spring is a soprano – warbling birds scaled new heights. I stood at my window and surveyed the world, a mondo green marble, the morning tubular, astral. All the vapours and mists and bad feelings I had about the farm replaced by the chorusing red-winged blackbirds and black-winged redbirds. Robins. Lilacs punched happy mauve and white fists into the bright air. I scrambled into my jeans and string belt and tie-dyed shirt and jacket and raced outside into the dandelions, grabbing my wicker creel on my way and tucking Malibu Barbie into her special pocket. She wouldn't miss the morel hunt for the world; soon she'd lounge in the doll-camper I'd buy with my portion of the morel spoils. For me, it would be silver go-go boots like Nancy Sinatra's. I'd seen them in Tipping Creek Ladies' Wear, a store that trafficked in dowdiness but somehow those magic boots blazed their way in there and would carry me into my new life.

No lake-chalk residue, no marl in my mouth on Morel Hunt Morning! I sang "Maggie May," danced in the dandelions when a brainwave spasmed my sun-warmed skull. I knew where the Environmental Science teacher lived – everyone in Tipping Creek knew whose house was whose – I'd leave a basket of morels on his doorstep with a note stating even though I couldn't collect pond scum samples I'd harvested something better, a gift of morels. I knew once he tasted those dusky delicacies, he'd boost my class grade. My mother didn't need to know. And even if she did, she wanted me to finish high school because she hadn't, because of her shame – me. The note to the teacher would also say I was grateful for his concern about my progress in class; the morels were a gesture of my gratitude. I thought of this more as a story than a fib. I thought of it as survival.

In my mind, I strode in the silver boots, diploma in hand, warm wind riffling my hair. I'd write out the cooking instructions for the teacher, and slip them in with my note, the same advice my mother dished out every year at the Farmers' Market: *Don't soak in water, it saps the flavour. Fry in butter or a light breading. Grill the small ones whole. Slice the large morels horizontal in half before frying. A cornflake coating, try it. Dry for stews and soups later.*

'Later' was its own fib, and my mother and I knew it. Our customers gobbled the morels right away, they told us. It would be 'one more', 'one more'. Until it wouldn't. We were spring's reigning fungus queens. We knew morels' secret places, the dusky recesses where they fruited, those tiny feasts of the shadows. One patch in particular was the very bonanza, thick with morels, the El Dorado of wild mushrooms. That patch held the taste everyone dreamt of all year, that nutty smokiness that brought a sensation of deepest peace, all troubles puffed away, mere spores in the wind. Fried in butter, a touch of garlic, there was no taste like those fleshy ridges with the souls of truffles. Spring's very soul. Tipping Creekers were so crazy for that taste they were even nice to my mother and I in our market stall; their fungal cravings snuffed the usual crunched looks they sent us, looks that meant, "Here comes the duo of woe, prodigal Sadie and her burden of Faith. Oh, don't think we'd forgotten."

My mother was in her bedroom, dressing for the hunt. She'd be placing her wig-hat on her head, then that dorky mosquito-net rigging she wore every year atop that. I thought it was strange that, for ladies, wigs, so scratchy and hot – I'd tried my mother's wig on – were a fashion. They saved the time and fuss of curlers and backcombing, I guessed. I wanted to feel the warm spring breeze riffle through my hair, no wig for me! I danced in the dandelions some more, keen to set out, especially with my morel gift plan I felt sure would score me points enough to pass. No one could stay mean after even the first bite; why would the Environmental Science teacher be any different? Those spongy little taste-bud wizards everyone longed for through drab winters would translate into kindness, even from him, at least long enough to ink me a fifty percent. I'd add a further note, showing my deep knowledge: *How to tell the difference between true and false morels. The false ones, with their look of charred brains or domed, lumpen hearts, sicken. The true ones fasten their web-like feet among decaying leaves on old logging roads, beneath brambles, near withered stream beds or swales.*

I wouldn't need to trudge into any bogs, thankfully. Morels were smart. They fastened themselves near enough for moisture but far enough from nasty, harrowing zones.

The screen door retched open. Out came my mother with her wicker creel, in her cotton shift, rubber boots, and broad mosquito-net headpiece, veil already lowered. Her face came to me spackled, as tiny dots. But I sensed she was as jazzed as I was. She'd caught the day's fungal fever too, the way her creel bounced sideways, taking playful licks at her hip. Everything about her, since Woodstock, was so rarely playful I soaked in the sight of her moving towards me in slow motion. Time tugged at every fibre of me; I needed to move faster. Farther. *So far* from Tipping Creek County, I'd sleep beautifully every night, and not just once a year.

"Let's go! Step it up a little, can't you!" I called to my mother.

She didn't say anything through her net.

We were officially on our way, that was all that mattered. From the shadows, earthen honeycombed mouths of morels beckoned us. We'd catch their vibe, their shrouded cloak and dagger ways. We'd trespass. Steal something on someone else's land. My mother said we only did it once a year out of necessity, the egg cheques weren't enough. Our buyers didn't know the best morels grew beyond our property line. That farm's owner, an American, hadn't been seen in years. Maybe he was in Vietnam. On his land, that one special morel colony, the happy hunting ground, knobby domes far as our eyes could see, perfect little grumpy families. That patch alone filled our creels to overflowing. And the morels there, plump, lush, fetched top dollar at the Farmers' Market.

Planks of lemony sunlight warmed my head. My mother's wig-hat and mosquito-net veil blocked this gift. After a few minutes of tramping, we reached the property line: a low, mongrel wall cobbled from pioneer-stone-fence remnants, newer crisscross snake-fence rails, and still newer barbed wire. Often,

I'd pondered who lived here before the pioneers; they never covered that in History class. So many gaps in history, so much shrouded. I could have found the property line in my sleep; I'd often tramped the perimeters of the farm, to know its edges, to imagine *beyond* them, beyond Tipping Creek County. A restlessness I couldn't shake.

The piled stones formed a stairway of sorts. My mother and I picked our way up and over with our creels. Soon the *Trespassers Will Be Prosecuted* sign was at our backs.

We hot-footed it for El Dorado, the old logging road, the thrill of booty pulsing strong. Man, I already felt the silver boots gleaming up my legs. I smacked a mosquito to death, but not before its poison pricked my cheek. Some bird shrieked on high. A stricken elm tree threw up its charred, bony arms.

Before us: pillage.

Earth stubbled with sheered-off morel stalks. A band of marauders had gotten here first. Earlier thieves than us. Every morel bladed, and recently, gauging by the fresh cut marks we bent to examine.

My mother's wicker creel thunked to the ground. "Who could have done this? The hunt is ruined, Faith."

I scratched my burning cheek. What would Betty Kennedy do? She'd keep her cool, press on. "We're not quitters, Ma! There must be more morels they didn't find." I tented my eyes against the sun, scanned a distant gully; elm trees had toppled, canted eerily, into it, their final resting place. We'd never needed to go there before. Now we did.

"Down there!" I called out. Why did my mother stand netted, frozen, her creel still toppled? The morning would slip away, along with our profit. Someone else's feet would slide into the silver boots.

I loped, gully-bound. My mother's urgent words at my back:

"Faith – no! Don't go down there! There's – *snakes!*"

"Might be morels, too!" I was so far ahead of her I didn't know if she heard.

The gully bottomed out. No more birdsong. A stream must have bounced across this low zone once; now the place had a waterless, hollow feel, ghosted. This was just the sort of habitat the Marl Harrower might hover in, but I couldn't stop – some essential thirst to know what was there parched my throat.

I halted in front of a lumpy little tower built from jagged stones. Not *so* little, maybe four feet high. Tombstone-lonely.

My mother's footsteps crackled over fallen leaves that spring's winds had aired dry. Her breaths amped rasps.

I took slow, quiet steps closer. The stone structure dictated a quietness. Its name came to me. *Cairn.* Mason jars with wilted flowers, some shrivelled, nearly to dust, arranged around its base. A few toppled. Brittle rose stems crisscrossed on the ground. There were jars of less-dead flowers. Fresh lilacs. Higher, a stone jutted out, and, looped over the jut, a faded Christmas wreath. And the strangest thing of all: a small rubber boot at the cairn's base, off to the side a bit, with dried flowers stuffed in it, cobwebbed. The boot was a vase. Very worse for wear. Nearby, trinkets niched into gaps between the stacked stones. A cheap toy gun. Tiny plastic fish.

I felt my mother's fretful presence behind me.

I didn't turn.

I touched a stone halfway up the cairn. It was cold. The sun's warmth didn't reach down here. Higher up, there was a weathered, hand-painted sign, hooked with a wire over a stone lip, that said *Bobby*. Was Bobby a dog? Pretty fancy cairn for a pet, but I'd read Americans were sentimental about their pets. The farmer must have buried his dog here. Maybe he was back from Vietnam, and had harvested the morel motherlode. It was his land after all. Maybe he was watching us now. Maybe he carried a hunting rifle. *Trespassers will be prosecuted.*

"Faith. Come away, please."

She was right. We needed to leave. But just as I swiveled to depart from the sad stones and sorrowful trinkets and dead flowers, a golden glint coiled in a recessed space between stones caught my eye. I reached in. A locket.

My mother's voice pitched higher. "Faith. Leave it, it's not yours."

I opened it. Two tiny gold spoons, each cradling an old photograph, fingernail-sized. The locket must have cost plenty to seal in the images so well, out in the weather. In one spoon, there was a little boy. In the other spoon, a baby, not newborn. A girl. She had sparse hair, ribboned. Her eyes not centred. Other than the off-eye, she could be any baby. I turned the locket in my hand and studied the engraved initials on its back, *S.B.*

"Put it back, Faith. Put the locket back where you found it."

But it was in my palm. I only knew one other person with an off-kilter eye. Me. I didn't care about the American farmer now. What would Betty Kennedy do? She'd chase down the truth.

We faced each other, my mother and I, our empty creels at our feet. I dangled the locket in front of her netted face.

"Raise your veil," I ordered.

She obeyed. The stream trickled back to this low place through her tears.

I'd stolen her bliss. But I had to find out. "You know about this grave – or *whatever* it is. That's why you didn't want me in this gully. You know about this *Bobby*, too. Who is he?"

My mother's words came quietly. "He's not buried here. It's a marker. I come here sometimes. I bring him things. Flowers, mostly. I loved him. Only knew him a few hours but some people

you just love right away."
I peered inside the locket. "That him?"
She nodded most woefully.
"What about the walleyed baby girl, dead, too?"
Her mosquito veil slid down, she adjusted it back up again.
"No. The girl is very much alive."
"And?"
My mother's face blanched chalkier than white lilacs, she looked so much older than someone in her early thirties. "The girl is standing right in front of me, Faith. She's you. *You're* her."
Why would my mother stash my baby picture in a pile of stones in some alien gully? Why wasn't it enlarged, on the piano? Isn't that where baby pictures lived, proudly bluing through time? Was it because of the shame, her bringing me to the farm? Had Della-Mae forbidden my baby portrait? Did her word rule even now? And what about the initials?
I turned the locket in my hand. "Who is S.B.?"
My mother choked back a terrible chord. "Faith, you still play with *Barbie dolls*, good grief – how *could I* – you weren't ready to be told, weren't ready for–"
My bones had ignited into full fire. "Ready for *the truth*? Keep Barbie out of this. I'm ready *now* and you'll *tell* me. How did we get here? In the beginning, I mean."
"A godless wind blew us. A surly man drove us in a van. Before that, there was a fuzz ball, blown in through an open window, opened the smallest crack."
"No more *riddles*! Plain English."
She flattened into a scarecrow. "*S.B.* is Shirley Bannister, your mother."
The day came fully unhinged. I became the crow. "*Ca-aaa-aaw*! Where has she been all this time? Hiding behind the screen like on *Front Page Challenge*?"

The scarecrow slumped down onto a rock while I stood, aflame, wings open.

"You want *plain English*, Faith? Your whole family died in Hurricane Hazel in 1954. *I lost my mother*, too. Every day I live with that wound that never heals, losing a mother. I reckoned if you didn't know, you'd escape that pain. I was trying to *spare* you, I was. Don't you *see*? Many others died too. Firefighters. I was babysitting you and your brother Bobby that night. I hauled you both out of the house but the flood swept him away."

"*Babysitting?* Why keep me if I wasn't even yours? Why drag me to this – *wilderness*? You were only a kid yourself! Didn't you want your *life*?"

Her face went turbid, like a book typeset in another language. She breathed hard; I waited. False morels ruled the land now. Environmental Science meant nothing. My teacher's opinion of me, nothing. Silver boots shuffled away into yesterday.

None of these things mattered when your own name hung in the balance.

"This is the plainest English I know," the babysitter sighed. "Any plainer and it'll sob itself out of me, it will. I promised your parents I'd take care of you. With Bobby, I failed. I wasn't going to fail you. And after what we went through together, I couldn't let you go. You're the only one who lived through those hours with me, the night the world ended. Faith, you became part of me, don't you understand?"

I failed to follow. "Nothing you've said holds water, *Sadie*."

"You're wrong, Faith. That's *all* it holds – water. Water and mud."

"Cullen Quick isn't my father, then?"

She shook her head. That alone made sense; he'd never played a daddy part. Always grooved where the wind blew him. Cullen might not have been steady but at least he wasn't phoney.

Then my – Sadie – plunged into pleading, like a convict trying to talk her way down from the gallows platform. "Faith, I was there when you took your first steps, a sight your mother should have seen; *I* saw it. Only me. And let me tell me now, Faith, you weren't easy. Often you *scared* me, you did. Such lungs, such *a fierce look*, and off on your own island with that Barbie doll so much of the time. You're scaring me *now*, Faith! I knew this day would come but–"

What a *tangle of women*. And one doll. The babysitter seemed about to plead her case some more, but didn't.

Time ticked. She sat, splayed, on her rock. Mosquitoes ravaged her face and she didn't smack them to their deaths. She'd grown into the rock.

I needed to un-rock her. "My name is Bannister, then?"

The sad rock didn't need to answer. I knew.

"Then you and I, *Sadie*, share *no blood*? Not a drop?"

The mosquitoes had flown, fed, left puffy blotches on her face.

"Not one drop. But Faith, I *saved your life*, I did. I hauled you out of that sinking house, then out of the floodwater's nasty sewage and silt, I held onto that boat for dear life – Cullen helped – he's the one who found us."

The woman on the rock said this. Her words stole the breath from my lungs. Could she not stitch together a more solid family story? I hurled my empty creel at my old babysitter, she ducked, and it flew past her, onto the old logging road.

"Sadie, you think *you saved my life*? You *trespassed* on it! You saw the sign back there – *Trespassers Will Be Prosecuted!*"

She looked so stricken, like she'd perish right there on that rock. For some reason a Frisbee soared across my mind, like a large, bright coin hurtling through lilac season. I supposed Sadie hoped for some pity from me. A baby crow stolen from its nest shows no pity to the thief! Let the babysitter deposit her own happy-Frisbee-memory in her Royal Bank of Secrets. I didn't want it anymore, fraudulent Frisbee. Let her go bankrupt. What would Betty Kennedy do *now*? She'd drill for deeper truth. I fisted a mosquito to its death. I drilled. Sadie spoke, flat tones at first, then with a rising reverence. Faith was my real name. Sadie from her rock said my family had a storybook life, before the hurricane. My mother, Shirley, elegant as Betty Kennedy. Forest, my father, handsome, suave. They danced, and sailed, wore fine clothes. Owned two cars, one, an Austin-Healey, like a dream rocket ship. She'd ridden in it, on her way to babysit us that night. I lived beside the Humber River, in the prettiest house, with seafoam appliances and a dumbwaiter, and a posh living room with a hi-fi, until the storm blasted every-thing to pieces. I had the loveliest toys, this darling carousel with horses. A mobile over my crib, dancing seals. My family had a dog. Frowsy little thing. Cute. Did I have nice clothes like my parents? Sadie couldn't say, she'd only seen me in my sleeper. Did I have relatives? Sadie couldn't say. Maybe in Eng-land. She remembered neither of my parents had siblings; my father had told her that in the Austin-Healey.

A sour current tore through me. I couldn't breathe, my mouth felt clotted with mud. Time buckled. And suddenly I *knew*; the Marl Harrower had watched this whole morning un-ravel. Had hovered above the cairn in full daylight. Malibu Bar-bie's plastic toes poked hard at my ribcage, alarm pokes, urges, prods. She'd felt it, too. Maybe *it* harvested the morels; maybe *it* controlled my babysitter. Except for Frisbee tosses, Sadie seemed often to live in a trance, even banging on her typewriter; maybe she was the Harrower's secretary, did its bidding. Maybe it dictated what to type, making her a puppet scribe of our lives, underwriting the version it wanted, ensuring we'd never break away. Maybe it controlled the whole county, and everyone knew, but if anyone tried to say anything their mouth clotted with mud. Sending them into retreat, to their popsicle-stick crafts. I'd drilled enough truth. Always knew this was a bad place. I'd been pushing against its edges, the farm's perimeter, for a long time. My small suitcase was packed and ready. And now I had a *real reason* to flee, my whole life here had been a lie. All along I'd been training for this moment, to heed the voice inside me, the one true remaining chord, sounding: *Faith! Run!*

I ran. First to the farmhouse, to grab my suitcase. My meagre savings in there too, allowance from my egg-shed work, folded in an envelope. Then I sprinted up the gravel road into Tipping Creek. Malibu Barbie's toes knocking against my ribs. The All Disciples Track and Field Meet was a month away, the drivers of the pickup trucks and beaters spewing wakes of dust as they beat past me must have reckoned I sprinted along the road in training for the school marathon. They must have thought the little suitcase I toted was some kind of training device, adding weight to boost my stamina. In fact, the suitcase weighed almost nothing, being made of cloth. I was training, all right, but for a much more epic marathon. Shards of new knowing beat through my brain, in tandem with my pounding feet. I'd had a storybook life, a real mother who apparently looked like Betty Kennedy. A suave father. A beautiful car. Then the life of the long dirt road, the chickens, the tortured years at All Disciples, the jeering taunts about my child-mother – who wasn't even my mother at all. Had Sadie Wilder *ever* meant to tell me the truth? I couldn't wait around to find out. A moment comes when a bird must fly on its own.

Some luck in Tipping Creek. Luck in that town, man, was a rare thing. There was a new ticket person, bored, inattentive, at the bus depot. I'd take the bus to Toronto, find where they filmed *Front Page Challenge* and throw myself on the studio's doorstep. Maybe they needed someone to sweep the floor. I'd breathe the same air as Betty Kennedy, the air of truth! I'd be near a lady who looked like my real mother. But the next bus out of Tipping Creek was bound for Sudbury. It'd have to do. If I lingered in Tipping Creek, someone would see me and I'd be dragged back to phoney farm, maybe chained inside the egg shed. I couldn't trust anyone; who knew who anyone really was? I boarded the bus. I knew Sudbury was on the road to Thunder Bay. I'd heard one kid from All Disciples say he'd head to Thunder Bay and work at planting trees as soon as school ended for the summer. I'd plant enough trees to travel to Toronto. Go north to go south. Not airtight but it would have to do. This day hadn't exactly swum in an ideal pool.

I slunk low in my bus seat, holding the locket. My suitcase on my lap. Malibu Barbie still in her special pocket. "I'm sorry you didn't get your camper," I whispered to the inside of my jacket.

Tired and hungry, I traipsed around Sudbury. I bought a sandwich, egg salad, only kind left. I asked a plaid-shirted guy in the diner how much farther to Thunder Bay. Seven or so more hours, no way I'd make it all the way to "the Lakehead" that day. I had enough money left for a cheap motel room. After that, it was hitchhike. No sense hitching in the dark so the plaid guy drove me to his uncle's run-down motel, left me there. That room leaked rain and gave me nightmares. Mostly I stared through the threadbare curtain, waiting for morning so Malibu and I could hit the highway.

Morning at last.

Edge of the blacktop. The day was windy, gusts of havoc that almost knocked me off my feet. Brief guilt swamped me, leaving Sadie alone back there in those fields of death. All those soiled eggs. The sickening, penned-chicken panic. But she'd *shafted* me. Man, how to reason through this morass? What would Betty Kennedy do? She wouldn't slouch there, on the highway, moping, I felt sure. She had more ingenuity, more grace, than that.

I triggered my thumb into the air and corrected my hangdog posture, hoping for a ride. Hoping, too, that they wouldn't send a search party after me. I was nineteen. Hardly a missing child, but still.

Some cars snorted past. Then I saw a droning speck far down the highway, a motorcycle. It stopped inches from me, blasting a warm cloud onto my hands. The driver said I should wear a helmet, though he didn't. He had a striking, narrow face, nice cheekbones. He strapped my small suitcase to a carrier contraption at the back of his bike. It took me a few instants to figure out how to climb aboard. I'd never been on a motorcycle.

We rocketed north, close to flying, his longish, nutmeg hair blowing into my face, tickling it. My own hair rippled into flags out from under the helmet. It was like being in the movie, *Easy Rider*. I almost forgot the disastrous morel hunt, the babysitter, my old life, as we bucked along the highway. We zoomed through rock cuts, a constant zipper in the wind. I could have cruised with the biker forever but he was only going to Batchawana Bay. Punchy, I clambered off his bike there, grateful to be so far from the false fields. I unhooked my suitcase. As I returned his helmet, the biker said, "See you on the flip side," and roared away. I'd liked feeling his ribs through his leather jacket.

The next driver barely clung to life. His pickup truck, a single, broken-down lung, wheezed towards my raised thumb. But a ride was a ride. We jostled northward; my driver with his gristle of steel hair fought with the wheel, as if steering through a

Vaseline sea. He told me his story. His wife had died in a car crash, his son was in jail, his daughter shacked up common-law. I paid for this ride with my ears, listening. Better to hear his story than to have him ask me questions. The poor grizzled soul so struggled to breathe; I worried he'd die right there behind the wheel. I hadn't learned to drive yet.

He wobbled me to Wawa, an outpost with a Canada Goose statue as big as a building. It jazzed me to escape his death-trap truck. Just before I closed the passenger door, his voice scraped at me, "Watch – your – (gasp) green – back."

Green back? American money? I didn't have any, hardly any of my own country's currency.

Airstream campers, towed by cars, slouched north. Pacers. Traiblazers. Faces of children, pasted to the campers' oval rear windows observed me loping along the verge. Several tongues stuck out at me, gross pink slugs pressed against the glass. This country had only one highway. I knew that from Geography class. One road all travellers must take.

The campers didn't want me, so I walked. I wondered if the nightmares would stop when I reached Thunder Bay. Where was everyone? My feet hurt. To keep myself company I talked to Malibu Barbie inside her travelling pocket. She knew, too, that we had to leave the ruse behind. A truck cannonballed past, spraying muddy water over me.

I tramped northward. Hewn rock faces glinted, severe, even the ones with painted lovers' initials. I thought of my real mother's initials, *S.B.* Fingered the locket in my jeans pocket to make sure it was still there. Rocks towered along the highway, walling it in, and I thought of Sadie Wilder back there on her rock, ravaged by mosquitoes. "Whilst *we* are moving on," I told Malibu Barbie.

The motels, with their round chairs like bowls on legs beside each room door, dwindled. I stood on a prehistoric slab with swooping birds hideous as pterodactyls. Felt the blisters alive on my heels. I wondered what Malibu Barbie and I would do if no ride came along, then I shoved that thought back into my pocket. I fingered the locket. The locket my real mother had touched. If only I could have been wearing the silver go-go boots, likely we'd have had a ride by now. And maybe my blisters wouldn't be as bad.

A moose floundered out of the bush and, startled that the trees suddenly ended, hauled its mass back into the dark fringe. More cars beat their way past me with loaded roof racks, one with those wedding flowers made from Kleenexes. More pink slug tongues against oval glass.

At last a midnight blue *something*, an eyesore on wheels that couldn't decide if it was a car or truck. It flew at rocket speed, then scorched to a halt inches from my dusty sneakers, spuming up gravel smoke. When the dust settled, I could read the words welded onto the side: El Camino. I wondered if that was a place. The rig's windows rolled all the way down. A radio belted out the saucy song "Harper Valley PTA." The driver's long curly hair rippled down from under his cowboy hat like a dark theme-park fountain. He sported a light blue leisure suit, jacket open, and a paisley shirt unbuttoned to the gleam of a bulky gold chain. No one in Tipping Creek dressed like that. He looked so copacetic in his machine, like it was the only place he wanted to be in the world. His gaze beheld my chest as Mama in the radio song socked it to the Harper Valley PTA. He stared hard at me. At last, spoke.

"Where you headed, Bambino?"

I tried sass. "Bay of Thunder. Head of the Superior Lake."

"Port Arthur? Why dint you say? Then Bam the Jam, jump in."

I glanced back into the El Camino's strange flatbed rear, where tarps were wrapped around something big, blockish. I settled into the front bench-style seat and admired the deep twist carpet. My small suitcase tucked under my knees. A Virgin Mary air-freshener dangled like a pendant from the mirror. The driver must be devout.

"Thanks, Mister."

"Vinnie Corio," he trumpeted like I'd won a prize. His machine sprayed gravel as we re-entered the highway's long grey thread.

He commanded the road, his intense eyes darting away from it long enough to green-light on me. The road again. Me. His inky five o'clock shadow made him swarthy, like a pirate. He might have been forty. Far from gasping his last like the earlier truck driver. He clicked off the radio.

I'd done it. I'd escaped those false fields. Keeping the air fresh, pure, Virgin Mary bobbed before my eyes.

"You got pluck, hitching alone like that," Vinnie Corio scanned me again with his traffic-light eyes. "And you got a *bella figa*, too."

It was nice of him to tell me I had a good figure. Which is what I figured *bella figa* meant.

Vinnie had a vendetta driving style, attacking the road like it wasn't only his personal enemy but also the enemy of his father and his father before him and all the Corios before that. He started to talk. Fast. He used some words from another language. He asked my name and I told him. Maggie May. Like the song. I couldn't let any search party from Tipping Creek County find me.

Would I help him scout for cherry tops?

I answered sure, if I knew what they were.

He made a snorting-pig noise. "Oinks. Fuzz. Get it? Dig?"

Finally, I dug. "Abso-cherry-lutely, Mr. Corio."

"You got a wandering eye. That'll make you a good scouter."

He'd noticed my defect. My cheeks burst tropical while he assaulted a marathon up-curve until the highway spilled open above a blue wedge of lake. It had to be Superior. He drew a lumpy, hand-rolled cigarette from his leisure suit pocket and flicked a lighter with a spur on it. He sucked intently on the sweet-smelling cigarette.

The blue opened wider and wider. It was like Vinnie forgot I was in the car. Finally, he remembered. He thrust the burning stub in my direction. "You want some?"

His swashbuckling style, exotic way of talking, gold chain, and the war he waged with the road made me want to be worldly. "Sock it to me, Mr. Corio!"

He shunted the burning lump over to me. I took the smoke into my lungs like he did. I coughed, hacked and croaked. Felt more like the rickety driver of the pickup at *Wawawatch Your Back* than a girl with a *bella figa*. The sweet cigarette was a pain in the lungs. I passed it back to him through the widening blue wedge.

Vinnie Corio switched on the radio. A divine, symphonic galaxy backed Jimmy Ruffin's aching question about what becomes of the broken-hearted. The north was a place of deep questions. Jimmy Ruffin's riddle wracked my core as I struggled through the sweet burning smoke to solve it.

Sadie Wilder was one of the broken-hearted after Cullen betrayed her at Woodstock. I remembered the day she returned, having hitchhiked back to Canada in her long dusty-rose dress with its grievous ruffle. She'd never have taken rides with strangers but she'd had no choice. I wondered who'd toss the Frisbee with her now that I was gone. But she'd broken *my*

heart, too, by not telling me who I really was. What would become of *me*? There was no answer to Jimmy Ruffin's riddle, only
sorrow that yawned more endless than that northern highway.

The lake went on forever, too, its transparent blue tinting to
green. "I don't know the answer, Mr. Corio."

"Answer? To what, Bella Figa?"

A bumpkin tear dribbled down my cheek. "To the question
in the radio song."

Vinnie thrust the burning lump in my face again. "Don't
worry about it, Bambino. Here, take another toke."

I inhaled, coughed harder, and pressed my back against the
seat. As much as the smoke hurt my lungs, it eased the blisters
on my feet. The rocky headlands were a testament to the broken-hearted. We were driving straight into the Bible. *The Book
of El Camino*. I studied Vinnie Corio as he held more gulps of
the cigarette in his lungs, scrunching his face like a man in pain.
He looked over at me and called me quiet. That sounded like a
riddle, too. Life in the north was one big riddle with pink slug
tongues against glass. Vinnie handed me the cigarette again; it
burnt so low I inhaled fleetingly, afraid of scorching my fingers.

My quiet alarmed *me*, now too. If I was *too* quiet, he might
think I was ungrateful for the ride.

"Where (cough) – you (cough, cough) – from, Mr. Corio?"
I passed him the hot stub.

Polishing it off, he tossed its tiny terminal ember out the window, and hoisted his broad shoulders into such a manic shrug
I wondered if I'd offended him. "What? You can't tell?" Words
he spat through his smoky teeth.

As Fresh-Air Mary was my witness, I could not. I was
queasy. If I couldn't answer the question, I thought Mr. Corio
might boot me out of his El Camino, disgusted by my igno-
rance, turf me onto the highway. It wouldn't surprise me if his

high-powered machine had an ejection seat.

"Sorry, I can't." Moths bashed my stomach wall.

Instead of ejecting me onto the road, Vinnie Corio laughed. For the first time, I noted a gold tooth dazzling the side of his mouth. The tooth matched his neck chain. Matched the gold locket I'd stashed in my pocket, the only real thing left of me, besides Malibu Barbie in her travelling pocket.

"Schreiber," Vinnie groused. "You asked where I'm from. That's my hometown. We'll pass it soon and y'know what? We're gonna fly right by. I'm done with that town and all the people in it and their little macaroni weenies. Especially my cousin, Gino Spadoni, that nark, flip him the bird, spit on his grave."

My mind was a sickening Ferris wheel. "He's dead?"

"*Naw*, he ain't dead. It's just a figure of speech, Maggie May."

"A *bella figa* of speech?"

Vinnie smirked and cackled a growly sound that reminded me of the John Deere tractor back in Tipping Creek County. Nothing ran like a deer.

"Yeah. A bella figa of speech. You're funny, you know, kid?"

I shrugged. The sun rode shotgun high in the sky, ambering the highway's scarf. A colouring-book world. We followed the yellow thick road, the pavement's Nordic roll. Great timber pelvises of trees blurred past. We blew by a hitchhiker, a stringy-haired guy, guitar case at his feet. Silently I wished him a superior life, a ride. I knew what it was like, having no ride.

Vinnie Corio fell quiet. After a while he asked if I had a crib at the Lakehead.

"Crib, Mr. Corio?"

"Digs. Place to stay."

I shook my head.

He asked what I'd do up there, for work. I told him plant

trees. I was only stopping in Thunder Bay to latch on with a planting crew. Then I'd head into the bush. It pleased me how rugged that sounded.

"They'll tell you it's one town, Thunder Bay," Vinnie Corio said, apropos of nothing I could loop together. "Amalgamation. But it's not, Missy. Never will be, just two ragged lungs coughed together with a mayor's seal."

I didn't know what to say. He'd dropped this like a stone into some curdled pond. The El Camino overtook a log truck lugging its fallen forest up a great whalebone incline. We were airborne.

"Smokey," I warned, and I was right.

Vinnie Corio dropped his speed like a ton of scrap-iron. He drove furrowed in thought. "Hey, you did me a real favour back there, scouting the Oink. I'd like to return the favour, Bambino, in a major way."

I waited for his major way while the doleful pecks of Sadie Wilder's typewriter lumbered through my fuzzed mind on that endless road. I wondered what she'd type now that I was gone. Now that I knew the truth she'd withheld. Maybe she keyed *The Last Will and Testament of a Truth Withholder*. Was withholding truth worse than lying? I was about to tackle this puzzle, tangled as Jimmy Ruffin's question, when the El Camino driver began puffing like a magic dragon.

"I got a proposition for you, Missy. A job. It'll beat the pants off planting trees. That's backbreaking, and seasonal. Over in a kick. Then what you gonna do? Take what I'm offering, you'll have more money and fun. And it comes with a crib – lakefront."

He had my attention. "What kind of work is it, Mr. Corio?"

"Vinnie. It's in the entertainment business."

"Groovy, Vinnie. Will I be in movies?"

"Not right away. But who knows where it could lead? It's dancing. You like dancing?"

I sighed, picturing myself, dancing in the dandelions yesterday morning, which felt like years ago, before the world as I knew it, ended. "Who doesn't like dancing, Vinnie?"

Some kind of silver bird plunged across the highway that I noticed, for the first time, had a number. 17. I was older than the road, a tubular, mind-bending truth.

"What's your name again, kid?"

"Maggie May."

"You'll need a new handle for work." He once-overed me again. "You could do okay. No one would notice your bad eye – the stage lights shine on other parts. You've got legs up to Alaska. That's all I saw of you at first, long flash of gams on the highway. Then I got closer. You're a brick house."

"Vinnie?"

"You're a bit sluggish, kid. You're *built*. Stacked. *Hubba hubba*, you know?" His hands left the steering wheel for a few seconds and bounced, cupped, in front of his gold-chained chest. The El Camino veered off course and my breath left me, but he grabbed the wheel and wrenched us back to the good side of the rocks again. *Brick houses? Stacked?* No one used these saucy codes in Tipping Creek County.

He attacked the road like before. Resumed his high-voltage talk fit for a circus master. "Endless gams, generous cans, a winning combination. So. You wanna dance or plant trees, sup to you –"

"Dance. Where's the dancing place?"

"My club. Right on the strip. Cumberland Street, Port Arthur. And like I said, you get a crib. Just down the street from where Neil Young stayed a few years back."

The prospect of sharing the strip with a star thrilled Malibu

Barbie, her toes poked my ribs, stoked pokes. "Far out, Vinnie. What're the hours?"

"Nights. You get the whole day free. All you have to do is stay out of trouble. No moonlighting at the St. Louis Hotel or the Nor-Shor or The Paradise Club or even slinging drinks at The Lotus. You work for *me*. Fifty bucks a week base salary. Plus tips, and on a good week tips can top base. You interested or what?"

The idea of so much cash blew my mind. I nodded, soft as a sweet herbal puppy.

"Gunshot, gunshot," Vinnie Corio blurted. "Wait, before we seal this deal: you got an old man down east?"

First, I thought he meant father in the Maritimes. "No, my daddy is dead. Just found out."

"I'm sorry for ya. But I mean, boyfriend you're running from, or husband? 'Cause I don't want no busted-heart drama in my club."

"I never even went on a date, Mr. – Vinnie."

"You're not knocked up, then?"

"How? Like I said, no dates."

"You're not running away from something, are ya?"

For a second, my throat constricted, a reflex memory of The Marl Harrower choking me at night, wadding my mouth with mud to staunch my screams. My new boss must never know about it. He might think me unbalanced. Anyway, I was far up the road now, into my new life.

I fibbed. "I'm just a girl making her way in the world."

"No prior offences?"

"Vinnie, I've got a heart of gold, like in Neil Young's song."

His face, a fleeting curtain of scorn, turned zany. "You're a bit different, arncha?"

A dark, prehistoric swoop right out of an encyclopedia sent

down this terrible wail, saving me from answering. Bam the jam the birds were ugly in the north!

Vinnie told me I was hired. That the kind of dancing I'd do would be new for me but the other girls would teach me. He added I'd find my *own style*, in time. "Keep it arty. We want the theatre aspect. That's what sets us above the other joints. Plus the sound system – those're new speakers in the back, under the tarp, they'll wake up the Sleeping Giant himself."

I couldn't think what he meant. Giant? "What are the other girls like, Vinnie?"

He blasted out a raucous, gold-flashy laugh. "They're real Girl Scouts. One big happy family, you'll see."

This cheered me; I'd never had a real family, now I would. I had the whole Canadian Shield by the tail. Superior lake in my back yard. A whiff of Neil Young's genius just up the strip. The promise of riches. No spruce seedlings for me! No more chickens or cups of swamp sludge. I dared to dream the end of nightmares.

It was twilight when Vinnie Corio delivered me to my crib, The Giant Snooze Motel. A motel like others I'd passed on the northern highway, low-slung Lego blocks, or fossilized trains. Like the one I'd huddled in, in Sudbury, only much jazzier. There was enough daylight left to see the motel's pinkish fake-stone trim, a Flintstone feel. The upbeat sign in the parking lot declared: *Modernly Appointed Rooms at Reasonable Rates. Fully Air Conditioned. Colour TV in Every Room. American Express. Chargex.*

Vinnie keyed me into a room, tossed five dollars on the che-nille bedspread, and told me to buy myself some pizza pie. Gon-dola's was decent. I had my own telephone, I could order in. There was nothing like this back in the fields of death! My new boss said I should work on my stage name, my 'concept'. I'd have two nights of in-costume observation at the club, then I'd be performing too. Short training period, paid sooner. "Show up at the club in costume tomorrow night, 8:00 pm. Sharp." Then he jabbed a finger at me, like he thought I might commit some misdemeanour, but only said, "Later, Bambino."

He *yabba-dabba-doo*'ed it out into the Bedrock twilight. Famished and weary as I was, I imagined all the interesting, Big-World people I'd meet in Vinnie's club. I clicked on the television. Black and white, not colour like the motel sign said. I'd earn so much cash I'd soon upgrade. I set Malibu Barbie on the television and told her our real life was about to begin. I could be whoever I wanted in the north. No one else would decide who I was from that day forward.

In my crib, I was content, munching the first pizza wedge, when my door nearly derailed from its hinges – fisted, insistent bangs. The knocker wouldn't be refused. Maybe he smelled the warm, dripping cheese. Maybe Mr. Corio forgot something. Maybe he'd meant to leave me some money for dancing outfits.

I opened the door to six, no seven, pairs of heavily lashed, black-lined blue-shadowed eyes. Curious. Friendly. Doll-like. Devilish. Bold. Cold. Colder. Meringues of hair lacquered with spray. The frothiest backcombed 'do's' I'd ever beheld. Bottle-blondes betrayed by dark eyebrows. The hairstyles made the seven heads enormous. Seven brightly painted pink and poppy mouths, some blowing smoke. Bright bubble gum snaps. All mouths on deck, in action. Must have taken these ladies ages to do their hair and makeup and that didn't include their long talons in shades of blood or candy tones. Mood rings adorned some fingers. Their necks decorated with chokers strung from shells or strips of black velvet ribbon. Their burnished suntans far advanced, for May.

Were these typical northern ladies? What a mingle of strong smells – hairspray, Orange Crush, coconut suntan oil, whiskey, French fries, patchouli, the same sweet tobacco Vinnie shared in his El Camino. These ladies were some kind of gang, painted prettiness, yet severe. Like *Lord of the Flies*, only with girls. With one exception, all brick houses. Their hot pants, curved high over tanned thighs, were fire hazards. The brick-less house wore a short, glittery silver dress and go-go boots that spurred envy in me. Her beauty ghostly, like Karen Carpenter. A vanishing wafer of light.

They looked older than me – the one with peaks of white-blonde hair like whipped cream and a hunting knife in a sheath looped to her frayed corduroy shorts might have even been the truth-withholding babysitter's age, early thirties. Freeze-framed in my doorway, they inspected me through smoke and popping gum. They muttered to each other: "fresh meat," "we better hope she cleans up okay," and "what's The Vin thinking?"

I wasn't liking this inspection by a band of very stacked racoons. Was *this* the big happy family Vinnie Corio told me I'd be joining?

One varnished lady spoke, full-voiced: "Are you *slow*? Are you just going to *stand there all spazzed out like that?*"

They flared forth, all scoffing giggles. Their heads bobbed up and down like painted horses on a carousel.

I was new, it behooved me to be polite. "Do you all work in the entertainment business? Who are you?"

Instead of answering my question, all seven of them slid inside my room, moving like a single smoky muscle greased with hairspray and patchouli oil. "I *thought* I smelled pizza!" one part of the muscle trilled. They descended on my Gondola's pie like famished lake gulls. Three of them took little flasks from their pockets, swigging between bites. Everyone except the wafer girl in the shiny dress. My stomach still panged with hunger but soon the box held only a few crusts. Wafer Girl studied the swag lamp as if it dangled a dispatch from some farther planet.

I asked my question again. They'd demolished my pizza, at least they could feed me an answer. The large-boned girl with sky-high hair threw me a crust: "Who do you think, Snow White? We're the Seven Freakin' Dwarves, the Welcome Wagon, and this place is *Shangri-Fucking-La.*"

Wafer Girl snapped free of her swag lamp hypnosis. "Gloria, for heaven's sake, ease up on her! She just *got* here!"

So Large Bones was Gloria.

Suddenly Gloria's jade eyes darted over to the television, to Malibu Barbie's straight doll legs mimicking the rabbit ears. Large-bones hooted loud laughter. "Girls! Our newbie still plays with *dolls*! Lord love a wolverine! I've zero time for *this.*" Her puffy head swiveled suddenly to Wafer Girl. "Dorothy, you bring her up to speed, I don't *babysit*. C'mon girls, let's blow this playpen."

Her babysitting snark stabbed into me.

A puff of patchouli and smoke, and they were gone, all except Dorothy. She floated down onto my chenille bedspread, barely dinted it, so spun from ether was she, with a voice from someplace sweet, not rude like her cronies.

I offered her a pizza crust, all I had left. She declined. She asked if I had a name.

"Faith," I blurted, forgetting my northern story. "But don't call me that, *please*. Call me Maggie May."

"*Got* it." Dorothy tipped the swag lamp into a sway like she was lovingly pushing an invisible someone on a swing. "Oh pocky-bun my brain! I need to impart some things to you, Miss

Maggie. First, welcome to *The Dimension.* I'm thrilled to my boots you've come to work with us." Her shiny dress glittered like raindrops in sunlight. She went serious. "I'm Dorothy, you already know that. I'm a regular rising star!" She rippled a laugh meant to mock herself. Went serious again. A pretty light blinking off, on. "Gloria shouldn't have laughed at your doll, that was harsh. The three flask-tipplers are Lois, Winnie, and Daisy. Lois, you'll have noticed, looks just like Cher, as in Sonny and. The gal with the hunting knife, Shirley, is our headliner. None of us can ever hope to soar that high."

I couldn't make much sense of this. I'd never met a lady who accessorized with a knife used to gut animals or clean fish.

"So, you're a dancer, too?" I asked the wafer of light.

She throated a laugh, reed-hollow, like the inside of a waltz, laughed so long I worried it would sap her strength. "Is that what Vinnie told you? Miss Maggie, we're *peelers.* Though I prefer to think of us as exotic dancers. All of us. As I always say, *Raza Unida.*"

I didn't speak wafer. My mouth must have curled in puzzlement.

"It's Texan," Dorothy explained. "Means: *We're all in this together.* We work, now *you* work, too, right across the street. The joint is closed, it's Sunday here. Here, Maggie, see for yourself –"

Dorothy tugged my small window's curtain aside. Against the dim, northern sky, a large, lit, rough building, some kind of barn, with a crude silhouette, a woman standing, her shapely legs planted apart, her arms raised as if tousling her hair and, other than little ledges to suggest tops of tall boots, nothing to indicate clothing. Small white lights pulsed along the roof's line, a string of beads having a seizure, and beneath that, a sign, in raised pink neon:

THE BEAVER CLUB

Under that, in palsied lights:

Headlining Fri Night – The Penalty Box

How had I driven with Vinnie Corio along Cumberland Street without noticing this circus of light? I must've been too dazed from the riddled smoke in my lungs; either that or I had eyes only for The Giant Snooze, the promise of a crib. Or both.

"I work at *that* seedy place?" I asked dumbly. "Vinnie called it artful – like theatre. That doesn't look like an art building, *or* theatre, at least how I'd imagine them."

Dorothy flicked a piece of gum into her mouth. Shrugged. "Vinnie's club has more 'theatre' than the joints over in Fort William. He prides himself on that. And his high-class clients. We get people from Bobby Curtola's circle. Foremen from the grain elevators. Railway bosses. You don't have to be Blaze Star or Gypsy Rose Lee but you'll need a stage name that fits with your act. Your 'concept', you know?"

I picked nervously at a pizza crust. "What are yours?"

"I'm Candy Cane," Dorothy said. "I make it Christmas every day. Daisy is Perpetu-a Motion, she's an expert pole-spinner. Lois does tricks with water, she's Tempest Tossed. Winnie is Itty Bitty Bang Bang. She plays with toy guns. Gloria is Chocolate Moose. Connie, Shay Grope. Shirley, like the big, blinking sign says, is The Penalty Box. When she storms the stage wearing her goalie pads over her G-string and her goalie mask, and a recorded track of Foster Hewitt's play-by-play blares, and starts her moves, the audience goes wild. Who wouldn't? Hockey and sex. That's this country."

I didn't know, hadn't been anywhere before bolting from Phoney Farm. And mainly I watched *Front Page Challenge*. Dorothy told me Shirley wore fake skates with tinfoil blades strapped over her high heels, and at the perfect moment she'd kick them off, send them sailing into the crowd. Guys who caught them raised them in the air, like trophies, kissing them. The Beaver crowd adored flying objects. Shirley was Vinnie Corio's cash cow, Dorothy said. Pulled in hundreds in a single show.

I had to stop the Candy Cane. "Aren't you and the other girls jealous?"

"Not at all. *Raza Unida*, right? Besides, we can't come close to The Penalty Box's talents and we know it. She fills the club – even the night Tina Turner played Fort William Gardens – and we go home with wads of dough."

That word again, *home*.

"Why aren't you over there, working tonight?" I asked.

Dorothy took a quick sip of air. "Like I said, it's Sunday. Club's closed." Then she swerved into a new, more unsettling Dimension. "Watch out for Vinnie," she warned. "He's a goon, a real juicer. Don't make him mad."

The Dimension had its own lingo. I couldn't keep up. "'Juicer', Dorothy?"

"Casanova, you know? Hustler. The Godfather of northwestern Ontario. Finger in the druggie pie out in South Gillies. Probably bootlegs amethyst." Dorothy's mood ring darkened as she swatted at a mosquito that must have flown into my room with the painted ladies. "And he owns *this* pit."

I marvelled at how one man could own so much. "Does Vinnie live here at The Snooze, too?"

"*Hardly*. Lives with his wife and kids in a palace with white marble pillars a few miles from here. Calls it Vinland.

Meanwhile we're crammed into this dive. He puts the tourists on the floor above us. *They* get the coloured television and cool air. He's around here all the time, though. Watching us. That's why we've got to stick together. *Raza Unido*, remember?"

A vehicle tore past outside, radio bellowing a song about Honky Tonk angels.

"What about you?" I asked Dorothy. "What's *your* story?" She looked wistful. A wistful wisp. "I'm only here for a squeak of time, long enough to save money for Vancouver. I should go practice my dance routine now. Almost forgot." She drew a handful of something from her purse sewn from suede patches. "I always carry extras. This is your uniform, Maggie May. The Basics. Make sure your string fits tightly, otherwise the money bills won't stay in place."

She threw a shiny handful on my bed. The handful split into three parts: a glittery triangle tied to string, and two spangled circles with tassels. Each circle a bit larger than a silver dollar. She also gave me a tube of something. Toothpaste? "Spirit gum," Dorothy explained. "It holds your headlights on, don't scrimp on it. Everything else, make it so it flies off easily. And have your 'concept' by the end of tomorrow. You don't want to rile The Juicer. He can be brutal."

A silver flicker, and she was gone. I glanced at the spangled, tasseled bits on my bed. I imagined the money bills that must hold tight against my skin, tucked under the string – my ticket to Toronto, to glamour. I clicked on the television, massaged my road-sore feet, and wondered whether the broadcast signal for *Front Page Challenge* reached this far north.

Through the night, wolves yipped. In the switching yard behind the motel, trains rearranged themselves. Ships fog-horned the lake. I heard some helpless, screeching prey being torn open by a pterodactyl bird. How it hunted in the dark I didn't know.

Night was busy in the north. The motel walls more like paper
screens. Travellers' snores reached me. Cries and groans of sex,
had to be, from some upper room. Canned television laughter.
A Frisbee soared all the way across Lake Superior; its airborne edge beaned me on the head. I awoke. A goon held a
knife-sharp shard of amethyst against my cheek, and ordered
me to write an essay on the topic of home. I failed.
Near morning I slept at last. My mouth clamouring silently
for food, but free of mud, at least.

The coiled locket, a delicate chain that once wreathed my mother's
neck, shone, lit by morning sun that shouldered through the
curtain crack. I owed that locket everything, for had I *not* discovered it, I likely wouldn't have stitched together the truth.
Sadie Wilder could have spun a story about the strange cairn
as a grave for someone's pet, nothing more. But I *had* found it
– them. Us. My brother. Me. The two tiny faces cupped inside
the locket. In this way my real mother had, from some other
dimension, helped me.

Light also sliced in under my door, a mouse could easily
enter my room through that wide crack. *Something* had. Something rolled in paper. A small knife. A note, unsigned: *Welcome
to Shangri-La. You might need this. Several of us carry them.*

The knife and note rattled me. I left them on the television
beside Malibu Barbie. "We'd better get cracking," I told her
black-lined eyes, which were distant, sullen, that first morning
in the north.

I had a little pizza money left. I needed it for toothpaste, a
hair brush. Food. In a dreary diner along the strip I ate a glum
toasted western sandwich, worried about my 'concept'. What

could I *do*? What was I *good at*? Crafts. I'd have to forage a concept from what I could gather, what morning's tide washed onto my new shore. One thing I knew, I wouldn't wear the locket onstage. How could I dance with the dead little boy between my collarbones? My real mother would have been ashamed of me, working at that seedy place. I wouldn't taint the one thing her hands had touched. I whispered to her that this job was only temporary, and someday, wherever she was, she'd be proud of me, and the rest of my real family, too, wherever *they* were. Heaven? It would take clouds of Vinnie Corio's lumpy-cigarette smoke to reckon on that. Since the cairn, I'd wondered if I'd believe in anything again, thanks to Sadie Wilder's deception. I wasn't even sorry I made crow noises at her.

I ventured into the tall weeds behind The Giant Snooze Motel and began to forage. There was a rusted-out washing machine. Worn tires. A turned-over boxcar. The maggoty carcass of some animal. Garbage. Out on the vast lake, whopping clods of ice tipped about in the swell, even though it was May. Small wonder I shivered. No concept offered itself up until I ranged closer to the grain elevators, then *Hallelujah*! Revolutions and ringlets and curlicues of castoff cord, twine, string, rope, and gnarled hemp strands. *Material*.

Macramé Maggie was born. After several hours of work in my room I'd fashioned a skirt, of sorts, from every knot I knew, loop knots, hitches, capuchin knots, lark's heads, reverse larks' heads. A bikini top sprang from double half-hitches, flower knots. A sort of headpiece, long ropes of hair. I was pleased with the concept. Sadie Wilder was wrong about not being able to launch a career from crafts. I was doing it.

The Beaver Club was its own island, fusty-aired, deep-throated. It bristled with the night's prospects, a dark circus. Smells of whiskey. Beer suds. Smoke. All of us in costume, around the round front table marked *Reserved 4 Performers*. The Candy Cane, decked in red and white banners, was seated sweetly beside me. Vinnie Corio drilled his cowboy boots along the floor and stopped in front of me, a girl made of string. He scrunched his five-o'clock-shadowed mug at me. "And *this* is? And *you* are?"

My hands trembled. My concept wavered.

"Macramé Maggie," I answered.

His gold tooth flashed, a reverse smile. "I scooped you off the highway, you better make it worth my while. And don't you lie to me again, Missy. I don't trust you now."

"Mr. Corio?"

"Your name, Maggie May, that's a load of guff."

His cowboy boots malleted to stage-side, into the zone with the vast sound system. How had The Vin discovered my name? My lower lip quivered; Dorothy was the only soul who knew, I'd believed Dorothy a friend, her and her *Raza Unida*.

I shot The Candy Cane a puzzled glare through my string hair. "The Vin came to my room," she said. "He grilled me about you. I was scared. I'm sorry."

The circus began. Vinnie Corio, in a metallic jacket with wide lapels, behind his giant bank of knobs and amps and hut-sized speakers and reels and vinyl records, took a bullhorn – a disc jockey manning a rocket ship of sound. In his horn, he bellowed things like, "Get a piece of this, Gentlemen!" And "Sock it to us, Baby!" He knew no one would leave until they'd seen The Penalty Box, Dorothy told me earlier that night. Men came from all over northwestern Ontario, she'd added, in winter, driving their pickup trucks over black ice, steering their skidoos through squalls, not to mention the steady flow of wayfarers on the country's one main highway.

Chocolate Moose strode onstage, wearing antlers and an orange hunting vest and matching G-string. She unhooked her horns, teasingly, and lobbed them into the crowd, then took to the pole. Tempest Tossed doused a bucket of water over her head, then hurried her hands over her slicked-down curves. Candy Cane turned her Santa hat into a lasso and strutted in her tall white boots that made her legs into long bleached bones. She licked the pole and made every night Christmas. Itty Bitty Bang Bang, a cross between a bird and naughty angel, un-latched her sequined wings and flung them into the crowd, causing a sparkling snowfall. Shay Grope was all leather and whips. Perpetu-a Motion did nothing but spin around the pole, before collapsing and playing dead. Vinnie, circus master, thun-dered through his bullhorn: "Only her majesty's face can revive our poor Perpetu-a." Wallets flopped open throughout the club. Perpetu-a returned to life, then spun her tassels for a full two minutes. Bizarre theatre.

Finally, the Headliner. The Penalty Box. *The Hockey Night in Canada* theme song. Referee whistles. Flying goalie pads, skates. The dancer's sublime scorn. Then the wallets, flapping open like so many whisky-jack wings.

So that's how it was done.

Before the next night's show, Vinnie Corio summoned us 'back-stage', a crude, stark room with a long bench, scrub buckets, and a pay phone. A tattered newspaper article tacked to the wall: *Russian Robot Lands on Moon*.

We slumped onto the bench. Everyone except Shirley, the headliner. Vinnie Corio paced in front of us like a coach before a key game. "Where's that lazy broad, Shirley?" he groused to us benched ones.

Connie spoke out. "Didn't you get the message she left at the motel front desk? Shirley's sick. Migraine."

"I'm sick *too*," Vinnie storm-clouded us. "Sick of excuses. It's a full house tonight. We need her. Go drag her over here. *Now!*"

Connie glamped out, a bolt of leather.

I'd asked Dorothy why our headliner, a local girl, lived in The Giant Snooze. The Candy Cane said Vinnie made all his girls live at The Snooze, some horse-feathers about keeping us together, a family in the service of art.

After a few long minutes, Shirley dragged herself and her hockey equipment to our grim huddle. She looked terrible. Connie sank onto the bench.

The Vin glowered at us. He hadn't yet donned his wide-lapelled jacket, and I couldn't stop staring at the ripped seams where the arms of his t-shirt had been razored off. He pushed Shirley down onto the bench, grasped her neck with both hands, and made like he'd thump her head against the wall, flashing his gold tooth. He ignored Connie's plea, "Stop it, Vinnie! She's sick, for God's sake." Vinnie released Shirley's neck. He told her if she didn't strap on her goalie pads and get stage-ready, she was done; then she'd get a *real taste* of the penalty box, all right, the one called unemployment. The rest of us would go down with her, our boss said, because we all knew no one came to see anyone but The Box, and he could re-place the rest of us overnight. All he had to do was cruise the highway and see what road kill he could find. He'd glared at me in particular, with these last words.

Shirley went pale. Her hand slid slowly to the hunting knife in its sheath on her belt, then away.

"Show time!" Vinnie Corio bulleted, then left the backstage room. We filed out into the club, to the big round table in front of the stage, where we'd sat last night. The idea was, when we were 'on deck' we slipped behind the curtains, made our entrance on cue, according to Vinnie's bullhorn, and emerged between the black curtains like we'd sprung from the very core of darkness, until the spotlight found us.

The Vin controlled the lights and sound. He'd slithered into his jacket and stationed himself in his stage-side kingdom of turntables and wires and amps and receivers and vinyl. The bullhorn readied in his hand.

It was a long night. I shivered in my hitches and knots, despite the crowded club's heat. I wasn't used to dressing so skimpy. The girls, haunted by Vinnie's earlier rage, didn't dance well. More like marionettes, jerking through their moves. The clients' sparse bills showed they noticed as well. There was a bit of heckling, even. Had to be why Vinnie kept bawling through his bullhorn about the *sen-sa-tional, the smouldering, the one and only Penalty Box coming right up* (even though more marionettes must lurch and spin before the headliner).

Holy *Front Page Challenge*, I was thankful it was still in-costume training for me. I could stay hunkered at the table and not expose myself. I wasn't ready to perform. Then more heckling from the house, more bullhorned promises.

Finally, Shirley took the stage. We sat, edgy, in our places, as the *Hockey Night in Canada* theme song began. Something was wrong. We saw that right away. Shirley appeared unsteady. She slogged, in her gear, onto the stage. She wasn't drunk, didn't drink, The Candy Cane told me. She smoked hash, helped her dance. Her goalie pads might as well have been hunks of iron chained to her legs. Her face looked like she was dancing for a crew of ghosts. I glanced over at Vinnie Corio; his vinegar aura told me he, too, noticed something was badly amiss.

Shirley swiveled her hips. Kicked one leg high as she could with the pad still strapped on. A 'skate' flew into the crowd, caught by a guy who made a show of fondling it against his beard. People laughed. *Shoots! Scores!* Her other 'skate' flew askew, landing at the front of the stage. Wallets unfolded slowly. Referee whistles shrilled. Shirley's face was a death mask. She grabbed the pole, spun around it, clumsily, still wearing the goalie pads and then –

I saw the blood.

Chocolate Moose saw the blood.

Perpetu-a Motion saw the blood.

Candy Cane saw the blood.

Shay Grope saw the blood.

Tempest Tossed saw the blood.

Itty Bitty Bang Bang saw the blood rivering down Shirley's bare legs behind the goalie pads as she spun. Then down onto the lit stage where it pooled, ghastly red.

Someone in the audience near us now saw the blood. The young regular in the toque who always came early for a front-row seat, I'd heard. Anyway, some guy hollered, "Holy Hell, she'd bleeding!"

The soundtrack kept playing.

The Penalty Box collapsed, heavy, in a heap beside the pole.

A confused rumble washed through the large, murky building. Then a tall, handsome Native man made his way through the club; he was Shirley's boyfriend, Dorothy had told me. He blitzed onto the stage, shouting, "Somebody call an ambulance!"

Vinnie Corio roared, "Get her off the stage! Now!"

Connie screamed, "Help her!"

The soundtrack finished.

All seven of us tripped over each other, clambering onto the stage, panicked cries from our painted mouths. We crouched, clustered, around Shirley. She was unconscious. Still more blood. A red pond, widening.

The boyfriend knelt beside Shirley and warned us back, wanting to give her some air. He loosened the bloodied goalie pads and tossed them aside, and hollered up the pole, "Where's that ambulance?" And grasped her still hand.

Shirley laid limp as a gutted rag doll.

I started to cry.

Tempest blubbered.

Perpetu-a wasn't in motion.

Dorothy the Candy Cane went ape. She stood over Shirley despite the oxygen warning, and wailed. "Shirl, please wake up! This fake blood routine isn't funny, oh no, not even a little! Shirl do it for us! *Raza Unida*, remember? We're all in this together."

"Dorothy, shut up!" yelled one of the girls, who knew who, chaos blurred them, but the command hit its mark. The Candy Cane's face whitened, and she crossed herself and prayed to whatever Dimension would listen.

I didn't know Vinnie Corio's whereabouts during this catastrophe. Gone to call an ambulance? But suddenly he was there, on the stage with us, a menacing, metallic streak. In charge, again. He ordered Gloria and the boyfriend, to carry Shirley offstage.

The boyfriend argued, saying it might be wrong to move her until the ambulance came, then stood, facing Vinnie Corio, their noses almost touching.

"*You* did this, you psycho thug," the boyfriend seethed. "You got her – she told me – you're gonna *pay*." He was about to land his fist on Vinnie's mug when two medics carted a gurney through the throng and scrambled, with the gurney, onto the stage.

The boyfriend backed away but the fury never left his face. After the medics lifted Shirley onto the gurney, he followed them, still cursing Vinnie Corio, towards the Exit door. Connie made to leave with them.

Vinnie boomed at her, in full-menace force. "*You* – stay here! You're on duty!"

Except for the rapid shuffling of the medics' boots as they bore the stretcher through the crowd, you could have heard a G-string snap.

Connie straightened to her full height, her pasties' tassels pendulums in twitchy swing. Then she did something chilling. Magnificent. She pulled her black whip out of its holster-like holder and cracked it down hard, spraying up a fountain of Shirley's blood. Instinct jolted us trembling ones backwards to avoid wearing blood. And, cracking her whip again, Connie blared. "You know what, Vinnie? You can kiss my *Royal Canadian Rump*!"

With those words Connie lowered her whip, it coiled in the blood, a grotesque red snake, as she hurried to catch up with the medics. I worried she'd freeze out there in the chilly spring night. I hoped they lent her a blanket, and let her ride in the warm ambulance.

Some man in the club yowled, "*Yeah*, you tell 'im, Grope, *sock it to 'im!*" And soon the whole house sent up cheers for Connie's bare, retreating back and *beautiful defiance*. Cheers, we all understood, were the same as *boos* for Vinnie. We hurrahed Connie, too.

The ambulance careened away into the night. We braced ourselves for Vinnie Corio to blow. It was easy to see he was volcano-mad. His neck veins were about to pop open like milk-weed pods, when suddenly he turned to Lois and Winnie. "*You* and *you*! Get a bucket from the back and vamoose this bloody mess. *Now!*"

Every soul in that seedy joint went quiet.

Trembling Lois: "But Mr. Corio, we got no towels."

"Then use your *own clothes*," Vinnie snarled. "But God forbid you should use your *brains*!"

Lois and Winnie scudded away to their unsavory task.

The crowd didn't care for how The Vin had turned on us, everyone could tell. But he was too far inside his own scheme to sense the disapproval vibe. He didn't seem to hear the 'aw, c'mon's' or hisses that spooked the smoky, blood-tainted air, so absorbed was he in trying to salvage the night's profits.

Winnie and Lois mopped tearfully on the stage.

Vin the Juicer, the goon, turned on me viciously. "*You* – Mac – Mag – *Whoever* the hell – start earning your keep, Missy! Get up on stage and shake your strings!"

He looked about to throttle me. Anyone with a shred of decency would have closed the club for the night. But the Beaver Club customers would go to Scott's Tavern or some other joint if he pulled the plug. He couldn't let one of his girls collapsing in a pool of her own blood be the night's final event. Something else had to happen.

That something was me.

The other girls beamed pity my way. Dorothy squeezed my hand and pressed something into my palm. Her mood ring. "Wear it," she whispered. "It's charged with *Raza Unida*." I skidded it onto my finger, whispered back thanks. I thought about the robot on the moon, where I longed to be at that moment. This wasn't a good night for a debut. I shuddered. I hadn't given any thought to music. I'd only been meant to observe.

As I took the stage, queasy, the blood's tincture lingering, Vinnie's circus-master jabber made me even queasier. "Ladies and Gentlemen" (though the only 'ladies' were the bar waitresses and us) – "What happened here tonight to our talented Penalty Box is most unfortunate, but our girls are art-teests, and you paid to see their art, so to reward your loyalty and as compensation for tonight's Headliner letdown I'm buying a round of drinks for the whole house." (The bartender revived.) "And I now present our newest talent, a crafty girl as wholesome as 4-H, but as you can see, with naughty intentions. *Macramé Maggie!* Or, if you prefer, *Knotty Maggie!*"

He remembered my name when it mattered.

My stomach convulsed. The lights exposed me. I gaped down at the staff table, the anxious faces. Bar waitresses, trays laden, moved through the shadows. I stood near the pole, the hot lights fired my fear. Told myself, *I am a brick house.* But I'd have to *do* something. If I lost my job I'd perish on a slab of rock, or be eaten by one of those pterodactyl birds. My long string-hair tickled my neck, urging me to stay in the game.

The club fell quiet.

"Sorry," I sputtered into the shadows, the blur of waiting faces. "I'm a little tied up in knots tonight."

Guffaws. Relief? Wrong. Mere seconds of cut slack. Then I heard a heckler in the darkness. "Get with it, string girl! We want *moves*, not stand-up comedy!"

From behind his control panel Vinnie Corio yelped at me, "Music?"

The image of Shirley, so still on the stretcher, strung itself through my mind. Was she alive? We had to *do* something for her. Even if my first show was my last. Even if those hideous birds ate me alive. I thought about how Connie had stood up to The Vin.

"'I Saw the Light'" I bally-hoo'ed over to the sound equipment.

Vinnie Corio snarked, "*Church music?* What the blazes?" but began flipping through his enormous vinyl library. He found a snappy version of that gospel great and, as I figured it was my terminal dance, I gave it my all. I swung my long strings and cords like a rodeo queen, copying the other girls' moves. I unloosed the string skirt, pranced and cavorted. At the song's chorus, I trotted to the edge of the stage and raised my arms in a sweeping gesture of invitation.

"All together now! *Sing it*, people!"

The open mouths of Vinnie's remaining girls formed red 'O's' around the staff table. Gloria broke into lusty song. Candy Cane piped up in sweet, angelic strains. Then the other dancers, the waitresses, still serving the free round joined in. The bartender, the burly bouncer, a biker in a pirate headscarf. Then others sang until every last soul in The Beaver Club saw the light and, in their enlightened states, tucked bills under my G-string, warming my torso.

"That was for our Penalty Box," I announced at the song's end.

Applause drubbed my ears. My cheeks burned.

Vinnie caterwauled into his bullhorn. "All right, that's it! Drink up! We're done here!"

While the men chugged and I plucked bills off the stage floor, Vinnie vanished into the shadows. Gloria hurried backstage to phone the hospital. A few minutes later Vinnie blasted back out of the shadows. "Return to your cribs," he gnarled at us. "This night is *fucked*."

Ignoring him, the girls shuffled backstage to hear the hospital news. I headed there, too, until Vinnie Corio growled at my back, "Go to your room *now*!"

His growl signalled, *bad dog*. I obeyed. I'd find out about Shirley over at the motel. I shivered my way out of The Beaver Club, across Cumberland Street. I jiggled my key in my lock, humming "I Saw the–"

Hands with freight-train force seized my fingers, my shoulders, and the key dropped. Nasty Vin-master's voice, his sour breath in my ear said, "Let's take a little *stroll*, Naughty Maggie!"

The night bit with chill. Except for my string getup, I was naked. My high beams shone no light. The long, wet grasses slimed my legs. Vinnie Corio's one hand clamped over my mouth as he dragged me through the weeds behind the motel, where birds swooped and things died and garbage got dumped. I squirmed and kicked to free myself, to knee the part of him that would hurt him worst, but he was wrestler-strong. I couldn't call out.

He dragged me to the lake, lowered me roughly onto a rock right where the dark roil met the shore. He meant to throw me into the icy waters of Lake Superior. I couldn't swim. I trembled violently. Vinnie Corio's huge, gaudy ring sliced through the night as he pulled me, still clamping my mouth, close to his face. He shook me. "Thought you were pretty smart back there, didn't ya? You made me look like a fool. What the hell you doin' with *church music*? You could'a *offended*, we got solid Catholic regulars –"

He held my head, like it was a pumpkin he could demolish with his bare hands, his deathly grasp. Made like he'd dunk me into the lake but pulled back at the last second. Then he released his hand from my mouth.

"They didn't seem offended, Mr. Corio. I– I– just tried to take their minds off Shirley."

"Not good enough, Bambino."

I barely had time to close my mouth before my head plunged

under water, cold, so very cold. His monster-claws held me under. Suddenly I knew, down there in that liquid frigid prison, I'd been down in that death-place before. It wanted me back. And Vinnie Corio was The Marl Harrower, or its northern partner. I'd die after I couldn't hold my breath. I fought hard against the assassin's claws, my last, desperate prayer, *help me, one, help me, two* –

He yanked my dripping head out of the water. "Don't pull that crap again. You made a mockery of me and my club. A *tapestry.*"

I sputtered, gasped. Words returned. He must have meant *travesty.*

"Got it?" He dunked my head into the cold void again, briefer, this time. He jerked me back up by my hair.

I sobbed. Heaved for oxygen. *"Got it!"*

Another dunk. "I can't *hear* you, String Girl!"

Back up into the night, from one grave to another. This was no riddle, this was death. I sobbed harder, sputtered. "I – *got* – it – *Sir!*"

He'd finish me, I felt sure. Instead, he dropped me like a bag of rotten fish onto the rock slab. Ripped away the bills still folded over my string, and pocketed them. His words guttered, if I told anyone about this, things would go badly for me. He staggered off, crazed veering steps, back towards the motel, leaving me paralyzed, a bawling heap on rock. Dripping lake mixed with my tears. I couldn't stop shaking. Couldn't quiet the terrible echo of being down in that drowning place before. But this time no moth – babysitter – *anyone*, to shake me awake.

How much time mouldered until I crept, wretched, through weeds to the motel? My teeth banged together so hard, so freezing was I, I worried they'd broken.

My room key was right where it fell, in front of my door. In my room, I shoved the dresser and every other piece of furniture against the door. Even after being dragged through the weeds, somehow both tasselled high beams held. I'd used plenty of spirit gum. It hurt when I pulled off the pasties. I dabbed my scraped thighs with toilet paper. I glanced over at the phone. Maybe Vinnie Corio had tapped our phones, he'd know if we called anyone. I eyed the hunting knife one of the girls had given me, if only I'd thought to carry it with me to the club that night.

I made a miserable pile of myself on the bed. Sadie Wilder's words echoed through the room, I was lucky to be alive. And she wasn't even here for me to agree with her.

Dorothy took me to an employment office in Port Arthur the next day. I didn't allow her into my room at first, too afraid to shove all the furniture aside to open the door. She kept hailing me from the other side. I made her talk to me through the smallest crack. Also, I worried Vinnie Corio had sent her to do his bidding. I low-shouted back to her, is *he* with you, did *he* order you here? She promised no. Finally, I moved the furniture enough to open the door. She was so thin, it didn't take much. The Candy Cane sugared easily through the crack of light. I told her I couldn't stay. She said to gather my few things, and I threw them into my small suitcase. The locket lived around my neck. I slipped my high beams and G-string into Malibu Barbie's traveling pocket with her; they'd serve to warn us against taking rides with strangers.

Dorothy didn't ask what happened after I'd left the club. But she understood I couldn't stay. She knew someone at Great

Lakes Power and Paper Company. I said, "Why don't you come with me? Plant trees with me?"

"*Look* at me, Faith. Do I look like I could lift a tree, even a sprig?"

She had a point.

Just before she left me at the office, I realized I still wore her mood ring. I started chunking it off my finger.

"No, Faith. Keep it. *Raza Unida.*"

She patted my hand so lightly, a spirit touch, then vanished.

My face welted with blackfly bites, my aching back harnessed, burdened with baby trees, my hands calloused from the shovel, ripped with bramble and slash. A dark mood, my mood ring. The bulky gloves they issued made me fumble the spruce seedlings so I stopped wearing them. While I bent at my toil, the locket nubbed at my neck. My new footwear was safety boots with metal toecaps, good thing, given how often my shovel hit rock or clay.

The foreman called for volunteers to work the roughest terrain, the high north track. "I'm not going to lie, kids, it's nasty up there."

A track far from Vinnie Corio. No road fit for his El Camino.

My fingers shot high.

A guy wearing a bandanna raised his hand.

"All right, you two," the foreman said.

My thoughts ranged wide and wild as my shovel shunted seedlings into scarred earth. How no hummingbirds hummed, there. Dorothy, the wafer-girl. The brief girl at my high school back in Tipping Creek. (Are *all* girls brief?) The small boot by the stone cairn. Sadie Wilder withholding the truth all those years. What right had she? The crazed panic of poultry, that mad flapping their only defence.

I thought about distant Toronto. And worried what I'd do after planting season.

On the high north track, ghastly things patrolled my shovel's progress. Those pterodactyl birds. Boreal buzzards. Vampire bats. A winged death squad that awaited my collapse. They scared me, but less than Vinnie Corio scared me, or The Marl Harrower.

I didn't talk to the bandanna guy. Didn't even care to know his name. Thankfully, he worked quietly, ten feet away, a moving, parallel shadow. Until one day he scared off a bear by yodelling loudly, badly. I had to say thanks.

"Sure," he said. "Sorry for the racket. I'm Warren. Warren Crouch."

I didn't tell him my name. No one here could know I dressed in strings, briefly, or that I'd worked for *that man* in *that place.* But my planting partner chipped away at my reserve, with his odd little inventions, like the extension he rigged, a wire arm like an upside-down letter 'U' attached to his seedling bag. From it, wind chimes. A plinking lullaby for this wasted place as through the heating days we imprinted two tiny forests in our wakes.

Planting season ended. Driving with Warren Crouch wasn't like taking a ride from a stranger. During our toil on the high north track, I'd grown to trust him. He knew what noises kept bears away. He let me live inside my quiet bubble. Time stretched itself, daylight made long, slow exits and dips but never fully left.

The sky, alive, pulsed with jewel tones. Slowly, I began telling Warren things. Not about the cairn, or what I'd discovered about my real parents, but general things, like how I'd found Tipping Creek County forlorn, and how my favourite television show was *Front Page Challenge*. I told him Sadie Wilder adopted me. He didn't find it a freak move for Malibu Barbie to travel with me. He didn't make mean jibes about my walleye. He only said we'd need more work after planting season. He knew a couple of guys pulling in top wages at a mill in Alberta. There'd likely be something for me to do there too, service industry. We piled the few things we owned in his Ford Torino and road-tripped it west, tree-planting pay cheques in our pockets. The problems of food and shelter weren't immediately pressing, and Warren was the only friend I had in the world. I'd go west for a while, I told him, but Toronto was my dream. "Sure, sure," he said, not unkindly. He didn't drive flashily, in rocket-spurts like Vinnie Corio. He was nothing like Vinnie the juicer, the goon. Warren had this steady core, and made no sudden, unexpected moves. He just steered the course.

We drove. The earth flattened out, the horizon, distant, fuzzed with trees. I kept notes, like a diary, only more scattered. It passed the hours. *A tree line, hazed. Another tree line, rubbed charcoal pencil. A westering line, crimson canopy in late-day sun. Another, washed out by a downpour, the wiper blades beating it back, a tree line seen as though under water.*

We drove. *A ravaged horizon, shorn of trees, clear-cut.* Sometimes I read my notes to Warren while he steered us west. He'd pointed out that my use of 'tree line' wasn't accurate in the strict scientific sense. I showed my gratitude for his plodding accuracy by feeding Neil Young to the tape deck with a single, decisive shunt. Neil's voice, like a lonely coyote, claimed a man needed a maid. I wasn't so sure. But the key thing was, each mile carried me farther from the juicer, the goon, the harrower. Fort Spindle, Alberta. I'd swapped one wilderness for another. But Warren *raging-loved* it. His words. And he earned so much at the mill, he called my waitress pay *chump change*. Other than essentials like food and work boots and Kotex pads there was nothing to buy in that settlement of scrappy houses huddled on two levels, mill at the bottom, so I stashed my *chump change* in my suitcase in a remote closet corner. Waitressing tired me, I'd stopped writing in my notebook, and opened it one day to find my last entry had been, Gads, *almost a decade earlier*. The workings of time revealed themselves: tree lines that in the end blurred into one long receding horizon. A notebook, neglected. To measure time, I might have counted how many plates of bacon and eggs I'd served at The Alpine Diner, hundreds? Thousands? But waitresses didn't have the luxury of measuring anything but condiments. Customers demanded speed; they hoovered their breakfasts and pedaled-the-metal to the mountains, or, in the case of locals, the mill.

And one morning I rose and it was 1981. And I was still a waitress. What about Toronto, starting my *life*? I should have been moving in smart, glamorous circles in that city, before Sadie Wilder kidnapped me to the wilderness, and not running in circles in The Alpine Diner beside a bleak highway carved through clear-cut ridges.

As time passed, I felt myself grow dumber. My vocabulary, shrunk, rarely extended beyond, "Can I take your order?" "How's your meal?" But I knew there was a word for my life in Fort Spindle. After work one day I consulted the thesaurus in the trailer that served as the town's public library. I found the word: *inertia*. But Warren saw our western life, with a truck and the small bungalow he'd bought for us, as living the dream.

"But our house is in the direct line of the mill's rotten-egg odour," I'd told him the day he signed the real-estate papers.

"Plug your nose if you don't like it, Faith," he'd carped. "And, strictly speaking, we only get the mill's full brunt with an east wind. And don't forget, that *smell* paid for our pickup truck loaded with options parked out there in front of this nice home it also bought."

That word again, *home*.

Our house: a shell, pre-fab, identical to most others in the town except for a few palaces up on the ridge. It always felt like a strong gust could carry it away. And if I managed to grow anything in our scruffy lawn, deer and elk gobbled it for lunch. The short, intense summers scorched the grass, that and the beer bottles Warren's mill buddies littered after their barbeques pushed me towards fully abandoning the lawn. Della-Mae McCann said once, long ago when I was little, *it's a sad day when a woman abandons her lawn*. I thought of Tipping Creek County's trim green swatches with their gazing balls and gauzy smoke trees. While I refilled the ketchup bottles at the diner I wondered what kind of flowers my real mother had grown in Toronto. Roses, I imagined, spilling over trellises.

Waitresses at The Alpine Diner drifted in like seed-pod fluff in the wind. Lighted down in town, earned some cash, then blew away to fancier jobs at the resorts in Jasper or Banff. Or blew back east. Vera Moxon and I were the diner's veterans, the coffee-pot warriors. Head waitresses. I dug how Vera wore thick, black eyeliner. Kohl pencil. The customers gave her less guff the heavier she swooped it on. I tried it, too, but it smudged terribly. I looked like one of those sad French clowns. At least I *thought* they were French. Had I gone to a good school in Toronto, I'd have known the history of clowns. The kohl only drew attention to my walleye and I was tired of rude customers joking about it. Vera never did, bless her. The closest she'd crept to mentioning my off-eye was to tell me that true beauty demanded a flaw. Vera was a mushroom philosopher. And she'd helped me find my feet at the diner. She shared all her serving tricks, and how to tell if other waitresses filched our tips. How to bend, when clearing tables, to stave off a sore back. How to save steps. What to do when the mill guys grabbed at us or hurled insults when their orders took too long or their eggs weren't cooked right. "'Diner' might be a nice word, Faith," Vera said on my first working day, "But *this* diner is a grind, a tricked-out truck stop. Better grow a tough hide." She helped me like Dorothy, the wafer-girl, The Candy Cane, had helped me back at The Giant Snooze.

Vera and I walked to work through acid rain. We held Abba dance parties in her trailer. She ate magic mushrooms while I drank cocktails that early summer morning of 1981, the television turned on, and cathedral bells pealed as Princess Diana rolled along in her royal carriage with her prince, waving to the common people.

More tree lines, blurred. Vera and I refilled the salt and pepper shakers while Terry Fox reached his end. She sobbed in my arms in the meat freezer after her friend was killed in the Edmonton tornado. Besides Malibu Barbie, who stayed in the camper I'd finally bought her, and Dorothy, my brief friend beside Lake Superior (whose mood ring my finger always wore) and Katie, my even briefer pal at Tipping Creek All Disciples Secondary School, Vera was my only real friend. Thank the psychedelic stars for her! Once, in the foothills, we hunted for morels but found none. Anyway, she only cared about one mushroom, the kind that transported her to other places.

"Can your special mushroom get me to Toronto?" I asked Vera, once.

"It's not the sort of journey you can program, Faith, like

buying a train ticket. You have to fasten your seatbelt, get ready for surprises, and follow the visions."

I'd had enough surprises for one lifetime. I wanted to be in charge, chart my own course.

"Why don't you and Warren get hitched?" Vera had asked me while Diana floated down the aisle in her billowy white dress. "You guys own a truck, and this house, and you've been together for donkeys' years."

Vera nibbled on her mushroom, awaiting my answer.

"Warren thinks marriage is for squares," I said. "Besides, look around this town – what do you see?"

She swallowed, pondering. "Everyone's divorced?"

"Bingo," I said. "Besides, I'm not spending the rest of my life in Fort Spindle. I've been stashing years of diner tips. Chump change builds."

Vera saw where I was coming from. She wished she'd stashed, instead of mushroomed, her tips. "But you've got to get from one day to the next, don't you, Faith; you need a method. Feeding the rednecks and tourists wreaks havoc on a woman's soul."

It did – wreak.

The mill's stench didn't help my morning sickness. Neither did the grease in the diner kitchen where I slung steak and eggs until my body's roundness told a different story than the other tray-bearers shuffling among the tables. That was when the tree line emerged lemony but bilious each morning. No one wanted a pregnant waitress in 1988. I watched soap operas in our small house and started to write in my notebook again. Vera brought me milkshakes. She asked if I'd hit on a baby name. I hadn't. None of the soap-opera characters' names held any possibility.

Sometimes Warren played guitar, he'd gone electric, his

angular chords kicked against my stomach, and I'd joke once
the baby arrived he'd have to switch to something softer, like
lute, or harp. Those were good moments, when we both
laughed. Like when Sadie Wilder and I threw Frisbee. Warren
was pleased we'd soon have, he said, a little Crouch.

"Or a little Bannister?" I'd quipped.

"Your call, Faith. You're the mother. Who knows, maybe
there's some law about it."

I thought about how Sadie Wilder had missed out on the
queasy mornings of bile, and the same tedious question in the grocery store: *When are you due?* The swollen ankles. Heartburn.
And the oddest thing of all, the acute longing to eat mud. Sadie
had sidestepped this whole adventure. It had been easier to steal
someone *else's* baby and drag that baby to the boondocks. If
she'd taken me to an orphanage, where some family better able
to care for me – maybe even a family with a pretty house with
seafoam appliances – had adopted me, right now I'd be tripping
along the streets of Toronto. I might have gone to college.

Sadie should have let me go. She'd made a promise to my
parents to take care of me, but did that promise hold after they
were dead? They weren't about to pin a medal on her chicken-
barn overalls. Just to make sure they *were* dead, that my old
babysitter hadn't made *that* up, too, I'd checked official records
on a trip Warren and I took to Edmonton, shortly after he
bought the fancy truck. He figured I'd want to go to the huge
mall with the beach and skating rink. But I asked him to drive
me to the public library, then a government office, instead. A
few weeks later I had official identification for the first time. I
might want a driver's permit someday. I existed in the capital-
B Big World at last.

There was a mystery to how the baby kicked; I couldn't place the motions for a long time. They weren't random, but regular, steady. Then finally the pattern came to me, the movements were exactly those of a frog I'd seen swimming, once – a live frog, not the gruesome dead ones in formaldehyde that had sickened me in Environmental Science class. No, this swimmer within me moved with measured propulsion, bent on getting somewhere.

My nightmares back on the farm paled in comparison to the frog ripping me open as it – she – stroked her way onto the world's cold metal shore. Warren, on the verge of fainting, had to flee the delivery room, despite his resolve to stay. Vera held my hand, as I shrieked and begged for the agony to stop, and felt sure this was death. She sang to me, George Michael's song about having to have faith. When the nurse turned her back, Vera offered me a magic mushroom. I wanted it, wanted *anything* that could launch me past the pain, but I worried it might hurt the baby even though the fierce frog didn't care if she hurt *me*. Gads, what an unfair equation. Seven pounds of fury – no question she was alive. After she finally reached the light, and the nurse swaddled her, I looked at my shaking hands. Somehow, still attached to my arms. My old mood ring shone a vibrant colour I'd never seen before, like honey, lit from below. Not honey. *Amber*. That was her name, Amber, I told Vera.

"That's nice," my friend said.

"I'll wait for a couple of weeks, see if it sticks," I added, knowing full well this was the girl's name. She'd be my Honey Stone.

I told Warren. The ring inspired her name.

"Your call," Warren said, still looking pale, unnerved, adding, "I like it."

"Amber Shirley Crouch."

"Not Amber Sadie Crouch?" he asked. "It'd be the same initials on her gym bag, Faith. And Sadie *did* raise you, like you told me."

I repeated the name.

"Good-o, then." Warren grabbed his thermos, and hoofed it over to his mill shift.

That baby looped me out. When I craved sleep, she craved movement, play. We lived on opposite sides of the clock. Fort Spindle had no daycare, so I stayed home with Amber. Vera brought gossip and potato chips from the diner. She guzzled rye on my sofa and marvelled – how could it be, just *how?* – Princess Diana married *seven years* already? It was like we just watched her wedding yesterday.

I'd sighed, burping the baby. "Tree lines, Vera. And diaper changes and birthday cakes and winters' cuffs in the head and before we know it–"

I couldn't even spin my thought forward, that's how exhausted I was, from the baby's endless needs.

People were always saying you make scads of new friends when you have a child, in playgrounds, at hockey rinks, pools. I was supposed to exchange recipes for baby formula with these other parents or join a support group for new mothers. I'd been reading Dr. Spock's *Baby and Child Care* at the Fort Spindle Public Library; another, much younger mother, baby jiggling on her knee, smiled at me from across the small, book-lined trailer. I was supposed to smile back. But I drew into myself in Amber's early days, became an island. I took up macramé again, made a fringed wall-hanging for her nursery. Tying knots and half-hitches, I thought about my *own* nursery, the pretty things Sadie Wilder told me about. A carousel. Seal mobile. The storybook house where I'd been a baby. I thought about my father's dreamy car. No redneck truck for *Forest!* This aching rooted within me, that Amber should have more than this cardboard house with its burnt lawn. This town with its polluted air. She should have the things I'd missed. If I couldn't have the storybook life I'd been born into, maybe *she* could. I had to find a way. Months passed, a year, and she began to toddle about. Warren and I spoke a basic language needed to shuttle us from one day to the next, grocery runs, vehicle sharing, meals. We quarreled after his mill friends, partiers, trashed our living room.

"I don't want those lowlifes around our little girl," I declared after they left, Amber finally asleep. Their heavy metal and hollering kept disturbing her.

"I pay for all this," Warren clamoured. "I *don't* pay for you to call my friends 'lowlifes'."

That did it. "All – *this?*" I brandished my arm across the party mess. "They made cigarette burns in the sofa. They could have burnt down our house. Don't you care about your own –"

"Sure, of course, I care about her," Warren said. "She's my kid, why wouldn't I? But you? Nothing we built here, I built, was ever good enough. It's like you've got some *story in your head* you won't let go. Yeah, *story*, of what a life should be like – and it's *not this.*"

On that point, we agreed.

☙━━━❧

The western experiment was over. Warren couldn't say I hadn't given it a fair shot. Seventeen years had unspooled like an unregulated ball of yarn. As for Fort Spindle, new bars and a bigger tacky clothing store, and something resembling a mall had happened, but the town remained as bleak as the day we'd arrived. I couldn't squander any more yarn. I'd thought myself more rugged, substantial, than the waitresses who blew, like dandelion fluff, through The Alpine Diner over the years, but I was only a bigger blown speck. I'd made no imprint on those gnawed hills. The constant *ding-ding-ding* of the cook's bell when our breakfast orders came up wouldn't remember me. Warren didn't need anything more. He had the mill. His friends. He played with Amber sometimes. He was fond of her, in an afterthought kind of way.

How many times could someone hit the *reset* button on her life? The dark force of Tipping Creek County had been the land itself, some sour spirit it harboured, that narrowed its people's minds. Made them Barbie-doll murderers, teachers who left their students, in the name of Science, down in a mud swamp. What stranded me in Fort Spindle was sheer *inertia*, a *nonthing*, a thing so passive, invisible, yet over time it packed its own wallop. When I lugged Amber and my small suitcase, together, onto the Greyhound bus – it was early morning, before light, Warren in his mill shift's final hour – I hadn't been able to tell Vera good-bye, that was the saddest part. As the bus lumbered past The Alpine Diner, framed by its large front window, there she was, bent over a table, pouring a steaming arc of coffee into one cup, then a slight, fluid pivot of her form, another cup. Her choreography thrown into bright relief beneath the diner's blazing lights; she'd made waitressing a ballet in that ugly place, an art no one appreciated, or even noticed. To those lumpen coffee guzzlers, she might as well be an automaton.

A moment later the twin tunnels of light the bus beamed onto the highway were all I saw, and Amber, stirring, warm, against my body, all I felt.

AFTER FAITH LEFT

The small things that end the world: eggshells; unwanted flutters of fingers; losing lottery ticket stubs; a fly caught in a web the size of the world; all the bossy little chiclets: *log in, do this, do that*; tick; tick; the way each shunt of the clock's minute hand will conquer a rubber boot.

After Faith left, the annual morel hunt fizzled to a trudging chore I undertook alone. I needed the money. I never did find out who scooped our morel harvest that fateful day in 1972. So many things stay mysteries, they do. The rest of my time was barn work and typing and, in winter, cups of coffee I'd brew for my neighbour Ivan Price when he cleared the snow from my laneway. "I was quite the live wire, once," I told him one blustery day. He just laughed. Like he couldn't fathom this. "I had grand dreams too," I said. He laughed again, not cruel, but like my words were pieces from a jigsaw puzzle he couldn't crack and would be best set aside. When I informed him the chickens, over the years, pecked the life out of me, he swallowed the last of his coffee and said a person had to put food on the table one way or another. I didn't tell him I hadn't had much of an appetite after Faith abandoned me.

Summers, the garden brought me meaning, taking flowers to the cairn, the memory of Bobby. And typing more letters to Faith – like throwing darts into the darkness. But beat doing nothing, it did. Twenty-three years I've had, to practise my typing. It reached a pretty decent level until my fingers started to wobble and stray. Once that began, wrong letters peppered the page, then grew thicker, like craven weeds in a field of oats. *Essential tremor.* Doctor's fancy medical name for my rogue hands. I didn't tell her I'd been dropping eggs. Only that my fingers floundered as if searching for someone lost in darkness. I ask the doctor why I had the tremor, being only in my fifties. "Sadie, it can strike at any age," she said. "More often after forty. There are a few drug therapies to consider."

I muddled along without therapies. As long as the letters I typed to Faith, and my testimony of the hurricane night, were readable, that's all that mattered. And that I could work in the chicken barn. But I worried about my hands. The wretched new computer the poultry company made me buy demanded agile fingers. There was a new policy – egg reports must be filed 'online'. With the typewriter, I took my best stab. But when it came to the buzzing box on my dining room table, what the computer delivery boy from town called a *mouse*, needed to gnaw on just the right corner. One wrong move and crazy things appeared on the screen. Good grief, that computer rattled my nerves. Had *no love* for it, I didn't. *Log in. Do this. Do that.* All the bossy little chiclets.

"You have '*dial-up*' now, Mizz Wilder," the boy dazzled, as if I'd won a jackpot. I'd have been better off trying to find the lottery tickets I bought, stuck them somewhere in a drawer, but which one? All dial-up did was tie up the phone line. Even after so many years, I couldn't stop hoping one day she might phone, Faith might. It would have been easy enough for her to get my number from Information. I'd tried to find her number in Toronto. I had them search for Bannister listings. Nothing. One day, after clearing the snow from my laneway, Ivan urged me,

"Sadie, you've got to give up on her, too much time has passed." But I didn't; that would have been giving up on my life. Finding her had to remain a possibility to dwell in.

No one could phone me when the World Wide Web flashed its doom across the monitor. Mostly I avoided the Web; it only brought sorrow, like Hurricane Hazel's 'anniversary' a few months back. As if I needed a reminder. Why would they call the night the world ended an *anniversary*? That's not the right word at all. Nitwits ran the World Wide Web. Wherever Faith was, I hoped she had a better job than being a chicken farmer.

After Faith left I let the yard grow even wilder. I didn't have the will to keep the outbuildings painted and patched either, or the windmill straight. And I didn't care what the Tipping Creek gossips might say. The only thing I attended to was the chickens, no choice. I needed the poultry cheques. I used the annual morel profit to travel to that city of disaster, Toronto, to find Faith. Year after year, no Faith. Somehow, I felt she lived in those streets, but I had only enough morel money for my bus ticket, food, two nights' lodging, plus paying Ivan Price to feed my chickens and collect the eggs. I'd hardly get my bearings – searching for Faith until my ankles swelled from walking, leaving flowers on my mother's grave – before it was time to bus back to Tipping Creek. In Toronto, I tacked notices on bulletin boards in grocery stores and laundromats, like my old 'Reliable Girl for Hire' posters. Tricky to know what to say – *Babysitter Seeks Lost Baby, Baby is grown up now* – that was a nonsense burger to the wider world. In the end, the notices I posted in that city of disaster only said *Do you know Faith Bannister, aged* [I adjusted this every year]? *If so tell her to call home, urgent.* Then my phone number. No calls. I sent letters to Faith Bannister c/o General Delivery, Toronto, Ontario. I didn't really think an address that scanty would find her, but who knew?

And typing the letters made my fingers feel useful, at least, all those winter nights on the farm. Typing them felt like sending tiny search lights across the snow.

The worst part of buying the computer was that it took the morel money for 1994, and made me miss that year's trip to the city. I didn't miss tramping the streets, but *what if, what if* – my hands juddered harder when I broached the possibility – the *only* year I'd missed, Faith might have walked towards me on Yonge Street? She'd be in her early forties. Still tall. Dressed in a stylish spring coat, likely. Faith loved nice clothes. Like her mother. Would I have known Faith? Fires of heck, I'd know her. Those eyes. Would she recognize *me*? Would she *choose* to? She knew where I lived; she could have come back to the farm, but never did she return. Not even a letter. Or Christmas card.

But another, unwelcome voice clamoured in my head: Faith is a ghost (it said). And it'd be about your lousy luck, Sadie, if you *were* meant to pass on the street the *one* year you couldn't make it to Toronto because the computer's cost stole your annual morel windfall. Universe, why are you such a miserable crossword puzzle? I ordered the unwelcome voice to *zip it*. I'd never know, and pondering only worsened my tremor.

After Faith left, *right* after, the neighbours hunted for her everywhere. Barns. Bush. Dragged the Lake of Marl. Trolled the highway south to Toronto, where our youth vanished. I beat my way through the bush for miles around, calling her name.

The only letter I received, besides bills, was from the poultry company. It wasn't even a proper letter, but an electronic mail message:

Dear Sadie Wilder,

We write again concerning your egg quotas, which, our automated tracking system shows, have decreased noticeably over the past year.

As you are aware these are competitive times in the poultry industry; as one of our veteran growers we propose the following strategy to increase your egg quotas to meet current standards...

Their 'strategy' was, cram twice as many hens into my pen.

Theoretically, this should double your egg count.

Criminy, what were they thinking? Those hens would choke in a blizzard of their own feather dust! They'd be too sickly to lay eggs. *Then* watch my egg count plummet. My shaking hands sent a letter to the Regional Poultry Association, about the cruelty of their proposal. Then, I think around Valentine's Day, 1995, I realized – *Huzzah!* – I could throw the letter into the World Wide Web and my protest against cruelty to chickens would reach far beyond Tipping Creek. I'd make the buzzing box on my dining room table work *for* me. I, Sadie Wilder, little spider from nowhere, creeping into the Web. Why not? The only thing making any advances was time itself. Bossing the bossy little chiclet back, ordering it to 'send', my most daring act since that night over fifty years ago, when I rustled about in Shirley Bannister's periwinkle dress before the world ended. Maybe this time I could do a better job of saving lives, if only chickens' lives.

The sad little rubber boot in the woods by the cairn faded, a chalky shade. Years of weather disintegrated the sole; water I poured from a thermos oozed right out the bottom, seeping into the earth. The flowers withered in no time. That sad sight reached me when I returned to the cairn, sometimes only hours later, with more flowers. Tomorrow, the day of the annual morel hunt, I'll fill the boot with fresh spring herbs. Tell Bobby I'm sorry. Again. Then after the market, I'll take the bus to Toronto. Search for Faith. Again.

***

Fires of heck, *sixty-five – me*? There must be some mistake, there must. Or was it a trick of the drugs I've been taking to quell the shake in my hands? I gave in. A new century, and that city of disaster, Toronto, where still I travelled every year to search for Faith smeared itself ever wider across the map, gobbling every barn and silo in its path.

CRESCENT AMBER

The small things that end the world as I knew it: a fresh tattoo on my mother's lower back; my two front baby teeth, left behind; a brief cheerleader; a bottle of Sea Smoke Botella Santa Rita Hills Pinot Noir; waking up Little Susie; missing my scarf.

Just *spectacular*. I finally got some *respect*, as swim champion of my high school, and The Mom-ster went and moved us, mid-semester, to another *country*. Crescent City. The Big Easy. It took me long enough to make a few friends at home in Toronto. Her pitch: "Amber, this is our big break, this job offer of mine. You'll finish your year at a much *better* school, Magnolia Arts Academy. It's all arranged; they pulled a few strings to get you in, it's a special school. Dwell in a little possibility for *my* sake, won't you?"

I knew they were wankers even before I met them, the Academy kids.

My mother always had this wild *sense of occasion*. Like, on my birthdays, if she could have afforded it, she'd have hired a plane to trail sky-writing, or a banner of congratulations. But her waitressing day shifts and nursing classes at College on the Bluffs at night kept things tight for us. She said with her new job at Bayou Care Center, our money woes were over. The day before we left Toronto to go live in the United States she suddenly spun around in our empty kitchen, and flipped her blouse high enough to reveal, across her lower back, a newly-inked tattoo: *I Dwell in Possibility*. The letters' edges inflamed, sore-looking, and *F-bomb* me, I wondered if body ink was the wisest move before a long road trip.

I stared at the words. They looked, like, about to burst into flames. I glanced at the calendar above the stove to ground myself, trying to find my *own* words. The calendar told me it was March 6, 2005.

My mother rolled her blouse back down and swung around to face me again, and beamed – "Emily Dickinson!"

"*Stellar*, Ma!" I longed to deke outside for a cigarette. Had the hot flashes she'd been griping about made her get inked? I'd never had a solid grasp on what made The Mom-ster do the things she did.

She wanted more from me. Flung the last of our cutlery into a box, making these loud, jangly noises. Not *receiving* more, she said, "palm trees, here we come!" She checked for the umpteenth time that her 'papers of triumph' – what she called her Nurse Practitioner diploma – were rolled inside her new Samsonite luggage. As for her personal life, she said, who knew? She didn't look half-bad for fifty-two. She checked to ensure she'd packed concealer cream in her cosmetics bag.

"My tattoo celebrates our *new life*, Amber!" she jangled. "It feels right to mark it, and I've done just that – with poetry. I've lost so many years; now I'm going to *chase every possibility!* Hand me that roll of packing tape, please."

I played packer's flunky. Was *I* part of her 'lost years'? The Mom-ster was forever *blurting*, never thinking how *I* might feel. She'd told me once her 'quiet years' were when she was *this silent island, her own iron curtain*. That must have been before

I was born. As long as *I've* been around she's been a *talker*. After her waitress shifts, her night nursing courses, if I was still awake, she'd cozy down beside me on our futon sofa: "Tell me your news, Amber. Tell me *anything*. You don't want to hear about bedsores, believe me." But it was always mostly her talking. Remarking on, like, how quiet I was – her *hushed little Honey Stone*. Gag, I hated when she called me that. I didn't *have* much news when there wasn't a swim competition. Her quiet years had passed, that was for sure. And *talk* my mother *did, too,* on our road trip all the way to New Orleans – during music, after music. She'd made this special mixed tape for our trip – *Anthems of Possibility*. As we left behind the snows of Ontario and wheeled our way south, she played this one song on repeat. Kelly Clarkson, "Breakaway," spreading wings, learning to fly, *blah, blah*. Sentimental mush, to *me*, but for The Mom-ster, some mush was more equal than other mush. Whatever, she was totally stuck on that song. We'd almost hit Louisiana before I had the chance to play my Nirvana tape.

Mile after mile, my mother talked. How this *dark force* used to clamp down on her, harrow her, until she overthrew it once and for all, by keeping her dream alive, staying open to possibility. How she'd made it to Toronto at last, when I was a toddler, how she'd lived these different lives, and now we'd launched into yet *another* life, thanks to her job offer in New Orleans. "You've got to keep forging ahead in life, Amber. *Raza Unida*, it's you and me together, Honey Stone, and *look*, the world just burst into green, technicolour right before our eyes, like in *The Wizard of Oz*" (the greening had actually been gradual). My mother prattled about how smart she'd been, getting her driver's permit (she drove with a spirit of frenzied intent), how wise we were to ditch our sad, used furniture. For our big move, we'd take only ourselves, basic clothes, toiletries and our desktop computer. An allowance of *two small memento items each, but don't get sentimental*. We needed to stay clear-eyed for our big start-over, she said. I couldn't help noting The Momster left behind the tiny cloth drawstring pouch containing my two front baby teeth (which would have taken zero space). I saw her throw the pouch in the trash, a tad ruthless. She chose Malibu Barbie, which was no surprise. She didn't mention her second memento. I took my swimming medal, and the *Edmonton Oilers* jersey from my father. It was toddler-sized; he'd pulled out all the stops on my birthday that year. My mother said I was too young to recall that birthday, but I do. She'd always wanted a flowered sofa. We'd buy one in The Big Easy. "We should get a better car, too, Amber. A *luxury* car. This beater won't last much longer. Once we get really settled, we can get a dog. You always wanted a dog." (I don't remember saying any such thing; she was having one of her *reveries*, obviously *wanted* me to want a dog.) The Mom-ster talked while I knitted in the passenger's seat, making my spot into a yarn cocoon. As the grass of Kentucky blued around us, my mother asked what I knitted.

"A scarf," I said.

She laughed so rigorously I worried we'd careen off the Interstate and our exciting new life would happen in a *ditch*.

"Ma – be *careful!*"

She held the course. Said I didn't need a scarf where we were going. We'd never have winter again. But I *liked* winter. It was a *thinking season*. I liked the skating rink under the canopy of white lights in the park near our apartment. The time our class took a trip all the way to Ottawa, and we skated on the canal, the wind icing our faces. Then we'd eaten those pastries, beavertails. I'd felt like a *citizen*.

My mother drove and I knitted, sad to lose winter. She

talked about her plans for us in The Big Easy. Who knew, she said, maybe we'd have our own house someday with seafoam green kitchen appliances and a hi-fi in the living room. When she granted me a word in edgewise, I said it wasn't called a hi-fi anymore. I said, too, we were headed right for *sea level*. Didn't that bother her? She'd always had water issues. She'd never liked taking me to tadpoles swimming classes. She tried to hide it, but I knew, by the way she got all twitchy. She never wanted to go with me to the beach on Toronto Island. But I asked her, right there in the car, how she felt about us living so close to water. Her fingers curled tighter around the steering wheel as if it somehow held the answer to my question. "I'll be too busy working to be aware of it. And a job is a job, Amber."

The world flattened out before us; stark white crosses planted along the highway, marking deaths, fed into the gloom. Belching refineries. We passed an overturned transport, a badly smashed car. Ambulance. Police cruisers. If my mother hadn't forgotten her jacket back in the truck stop when we'd refueled, and we hadn't had to go back and get it, that could have been *us*, the wreck. Or if we'd left a tad sooner that morning – a minute, or two, or five – our lives might have been completely different.

"I used to be quite the macramé virtuoso," the Mom-ster brayed, pulling out into the passing lane like some Formula One racer. "A crackerjack."

I white-knuckled it. Dwelt on the word *crackerjack* to take my mind off dying, *crackerjack* sounded so – *old world*. Luckily, we didn't become white crosses, we lived to spread our Kelly Clarkson wings.

My mother was right; I *didn't* need a scarf in that muggy crescent bowl with its supersized shrubs and sodas and nasty creepy crawlers. City of sinking graves. I wore the black scarf anyway, for a while, in mourning for Toronto, for winter, for my school. The scarf was a buffer zone. I hated Magnolia Arts Academy from the first moment, when Principal Dyan Chandler, with her Dolly Parton vibe, stood me in front of the whole class and announced, "Amber is 'international', isn't that *exciting?*" Her news generated about as much buzz as a dental appointment reminder. I'd stared dumbly out into a gnarly sea of plaid shirts, perfect-girl hair, mostly blonde. I wanted to say "snap a picture, it'll last longer," as they gawked, their cold eyes scanning me from my Doc Martens up through my black jeans, then higher, above my black scarf to my pierced nose. After only a few days it became pretty clear they were a bunch of Emo-heads – so *sensitive* – whose parents used to listen to The Smiths, but now that those same parents drove BMWs, they didn't know what to do about their music. At recess, when I just wanted a minute of peace, and to steal a smoke under this monster oak at the edge of the grounds, a few Academy kids sidled over and badgered me about how I talked. "Aboot! Aboot! You talk funny, Amber Crouch. You say *aboot!*"

I never did. I've always said *about.*

Our apartment off Magazine Street, I had to admit, had funky attitude. Old low-rise building. We lived on the second floor and had a tiny balcony with pretty scrollwork. This huge kitchen island now ours turned into a 'talking island' for The Momster pretty fast. There was a giant walk-in closet in her bedroom, which clinched the deal. When she wasn't working her long shifts at Bayou Care Center, my mother loved to perch on a bar stool at the island, stroking its smooth granite surface, sipping good wine. "No cheap wine in our new adventure," she'd proclaimed. Wearing something bright, she looked like a giant tropical bird. *F-bomb* me, how she held forth about our brilliant new lives. She'd bought this huge flowered sofa with her credit card: "It's very *southern*, Amber. Vibrant!" I stubbed my toe on it often, that's how much it filled the room. She bought an antique desk with claw-like legs for the computer we shared. New clothes for herself – *dating outfits*, she called them. During my mother's shopping spree over several weekends, she asked what I wanted. School threads? She'd noted how the Academy kids dressed "very high-end." Just yarn, for knitting, I told her. Wanted to add cigarettes, but I couldn't. Smoking had to stay a secret. When I asked The Mom-ster about her job, she remarked, "It's a learning curve Amber, I *will* say that, a *whopping* curve. Thankfully, Charity Sparks, Head Nurse, took me under her wing. She has a daughter your age, isn't that nice? And kind Ivy Huckster at the front desk. Ivy gave me the skinny on how everyone calls the Center's Director, Mickey Chandler, *The Care Emperor*. And Sherry Rummage, the nutritionist, urged me to try this Internet dating site."

I hadn't needed to hear that last bit, about dating.

My mother asked me about Magnolia Arts Academy.

"There's *no* swimming pool, Ma, *no* sports program. Only *dance*, drama, writing, or drawing," I groaned.

"That's because it's an *arts* high school, Amber, it's *specialized*."

F-bomb me I was *aware*. How would I keep up my aquatic skill level? The Mom-ster had no answer. She reminded me that I'd only been accepted at the Academy because some strings were pulled. Her boss, Mickey Chandler, was married to my Principal, Dyan Chandler. Mickey prevailed upon his wife to take me as a student. My mother asked if I'd made any friends at the Academy. I hadn't. Her tongue clucked. "That *will* change, Amber. In fact, a *wicked brainstorm* just struck me. I just have to check out something at work."

I missed moving through water. Front crawl. Butterfly. I

needed to swim. I needed a smoke. Water, smoke. "Smoke on the Water," this old song my dad played on his guitar. After our arrival in New Orleans I sent him an email update with our new address. He mailed me cheques when he remembered; I was running low on cigarettes. I told him my new school blew. Reminded him Canadian dollars were worth much less in America. I left out that The Mom-ster had gone all born-again cougar, and was dating men from an Internet site. That scared me to my bones; what if one of those guys was a serial killer? I didn't tell my father that every time she went on a date, lofting a heavy hairspray and perfume wake as she swanned out into the firearm night, I'd whisper to the flowered sofa: *just come back*. I didn't tell him every day I felt like the dude in that painting we studied in art class, *The Scream*. And the only place I could chill in New Orleans was on our balcony. I told him a nice, older lady with beautiful ebony skin, Mrs. Celestine, lived downstairs on the ground floor and when I was on the balcony and she'd be outside pruning the flowering shrubs, she'd holler a friendly greeting to me. *Hello up there, Canadian girl*. I didn't add she'd sometimes chime out, *your secret's airtight safe with me*. She meant my balcony smoke before The Mom-ster came home. That was an awesome, neighbourly thing Mrs. C. did for me.

Even after my mother bought us a computer I wrote my father real letters. I liked picturing them hurtling westward through space, with my writing on them. I'd tell him my latest swimming prize. Other brief homespun anecdotes, like how my mother got riled if I swore, so I had to invent my *own* phrases, my favourite: *Damned Skippy!* Or, when things weren't going as planned: *Ah, Beavertails!*

I learned early on that a letter, whether delivered by email or written on paper folded into an envelope, sealed, and stamped, is mostly about what you leave *out*.

My mother found this black cat with a chewed ear near a dumpster a few weeks after we moved into our apartment. Ponty, we named him. Short for Lake Pontchartrain.

"Now we're a family," she said. "We have a cat."

I'd have preferred a goldfish. No litter box to empty – this soon became my chore – and I'd have liked checking out its laps around the bowl.

We'd been in New Orleans for almost two months when I asked, "And how is your job *now*, Ma? Any easier?" For the first time, I noted saggy half-rings under her eyes.

"Still a major learning curve," she sighed.

Half-rings. Learning curves. Crescent City. *Curve* was like *crescent*, a sickle struggling to make it all the way around, like a moon that ached to be full, but never could. Something hobbled it, held it back.

This was my mother's wicked brainstorm. The Head Nurse at Bayou Care Center, Charity Sparks, had a daughter who went to my school. Sienna Sparks. The two mothers set up sort of a teenaged girls' play date for Sienna and I.

"*Hey* Amber Crouch," this blonde cheerleader-type in tall boots clocked right up to my locker, as I stacked books on the top shelf. "Your mother talked to my mother, and we're supposed to hang out, or something. I'm Sienna. Sparks."

She must have been among the sea of cheerleader faces and plaid shirts the day Principal Chandler introduced me to the class, and that was how she recognized me. Her mouth launched a pink planet of bubblegum that popped on her button nose. She scrambled the planet back onto her tongue.

"Can you talk?" Sienna Sparks pressed. "Or does that *thing* stabbed through your nose prevent it?" She laughed, and I didn't like her.

"You wanna try, or what? Hang out at my house after school? I live in the Garden District. You can come over and tell me about your grunge style. We can watch *The Princess Bride*, I have it on video."

Damned Skippy, I hated that movie. As far as I could tell, Sienna Sparks and I shared zero in common. But I'd promised my mother I'd try. She'd emailed me on her break at the Care Center; I'd read her urging little beads, in the computer lab during my spare period: *Amber. Remember. Friend. Try. Promise.*

Sienna turned her lips into a small Armani purse like the one The Mom-ster had bought, to take on her dates. "Sure, why not?" I said. We scribbled our phone numbers and addresses on scraps ripped from notebooks.

The change-of-class chime, a lullaby pong so the sensitive, thoroughbred students wouldn't be startled.

"See you then!" Sienna chirped.

"Damned Skippy," I chirped back flatly.

Her perfect eyebrows flipped into puzzled mode. "Damned Skippy? Why do you say that? What does it mean? Some *Canadian thing?*"

"It's just my own expression when something's about to happen, like, us, hanging out. It seals it."

"*Aboot*," Sienna laughed. "You're darkly cute, Amber Crouch."

The tall boots clocked away.

I survived the movie night at Sienna's house with its mahogany and Persian rugs and spinning ceiling fans. Dying for a smoke the whole time. The two mothers, apparently, declared Sienna's 'befriending' of me a success. Oh, *spectacular*, like Miss Cheer-leader bestowed this great act of kindness on me. Most likely I was a pity friend. I needed to reciprocate, my mother declared. She had a date on Saturday night. I should invite my new friend Sienna over that night. The Mom-ster strutted around our kitchen in a red leather skirt, lacy black tank top, and platform sandals. Her hair backcombed. Cheekbones blooded with blusher. She always looked retro, somehow, even when I was pretty sure she didn't mean to; it wasn't just that old mood ring always on her finger. A side effect of being fifty-two, maybe.

"There's frozen pizza in the freezer," she said.

Where else would it be?

"You girls help yourself to anything. And don't be a fun sponge, Amber. Make it an *occasion*!"

Ah, *Beavertails*, I'd wanted a quiet night at home. Knit. Smoke. Headphones. Music. But The Mom-ster was so *intent on it all*. I couldn't disappoint her. A dark thought darted through my head, just for a second, that inviting Sienna over served as a – babysitter fix – no, that was silly. I was seventeen, I didn't need a sitter. No sitter hadn't stopped my mother from going on previous dates. If anything, I was the one keeping the home-fires burning, the cat litter changed. I hung out alone in our apartment all the time. *Think, Amber*. Things sounded pretty intense at Bayou Care Center, she'd raised the stakes with Sienna and I being, like, sudden best female friends. As if. That *must* be it; my mother new at her job, on a temporary work visa, needed brownie points. She didn't want to disappoint her immediate supervisor, Charity Sparks. And I didn't want to let my mother down. When disappointment struck, her face be-came this whole *awful thing*, like, a big candle, snuffed out. *Ah Beavertails*, that tanked my spirits. That's how my life became a hamster-wheel of disappointment management. And what made it worse was when my mother dressed beyond the nines to go on dates, her candle-face glowed so brightly despite the tacky blusher and mascara caked on her crooked eyes, she became this tall human candle and all I could do, all *any*one with a heart would be able to do, I felt sure, was cheer for her.

Soon enough, Sienna Sparks sat, like a princess on her throne, across from me at the kitchen island. The pizza heated in the oven. We acted formal, like two young ladies at some Victorian tea party. I was striving to be a good host. I knew this 'occasion' would be reported to my mother's supervisor, Head Nurse Charity Sparks. A poodle barrette, of all things, clinched back my guest's blonde strands. It fit her cheerleader vibe in this weird, quaint way. I thanked Sienna for wearing her poodle just for me.

"The barrette belonged to my grandmother," she said. Altogether missing my, like, subtle jokiness.

I lit candles. Put on some dinner music. Hole. While Courtney Love belted out "Olympia" Sienna poked around the apartment. "I've never known anyone who lived in an apartment," she said. The fact that I hadn't nosed around *her* house held no currency.

I heard her in the living room, mimicking Courtney Love's wails. No more Victorian young lady.

"Pizza's ready, Sienna!" I called to her. "Come get some!"

Sienna posed in the kitchen doorway, holding forth a bottle of my mother's red wine. "This goes well with pizza. There's tons of it in there." She jerked her ringed thumb back towards the living room, to my mother's large wine rack. Before I could say anything, she'd opened it (screw top), and declared it needed to breathe.

The Mom-ster *had* said help ourselves to anything. She'd said make this an occasion. Later I'd rearrange the bottles to camouflage the gap in the rack. I cleared space on the cluttered kitchen island, shoving aside bills, my mother's cellular phone she'd forgotten, my knitting. Sienna asked about the jumbo pile of yarn. I told her I was knitting the longest scarf in the world. "Hey," she said. "This is New Orleans. You don't need a scarf."

"That's what my mother keeps telling me. It's just a hobby, Sienna."

We guzzled the wine. Ate pizza. "You're a weird mix, Amber Crouch," Sienna said, her mouth full. "Doc Martens, nose ring *and knitting*? But you're okay. You know what *my* mom says?"

I gnawed on a crust. "No, what?"

Sienna's mouth pulled down long strings of cheese while she hoisted the pizza slice high. "She says, 'girls' friendships remain one of the world's great mysteries'."

Ah *Beavertails*, so like an adult, speaking in riddles. And I thought it was just *my* mother. I raised my goblet, a toast. We clinked, then gossiped about kids at school. The other day Sienna saw me talking to Bo Lockhart, Head Boy.

"I wouldn't exactly call it 'talking'," I countered. He'd sidled up behind me at the Student Art Fair. All those variations on *The Scream* a total snore except one, where the screaming dude wore a Ramones t-shirt and behind him, instead of that nauseating river swirl was this perfect aqua swimming pool and beyond that, a city skyline I'd squinted into Toronto.

Suddenly, I'd heard his voice behind me: "Wad you think of it, Canuck Girl?"

I'd turned. Head Boy, all hipster and MTV. I loathed how he said *Canuck Girl*. Like I was some third-rate action figure. "What do you want, Bo? I was, like, just here, appreciating this painting."

Bo had taken a step back, away from me. "I was only asking

your opinion about this painting you've been staring at forever. Personally, I think it denotes a degenerate mindset."

I told Sienna this. She took a long swallow of wine. "Heavy. What did you say, Amber?"

"I informed him I *liked* the painting. I didn't see him after that. I guess he went home, clapped his Bose headphones over his ears, and listened to Weezer."

I couldn't smoke in the apartment, but the wine was a nice buzzy substitute.

"You remind me of her, Amber."

"Who? Who do I remind you of?"

Sienna cracked up. "*Hooo – hooo –* you sound like an owl."

I laughed, too.

"Love," she said. "Courtney. Like, she's actually pretty but cheats her own natural assets. She's turned herself into a train wreck when she could look so sweet." Sienna drained her glass.

I followed suit. It seemed like the right thing for a host to do. The wine fogged my thoughts. I couldn't tell whether my friend had complimented or insulted me, or *what*, exactly, was her point? Sienna didn't grasp Grunge: that Love's stage presence kicked against perfect all-American cheerleader types like – Sienna.

I blinked back the urge to debate. Sienna was my guest, after all.

We demolished the pizza. Hole ended. Sienna began dancing to some music only she heard. Her cheeks glowed. "I just had this *genius idea*, Amber. Let's make our own girl band, just the two of us."

I reminded her that neither of us played guitar. She swatted her hand, a blow-off gesture, made this *Pffft* sound. "We'll *learn*, silly! How hard can it be? I bet we can score coaching from the music teacher at Magnolia and he's hot. In the meantime, we can figure out our costumes –"

I'd no idea where she was headed.

"Ah Amber, I'll break it down for you. I caught a glimpse of your mother off-duty, super-cougar, leather, low-cut slinky stuff. *Makeup to the hilt.* Like, she didn't know she'd missed Mardi Gras, still wandering around after it ended. She was in the drugstore near my house. I recognized her from *We Care in Spades*, the newsletter my mom brings home and leaves on the coffee table. Your mom was in the *New Staff* column. I'll bet she has lots of killer clothes. Let's borrow some for our band."

Sienna's Mardi Gras comment was low but she could say it because her mother was my mother's boss, and because Sienna lived in a fancy house in the Garden District. She waited for me to hurrah her clothes-borrowing scheme. The wine slugged me into snail mode while it turned my guest into the energizer bunny. Before I could protest – because even wine-headed, I sensed a wrong – Sienna tugged my hand through the living room, around the big, flowered sofa, and into my mother's bedroom. Kidnapped in my own apartment.

Sienna was used to getting her own way and I, drugged under her wilful spell, existed in some reality television show I couldn't turn off. Sienna dove right in, rifling through my mother's closet.

"We've got no business in here." I'd only seen The Momster's closet once, when we looked to rent the apartment.

A tiny, stern face stared down at us from a high shelf. The face creeped me out. Malibu Barbie dressed in her zebra-print bathing suit, her legs extended straight out forever. Sienna saw it, too. "*Freaky.* Imagine never being able to bend your knees."

It was just my mom's old doll, I told her. The wine unsteadied me. I clutched the doorframe at the closet's entrance. "Si. Please. This closet is a closed country. We've got no passports."

"This is so *rad*," my new friend gabbled, ignoring me. "Check this out, Amber! It's a theme park in here! A Mommy-Mardi-Gras, Cougar Disney World!"

She made it sound like Dizzy World.

Glumly I gazed inside. Theme park wasn't far off the mark. Clearly my mother's closet was an *occasion*, and a big one. She'd shopped her brains out on the weekends since our arrival in New Orleans. Not just furniture, stereo, and used vinyl records. A new wardrobe. Her closet even had *signage*. Hand-lettered: *Work Zone* (nurse hats, etc). *Retro Zone* (geometric patterns, human versions of Malibu Barbie's outfits). *Fun* (black, lace, leather, pleather). I half-expected a zone called *Outfits for Dwellers in Possibility*.

That was the tidy part. The floor was another story. Clothes swirled in mounds like cleft entrances to caves, soft tangled folds of fabric up to our ankles, higher in places. Emptied-out bags from T.J. Maxx, Saks. Floored lingerie – fishnets, red bras, filmy thongs, black bras, camisoles, tangled leggings with studs, a boot poking through one heap like it had washed ashore.

Sienna seized a lace thong and shot it like a slingshot. Her words slurred. "*Dude*! It's like a ransacked Victoria's Secret store in here!"

Stellar. Your friend just saw your mother's underwear, your *fifty-something* mother's *thongs*. "Come on, Sienna. You've seen it, now let's boogie back to the kitchen. We'll open more wine if you want." (The wine had become the lesser problem.)

She left off with her rifling around long enough to gleam her teeth my way. "I like the wine idea, Amb. Hold that thought –"

Then she looped back to snooping.

"I don't *wanna* have a girl-band, Si!" I knew my tone was childish but I couldn't help it.

She swatted me away like a common housefly. "Hey, Amber,

wine makes you whine. Listen, we'll rock the music world. We'll *kill it!* We'll be better than Hole! We'll call our band – *Sienna Amber!*"

"*Amber Sienna*," I countered thickly. "Since we hatched the idea at *my* place."

Sienna tossed thongs and bras and whatever else her greedy paws grabbed, into the air. It rained lingerie. My weak, "Oh no, *no*, don't do that, don't throw those" drowned out by the glee from her grape-drenched mouth. "Oh wow – this is just *too rad!*"

Then Sienna Pan-Freaking-Dora shoved aside an old fur coat hanging under the *Retro* label and discovered, shelved behind it, a small box covered in leopard-skin paper. Its label neatly printed in fading marker pen – *Macramé Maggie*. Underneath that, smaller print: Thunder Bay.

"What's a Thunder Bay?" she asked, fingers floating over the box's lid.

"A place. North. Canada. Now, for the last time, Si, please put it back."

My friend's face was so blissed I worried she'd burst with joy and splatter the balloon bits of herself everywhere. "Are you kidding, Amber?"

Nausea surged through me. Tears shoved at my eyes. I grabbed the doorjamb to steady myself.

Sienna opened the leopard-skin box. "Oh! Ho! *Ho!*"

"Stop it, Si! Izz not Christmas – put it back. Please."

My words were pointless. Sienna tore away the tissue paper in the top part of the box and dug in. "Christmas?" (She said it like Krizz-mess.) "What's Christmas got to do with it?" She drew from the box a string, fashioned from macramé, with a triangle stitched into it. It was yellowed, like something from an antique shop. Sienna shrieked, full glee, "Holy Prime of Miss

Jean Brodie!"

The closet reeled before my watery eyes. "Miss *Who?*"

An annoyed glance from Pan-Freaking-Dora. "Just some old book my mom read. But never mind that, Amb – this is so much better!" She removed two small sparkly disks from the box, each disk the size of a healthy rose petal, a tassel sprouting from each. Like the triangle string, these bore the whiff of art-facts.

"Earrings?" I asked.

Sienna howled like she'd been fed laughing gas through some invisible tube. Apparently, I was, like, the funniest comedian ever.

"No!" she pealed, recouping her breath. "You really don't know what these *are*, do you, Amb?" Without waiting for my answer, she placed one tasseled piece over each of her perky cheerleader boobs and bounced, tossing the tassels into a jiggling dance. "They're *pasties*, silly. Exotic dancers wear them, let's just say it – *strippers* – and the other bitty thing's a G-string."

F-bomb me, I was confused. "Maybe they're from an old Halloween costume of hers, Sienna?"

My friend made that *Pfffft* sound again, and rolled her eyes, which told me how lame she found my theory. "Naw, they're *real*, Amb – they've got this whiff of auth – *authenticity* – hey, watch this!" Then Sienna flat-out showed off. She was *born* for it. Still pressing the sparkly discs against herself she shunted her right shoulder into the air and jumped along with it, not seeing where she leapt. Sienna could jump, all cheerleaders could.

She banged her head on my mother's closet shelf. Hard. The pasties fell from her hands onto clothes heaped, mangled, on the floor. She blacked out, went down, her fall padded by The Mom-ster's messy world.

It was like I watched some awful reality television show except it was my life. I gawked at my friend down there, crumpled on a mattress made from my mother's lingerie.

The first time I'd seen Sienna Sparks quiet. Panic clenched my ribcage – what if she was in a coma and never woke up? What if she was *dead?* I shook her. "Si– Si–"

She didn't move. *Stellar.* My friend, dead in my mother's closet. I joggled her shoulder. "Sienna – talk to me – *please.*"

There had to be some Goddess of the Closet because Sienna began to moan. Then her eyes batted open. She seemed confused, groaned she might be sick. She rubbed her head where it had struck the wooden shelf.

"We're in some major hot water, Sienna! But at least you're alive. Can you sit up?"

My friend sounded a stretched *urrrh* then blasted the lumpy deep-pink contents of her stomach over some twisted white garment of my mother's. *F-bomb* me. I'd have to deal with that mess later. First I needed to get Sienna out of the closet. I had no idea what time it was, or how late my mother would be out. Maybe her date would be a bust, and end early.

"Wait here," I told Sienna, who looked seriously stunned.

I left her collapsed in the pink lumpy stuff and crashed about in the kitchen, bruising myself. The wine made me clumsy. I fetched a small towel, some ice cubes, and a garbage bag. Dumped the white garment covered with Si's sick into the bag. It was a sundress, halter-top style, ruined, most likely. Red wine stains.

I dragged Sienna out into the living room, stubbing my toe, and helped her onto the flowered sofa. I placed the homemade ice pack I'd fashioned with the towel and cold cubes, where she'd hit her head. She winced. I felt a bump.

"I have a bobo," she said.

"Yeah, Si. Keep this ice pack pressed against your head, it

should help."

My friend pressed the pack, then cast her dazed eyes around the room. "Lotta flowers."

I guessed she meant the massive sofa beneath her.

"Yeah. Flowers, Si, and please don't get sick on the sofa. I'm already so doomed."

Ponty meowed, shrinking himself into frizz under the computer desk.

"Sienna Amber," she murmured, closing her eyes. Her face wore this stoned smile. I figured the ice numbed the pain, or the wine did.

In the kitchen sink I scrubbed the white sundress, my efforts not promising. I balled the dress inside another plastic bag and put it in my bedroom closet. The plan was to smuggle it to the dry cleaner's. I cleaned up the rest of Si's sick in the closet, thinking how the leopard-skin box must have been my mother's *other* memento brought from Canada. When had she worked as a stripper? I bet she left *that* off her job application. But why keep *those* bits instead of my baby teeth? Would Mrs. Sparks hear about my mother's *work history*? This was not good. Sienna seemed to rest, dozing. But suddenly I remembered how, when I was really little, I fell down the steps of our house in Alberta and struck my head. My parents' alarmed words cobwebbed my memory: "keep her awake." *Ah, Beavertails*, that's right. People who hit their heads weren't supposed to sleep or they might never return.

I rubbed her arm. "Wake up, Sienna. Wake-ee, wake-ee!"

My friend groaned. "Tired. Need sleep."

"Oh, no you don't," I told her.

I thunked over to the stereo and slid one of my mother's vinyl records onto the platter. "Wake up Little Susie." After pumping the volume, I darted back inside The Mom-ster's closet. I returned the G-string and pasties to their box behind the fur coat and tried to recapture the exact chaos of the heaps on the closet floor so she wouldn't suspect an invasion.

I needed to squirrel away the empty wine bottle and wash the glasses. First I started clearing the kitchen island, which was strewn with pizza crusts and girl-party mess. I considered hauling Sienna onto my bed and staging it like a sleepover. I must have caught my mother's 'possibility' bug because I dared to think I might pull this off. I dared to breathe fully. The main sticking point – Si's injury. How to explain that?

She moaned on the sofa, then I heard something like 'eeep'. I guessed 'sleep', so I woke up little Susie louder, maxing the volume.

I returned to the kitchen, to my party-deleting chore.

The breath slapped right out of me with the shock of my mother, looming large in her platform sandals. "Turn that music off, Amber! I could hear it from the street. The last thing we need is a noise complaint. Why are you playing that? You *hate* that song."

A loud hiccup bolted from my mouth. I ran jagged steps into the living room, silenced the song, then returned to the kitchen, to the giantess on her golden platform. "Mom – you're home early. You scared me."

She was alive, at least.

Switching on the overhead light, she made a scornful goose-honk. "*Scared* you? Who *else* would I be?"

Her voice sounded fogged. Her makeup was creviced, her lips faded. She looked like she'd escaped from a carnival. I didn't know if this signalled a successful date, or not. She dropped her clutch purse on the kitchen island while scanning its candlelit surface: the empty wine bottle, her forgotten cellular phone, dirty plates. Her bracelets tinkled against the glass as she turned the bottle slowly.

I awaited my sentence.

Instead she read the label out loud. "*Sea Smoke Botella Santa Rita Hills Pinot Noir, 2002.* How was it, Amber?"

I shrugged. "It was okay." I'm surprised she hadn't noted *two* empty glasses. A rash of fresh worry about Sienna on the living room sofa prickled my skin. She was awfully quiet in there.

My mother set the bottle back down on the island. Her off-kilter look suggested she'd had a few drinks herself. "With just that hint of cassis, no?"

Again, I shrugged. "Yeah, I guess so. It went good with the pizza."

My mother scowled. "It went *well*, Amber. It went *well* with the pizza."

"Okay, Mom."

Sienna let out a loud, lurching cry of pain from the living room sofa.

"Jesus and Janis Joplin, *what's* that?" my mother sharked. "*Who's* that?"

"Uh – Sienna, Mom. You said I should invite her over, so I did."

"Why is she making those distressing noises?"

"She had a little accident, Mom."

The Mom-ster clip-clopped into the living room with as much speed as her platform sandals permitted, me scuttling in her wake. The ice pack on my friend's forehead had melted, cold water trickled down her face, her spazzed eyes beheld my mother.

"Good lord, Sienna! What happened to you? Should I call 911?"

At that moment, my mother didn't seem like a nurse. Weren't nurses meant to step up in emergencies, take control, and, like, calm everyone?

My version needed to get out first. "Sienna and I were practicing some dance moves for the school drama festival. She bumped her head on the bookcase and, like, drank a bit too much wine – and maybe I did, too." I burped.

Sienna flashed this broad, creepy smile. "Evening, *Miss Jean Brodie!*"

My mother grabbed her own face like she planned to rip it off. "Amber! Call Mrs. Sparks *right now*. Sienna is hallucinating – she must have a concussion – she doesn't even know who I am. *Hurry!*"

I punched in the Sparks' phone number, my fingers quaking. After the call, I whisked away the empty wine bottle, glasses, and the rest of the pizza debris. Snuffed the candles. I thought about how a crescent is a failed circle. The wine shunted my thoughts all over the place.

I returned to the living room, taking studiously straight steps. The Mom-ster roosted on the sofa's edge, muttering words of comfort to Sienna. *Honey this* and *Honey that*. She'd snugged a blanket around poor tragic Sienna. Already I knew I'd take the fall. Sienna's mother was my mom's supervisor.

Sienna got *Honey*. All I got was a mile-wide glare. "*Well*, Amber?"

"Mrs. Sparks is on her way." I hiccupped. Shivered, then leaned, weak, against the living room doorjamb. Our apartment was damp. I was the one needing the blanket, not Sienna. While my mother *honeyed* Sienna some more, I scrambled to my bedroom, fetched my black scarf, and wound it around my neck, which would no doubt soon be wrung. I slumped back to the living room.

My mother rose, more nurse-like, and squared a fresh ice pack on Si's head.

"She smells like a booze can," The Mom-ster snarked.

I knew better than to say, *so do you, Mom, and you look like a trashed panda with your smudged makeup.* Knew better than to remind my mother she'd told me we could help ourselves to anything.

Life was letter writing in action, more about what you left out.

"Well," my mother intoned, a funeral-bell well. "I see I can't leave you home alone after all, even though you're seventeen. Just when I began to have a possible *life.*"

Tears stung my eyes. It wasn't my fault. Not the wine, the closet, the bashed head, sundress mess. I considered telling my mother this whole night was Sienna's doing, but what good would that do? Charity Sparks would call the shots.

Just then I noted something new about my mother – a red welt like a leech attached to her neck. No, not a leech. A love bite. If this night wasn't bad enough, she'd dated a vampire.

Sienna's mother would storm in on us in any second. I tramped off to my bedroom again and feverishly rooted through my drawer. My skull-and-crossbones scarf surfaced. I blinked back tears and give it to my mother in the living room. "Put this on – it'll hide the mark on your neck."

She looked puzzled at first, then blushed, and obeyed.

The doorbell. Sparks were about to shoot across our apartment. Our cat scuttled away, a quick blaze of midnight, and hid behind the drapes, not wanting to lose his tail when the axe dropped.

CRESCENT FAITH

The small things that end the world: snagged pantyhose (a tiny thread-ladder that loses points); bedsores; little blunt-nosed fish with morel gills; a free-floating gold tooth.

My supervisor, Charity Sparks, a former Miss Baton Rouge (1984) was still beautiful, though a beauty that bolstered the cosmetics sector. She summoned me to her office, no doubt to discuss the fallout from our daughters' fiasco last night. Her eyes ice-picked the small white X, crisscrossed, on my neck. She moved down to my snagged pantyhose, a large white, ladder below my knee, courtesy of the ratty bus seat. The bus, late, snarled in traffic. Bayou Care Center's *Impeccable Staff Comportment* policy worked on a points system. The person with fewest lost points won Caregiver of the Month. A merit bonus. My ripped panty hose and tardiness made a diminishing math.

I stood before my supervisor, trying to steady my breathing. No one would've guessed Miss Baton Rouge 1984 and I had been having coffee, and taking Pilates together. That was over. If only Amber hadn't lost her cool last night, when Charity griped she should have known better than let her daughter pal around with a foreigner, "a reckless little punk-ass northerner." If only Amber hadn't shouted back at my boss: "We're not

foreigners, you fake-blonde, stupid witch! We're *Canadians!*"
Charity could fire me. My temporary work visa depended on
more than impeccable comportment. It depended on moral char-
acter. My daughter's, too. Bayou's promotional video went on
about what *good people we all are*, upstanding, compassionate,
how your loved ones will be placed in the most caring hands.

My supervisor rucked her face. "Faith, we won't speak
about last night, other than to say, seek counselling for your
daughter. The Care Center doesn't look kindly on juvenile
delinquency in staff families. I could have laid charges, given
my Sienna was drugged and injured under your roof. But you'll
receive a bill from Emergency. I had to rush her there."

"How is – Sienna?" I faltered.

Charity staged a gloomy pout. "In shock – hardly a surprise.
Missing school. Concussed. I had to have my sister drive in
from Shreveport to monitor her. But we must move on, Faith,
so move on we *will*. You're late as it is."

She passed me a computer printout, my shift assignment.
The janitress had called in sick so I'd need to change the sheets
in Care Zone Three. The new ward assistant, Orderly Lucky
Mason, would help. Bedrolls. Meds. Today was Arts Day. I remembered. Malibu Barbie readied in my satchel. I'd been trying
to amuse the patients by acting out some little pantomimes,
starring the doll. They preferred re-runs of *The Lawrence Welk
Show* on the lounge television.

Lucky Mason was a kind, doughy man of about thirty. His
uniform rumpled and soiled, like he didn't own an iron, or
washer. *He'd* lose points, too, but I didn't remark on this. We
worked well together, rolling bodies over to stave off bedsores.
My tight white dress tugged and rode higher with my movements. Traditional nurse uniforms were part of the *Old-World-
Comfort Experience* Bayou Care Center sold. Time travel.

Mickey Chandler's fantasy. "Damn it, a nurse should *look* like a nurse," he'd exhorted on my first day.

Bodies rolled, gently. My thoughts roiled, furiously. Amber was *no* juvenile delinquent – she *knit!* I thought about my date last night, at the roadhouse out by the shrimp shacks and pawn shops. The roadhouse and its setting were grainy and edgy, racy, like a *noir* movie. I was glad I'd taken a taxi. I couldn't afford a driving-under-the-influence charge, or to have my car vandalized while meeting CLARK KENT, hunkered at the bar, wearing a cowboy hat, western shirt, Wrangler jeans, and cowboy boots with spurs, just as his email said. And he'd insisted on using our on-line monikers, not our real names. Making us CLARK KENT and *Macramé Maggie*. It had been an earthy, promising date. After a few beers, then bourbon, we'd necked in his truck, like I imagined high school kids surely still did. Kids at All Disciples used to snicker about 'love bites'. Other than calling what he did for a living, when I asked, "a mean junkyard dog of a job," CLARK KENT hadn't wanted to talk work. This suited me. I hated nurse jokes. Neither of us had posted our photograph on *The Big Easy for Singles*. I couldn't risk a photograph in case a family member of a Bayou Care Center patient recognized me. No one wanted a cougar-caregiver, just like no one wanted a pregnant waitress in 1988. As for CLARK KENT, his deal, why no photograph of him, I didn't know. Most likely scenario, he was married. Whatever. I didn't want a husband. I only wanted to feel what it was *like*, a date, an activity that wasn't work. Warren Crouch and I hadn't really dated. I'd missed out on so much because my babysitter kidnapped me to the wilderness all those years ago, and had the gall to marvel that I was alive. But I *hadn't* been, not in the fullest sense.

After the Sienna-Amber fiasco, life tilted. Going to work set me on edge. When Charity Sparks handed me my daily shift assignments she eyed me like I was an insect, a white-clad roach, her look laced with doubt at my ability to complete the tasks. She waited for me to fail. *Counted* on it. As for Sienna's injury, Amber told me her (former) friend had been showing off cheerleader moves, the splits, and hit her head on our kitchen island. The wine was Sienna's doing, my daughter said, though reminding me I *had* encouraged them to help themselves to anything. "Anything *legal*," I added later. Not that it mattered now. We were in the supersized doghouse, Amber and I. Big and *not* easy. I'd only wanted her to find a friend. Charity Sparks likely reported Sienna's mishap to Mickey Chandler – a tangle, since Mickey's wife was the Principal at Amber's school. Amber struggled as it was, barely passing American History. Sienna cold-shouldered her – in hallways, classrooms, the library – after that night. "It wouldn't be so bad, Ma," my daughter lamented, "except everywhere I turn – there's *Sienna*."

Sunday morning at the kitchen island, Amber knitting – more black yarn. She stilled her needles and turned to me. "Ma, why don't you just get another job? Lots of places are crying for nurses, it's all over the newspapers."

But it wasn't that simple. I'd need a work reference from Charity Sparks. Bayou Care Center had sponsored me. My work visa was tied to them. I'd explained that to her before.

Then Amber said something strange. "Maybe you have other *talents*, Ma? *Other* lines of work *different from nursing* you could tap into? Like, from your *past*? You may be a *bit old*, but you're still in pretty good shape. Maybe if you found the *right place* for a mature –"

She seemed about to say more, then stopped.

Something in her voice, I couldn't parse it. *Scorn?* Amber wasn't a scornful girl. She could be saucy but it was surface sauce. She could be moody, could be *a real Miss Piggy* sometimes, but it always passed. Her ripped black jeans and pierced nose and wraith look hid, basically, a sweet kid. What brought this edge?

She returned to the Amber I knew. Her young eyes brimmed, hopeful. "We could always just pack up, Ma, move back to Canada. Go home."

"Amber. *No*. And *no*. I'm not waitressing again. I didn't go to college for that. And we're not letting the people with power over us, the Sparks and Chandlers of the world, defeat us. The word *quitter* isn't in our dictionary; I tore that page out long ago. Besides, we have a flowered sofa. We have a cat. Now go study your American History. It'll be Monday again before you know it."

That's what I told my Honey Stone. She set aside her knitting and slipped away to her bedroom, to study (I hoped). Washing the breakfast dishes, I couldn't shake my daughter's strange remark about *other lines of work*, her tone. The insinuation. That was it. But angular, misdirected, like tonguing a phantom tooth, removed long ago. I'd never liked the expression 'sea change' – we were people, not fish – but that's all I could think, reflecting on my daughter and I. The Sienna fiasco caused a sea change, and things weren't the same. Like the day at the cairn, with Sadie Wilder, when I'd cracked open the truth about her, about me. Had Amber plumbed some truth about me? It would never be that I wasn't her mother. My body still bore the marks of birth.

I craved space. A Sunday drive would also be good for the car, which had been parked for months in the old wooden garage behind our building while I rode the crowded bus to work. Suddenly I realized how *closed in* I'd been feeling, at work, at home. I knocked lightly on Amber's bedroom door, and told her I was going out. Among the papers and bills on the kitchen island I found a map. I planned to explore some parish or other, far from Bayou Care Center. I started the car and studied the map. Set myself in a general direction, listened to my lower back, and dwelt in possibility. Maybe Amber and I just needed a quick break from each other, and after my drive things would be smoother. Absence made the heart grow fonder. Or so they said. I wondered how Sadie Wilder felt about *that* adage. I hadn't thought about her for a long time. Building a new life for Amber and myself proved an all-absorbing project. While revving the car's engine a bit longer, I pictured Sadie's sad life, up north, among the chickens. I couldn't imagine her in any other landscape.

It hadn't been raining when I set out on my drive, Janis Joplin on the radio. Time plucked another little piece of her heart. It was Sunday, the service road empty. The rain thickened and my car began to steer badly. Boarded motels, shrimp shacks, and pawn shops quivered in a liquid blur. My worn tires shunted me, herky-jerky; water rose from the ditches. The road filled with water. I yanked the steering wheel this way, then that, like a doomed sea captain. *Faith*, I told myself, *you picked a barbaric day for your drive*. Another slice of Janis-heart shredded through ratcheted radio static. More water clotted the way forward. This was no mere flash shower. This torrent issued from the very maw of Moby Dick. It hurtled its force against my windshield. The wiper blades I'd needed to replace long ago battled to shove aside the deluge. Pulling over wasn't in the cards. There *was* no 'over'. No shoulder visible. Forward in some fashion seemed the only option. I did my best to navigate through the water blizzard. I feared a swamp invasion, that any second, alligator fangs would burst through the bilge, and puncture my cheap tires. Regrettably, I'd passed on the alligator-proof tires.

Water lifted my car. Punting it about in jagged bursts. My worn wipers couldn't *swip swip* fast enough. I pumped my brakes, driver's instinct. The flood's monumental current pushed in through the cracks around my passenger door, weakened from Amber slamming it whenever I'd drop her off at school back in Toronto. I took wild stabs at where the road should be. More water rose inside my car. My feet submerged in murky bilge. Hydroplaning didn't begin to capture what was happening. This was some serious automotive voodoo.

Sodden silvered ropes, like furred, hazed pendulums rose before my eyes. Cordages of white pantyhose. Tiny brown fish like swimming morels, blunt nosed. Then something gold – a tooth. A hunting knife sliced through the deluge. Hanks of moss-nooses swayed from trees. Rod Stewart belted "Maggie May" on the radio while I remained marooned inside this geyser. My car tossed like a giant's plaything, the dashboard slimed with moss, algae, and brackish swamp water. Right in the stew of it, some repulsive thing like green knitting with teeth paddled around my knees. Perhaps I'd been swept into the Mississippi River. A girl did the butterfly stroke, as if projected onto a giant, watery screen where my windshield glassed across. Her hair rippled like a long black scarf, out behind her. She swam with assurance, her movements precise, choreographed, but she'd grow weary in the force of this. Strange how my windshield had become a wavering screen in an underwater movie house. A face appeared, lovely, brunette, smiling through the water – Betty Kennedy, Angel of Calm! If only she could save me. Then a face from long ago, like a frozen mask, blued around the eyes, cloud-hair undulating in the silver haze – Sadie Wilder – her face, hands. Where was the rest of her? She must have grown out her hair after I left. She was writing something on swatches of bleached seaweed stitched to form a scroll. How could she write under water? While I struggled to steer, she turned the scroll so I could read, a strain, she always had tiny handwriting. Looked like, *Let me explain.* But the letters dissolved in the tempest, her face, hands, too. Dissolved into a speedboat spurting across the watery screen, Warren Crouch. He waved at me like he was on vacation, a pretty young girl in the boat with him.

A hideous alligator head butted my windshield, its gloating glare nasty, hoggish. Vinnie Corio leered. (So that was *his* gold tooth.) I read his swampy lips – "Not good enough, Bambino." Of all things, he'd followed me here? *No, I won't go down into that dark place Vinnie, you Juicer, you Goon.* A splat of mud against the windshield, like someone threw a dark snowball, obliterating all vision for an instant, until a new flood surge shoved it aside and the watery slideshow returned.

That girl again, the swimmer, arcing graceful butterfly strokes, shimmered before me. Amber. How long would she be able to swim like that?

A new, smaller shape spindled before my eyes, Malibu Barbie and her sad, twisted neck. The duct tape I wound to reattach her head wouldn't hold much longer in all that water. Barbie couldn't swim, either.

My hands still clamped the wheel. Sloshing in the passenger seat where Amber used to bend her skinny legs, my open purse – identification, work visa, ruined. A tampon I'd carried for two years, just in case, mashed into a snowball. My mood ring turned a deep, malignant violet. The mood you're in when you die, it seemed. I couldn't breathe. Like my nightmares back on the farm.

"*Wait,*" I sputtered, out loud. "This is *bullroar.* I'm an *optimist.* I'll survive this crazy flood. I won't be locked in that dark, drowning place again. Where's the Supervisor of Possibility? I have something to say to you. Just tell me! What do you want me to *do*?"

A murky surge billowed around my ankles, ebbed. As suddenly as the water rose, it subsided. I could see the road again. I pulled over to the mossy shoulder, braked. I felt my hair, half-expecting hanging moss, but it was my hair. My limbs were still jellied from what had just happened. Gads, what *did* just happen? Panic attack? Out-of-body experience? I didn't really believe in that stuff. But things were different now. Had Charity Sparks placed a voodoo curse on me? There was nothing like this in my nursing textbooks. Was I having a nervous breakdown? How would I drive home in such a shaken, spooked condition? What if the frightening spell happened again? For once I'd remembered to bring my cell phone.

The contents of my purse were strangely dry. Like nothing had happened. But *something* had. I reached inside my purse for my phone. Trembled in the Auto Association's number. I called for a rescue vehicle to find me at the edge of some vast swamp.

"We'll need more exact coordinates than that, Ma'am," said the fellow who answered my call.

Shaking, I looked around. I saw a stilt-like building, barely holding itself up. "Crescent City Auto Trade," I said. "Right beside Louie's Tackle and Bait."

While I huddled behind the wheel, waiting for the rescue vehicle, the images that had bombarded my windshield replayed in my mind. But one in particular stood out: Sadie Wilder's face, its deathly look, those alarming blue rings around her eyes. When had she grown all that long, white old-woman hair? Once, I read hair grew after death. But she'd been writing on her seaweed scroll. She wanted to explain. All these years later.

Suddenly I imagined something for the first time: Sadie

Wilder dead. Maybe the cosmos had special-delivered this news through the hallucination on the road. She *couldn't* be dead. I couldn't imagine her that way. I'd needed to sever myself from her that day at the cairn. She'd hidden who I really was. But wherever life took me, however often I started over, the fact of her existence pumped the blood through the jagged tale of *me*. I'd learned that day at the cairn that we shared not one drop of blood. But there was kin-blood and there was story-blood. I'd left her there, crying, on the rock. That was no fit ending to a story.

Absence made the heart grow fonder? Then *my* heart was the slowest learner in history. I thought of the consuming toil, worry, patience, that had gone into raising Amber and she was only seventeen. Sadie Wilder took care of me until I was nineteen. She'd done her best, done *everything* after Della-Mae was gone. She learned to drive. She ran a farm. And only in her twenties, still a girl. Scanty gifts under the tree at Christmas, scanty birthdays, but *gifts*. I sat, shaking, in my car, remembering something she'd said that day at the cairn: *Some people you just love right away.* She'd meant the little boy, Bobby. My brother. His sad rubber boot moldering by the cairn all she had left of him.

How long had it taken her to love *me*? Sadie had written words on the seaweed scroll moments ago back on the watery windshield screen. She'd wanted to explain. *What*, though? About those who you *don't* love right away?

Then, something broke in me. The Auto Association guy found me, sobbing in the driver's seat. He told me an isolated service road far from anywhere wasn't the best place for a lady to be driving by herself. Then he plucked a large, clean handkerchief from his pocket, passed it to me. "Ma'am, it's all right. We'll get you back home safe. No need for crying."

But there *was* need, all the need in the world.

INFINITY SCARF

The small things that end the world: returning agency to the students; assassin bug; brief news flash, *Macramé Maggie* can't come out to play today; a tiny blob of sweet and sour sauce on a mother's lip, unbeknownst to her; a flying bible; slick little eyes on high; spiders.

When my mother returned from her *outing*, which, I figured, was code for *date*, she looked like she'd been crying. When she cried, the whole world melted down, at least that's what it always felt like. She cried like she lived, *with a sense of occasion*. I didn't have the heart to press her about the leopard-skin box, and the bitty pieces inside. *Ah, Beavertails*, I was euchred anyway; if I asked her about it, she'd know I'd been snooping in her closet. She might even ground me. I'd started hanging out with this boy, Ike, from Lafitte Composite, the high school down the street. We talked, shared cigarettes, that was it. Ike Hanratty wasn't the sort of boy I'd be bringing home to meet my mom any time soon. But he was cool. He was company. I'd been just about to email him on the computer in our living room when my mother blew in, teary, mascara-smudged. What had happened to upset her like that? Had her date gone badly? Had the man done something awful to her?

"How was your *outing*, Ma?"

Her throat muscles jolted. Her voice came out pinched. "Rainy. It rained, Amber. *Heavily*. Please, could I use the computer now? I have to search for a – possible obituary."

So that was it. She worried one of her friends had died. Maybe Vera, her waitress friend with the Cleopatra eyes. I remember Vera, eating her funny mushrooms I was never allowed to taste. The Mom-ster often told me I couldn't possibly remember all those things from Alberta, because I was too little. We'd debate that. I hoped it wasn't Vera. I liked her. My mother put on this sorrowful record she played whenever something ate at her, *Pachelbel's Canon*. I never understood how that piece cheered her. I gave up my computer time; The Mom-ster was very insistent about needing it. *Ah, Beavertails*, it blew, sharing a computer with your mother, I'd told Ike. I'd email him later.

The Mom-ster clattered madly on the keyboard for a few minutes. Then she logged off, and poured herself a glass of wine and settled at the kitchen island.

"Did you find the dead person you were looking for?" I asked.

"No," she said, adding she'd decided to retire our car, it had served us well, but she didn't plan on driving it anymore. We'd both been taking public transit, anyway.

Before my mother returned from her outing, I'd been doing a little computer sleuthing of my own. Her dates worried me; only I had her back. No one else, except maybe Ivy Huckster, at work. But Ivy had her own family to worry about. I'd logged onto the dating site, *The Big Easy for Singles*, to track The Mom-ster, in case something happened to her and I needed evidence. I'd had these dark moments, very dark, when I thought all her *dwelling in possibility* could be, like, dangerous. I made a couple of failed attempts at her password. Then it came to me. *Damned Skippy!* I pattered *Macramé Maggie* onto the keyboard. My mother's profile popped up. No photo. I wasn't surprised. So squeaky clean, where she worked. She couldn't risk it. And they watched her, big mother (Charity Sparks) and big brother (Mickey Chandler). On the site, she'd compensated for no photograph with dorky little tags to describe herself. *Exotic. Seasoned. A taste of the north.* I looked at her chat threads. She'd flirt-yacked with a FUNTRAIN. Her most recent patter was with CLARK KENT. His patter: *he enjoyed their date, he found her walleye sexy. He'd like to get with those crazy eyes again, maybe another love bite?*

Gross. Not on *my* watch, he wouldn't.

I bit him with words. Used his regular email address so what I wrote wouldn't appear on the site's chat chain. The Mom-ster didn't need to know I was making an intervention for her safety.

Mister. Stay away from my mom (Macramé Maggie). Or else. Go bite someone else [send].

Or else *what?* I didn't have a clue.

Ah, Beavertails, how *are* we supposed to take care of each other? I had no inkling. All I knew: I needed a smoke.

My mother's key click-turned the lock. She was home. I logged off at the speed of a scampering mouse, a shadow, a flash, gone.

My school launched this new social media site. *Dashboard Confessions.* Principal Dyan Chandler *rolled it out* – she was always *rolling things out* – with this ginormous cake and crashing music played by the Academy concert band. She made a big speech about how Magnolia Arts Academy boasted the city's first student-centered site, *returning agency to the students* by letting us run the site. The Emo-heads couldn't even find an original name for it, had to rip off that gaggy band, *Dashboard*

Confessional. Soon after the site was *rolled out*, the hipster-boys with their messenger bags and the gum-snapping diva-girls scuttled past me in the Academy hallways. Jeers javelined my way. "Hey, Aboot-Girl Amber, how's your Cougar Slut-Mommy Ho, your Mama Jezebel, can we borrow her tit tassels, pretty please?"

Jezebel? F-bomb me, I was marooned inside some Nathaniel Hawthorne nightmare. I staunched my face. Those toxic morons weren't going to see me cry. During my spare period in the library, I logged onto the school's site. Scanned the cheap, nasty posts about my mother. *Nurse Tit Tassels. I need a nurse. Can you call your mommy, Amber Crouch?* It had to be Sienna Sparks spreading venom. The first posts were dated the day after her concussion. Her 'bobo' had kept her home from school, but not off-line. I couldn't even tell anyone about the mean posts. Principal Chandler would spill it to her husband, the Care Center's Director, Mickey Chandler. Boss of Charity Sparks. Boss of my mother. Of me. Of the amount of food in our cat's bowl. A serious downwards ripple effect.

Along the History Hall I flurried. Sienna's boots clomped behind me, closer. She had a distinctive clomp. Then I heard her chirpy-girl voice. "Amber, wait! I only posted that as a bit of fun. Let's be friends again, my mom might thaw eventually, okay?"

She cheerleader-twirled out in front of me, meant to roadblock my advance.

I deked around her easily. "You're dead to me, Sienna Sparks. Only the blow-flies want you now."

I walked straight down the History Hall. I didn't cry. Who knew why our mothers had ever thought we'd be friends? Sienna was a bottomless pit of princess, and I, a lesser star, a foreign freak.

Some day I'd name an insect after my former friend. Two-faced hornet. Jumping voodoo cheerleader. Maybe just Assassin Bug. Sienna Sparks was history, past tense and I, tense, passed her.

I don't know why but at that moment I decided I'd knit another scarf, not another furling banner, but a style I'd seen in a magazine – an infinity scarf. Closed loop. A fully rounded circle. Banners were *so yesterday*. I'd switch from black yarn, too; life was Tombstone Arizona enough lately. The new scarf would resemble one of those inflatable rings children use in paddle pools – a water donut, swim ring. I'd look for a light greeny-blue yarn, swimming-pool colour.

And I'd find a local public pool and do laps after school, if Ike didn't want to hang out. I couldn't believe I'd been swim champion of my high school back in Toronto. It seemed like an ice age ago. My medal hung sadly in my bedroom. Such a long time since I'd done laps. It might clear my head, moving in that pure element again.

"Ivy and I had the nicest lunch the other day," my mother said.

We were eating supper out of a box, she and I, pecking away at it with chopsticks in my case. The Mom-ster, across from me at the kitchen island, struggled with a spoon. All the forks were dirty. She was cutlery-challenged.

A noodle slithered off my mother's spoon. "Since you seem so *interested*, Amber, I'll tell you about it. Ivy and I took the Krispy Kreme donuts left from a staff meeting to the Center's lush emerald lawn. We benched ourselves beside the heritage garden. Louisiana quillwort grew there, voodoo roses. Sunlight glinted off the beaded chains draped from Ivy's glasses in such a lovely way. She looked like an angel of calm. We agreed we should have lunch outside together more often. Ivy probed what was bothering me. She's intuitive, you know? I told her that morning I'd found a pamphlet slid through the crack of my locker in the Care Center's staffroom: *Employee Assistance Program. Help for those with Juvenile Delinquency among Family Members.* Charity Sparks no doubt delivered it. A strike against *you, Amber.*"

"I'm sorry, Ma. That blows as a start to your day. What did Ivy say?"

My mother finally managed to swallow a bit of the meal that kept eluding her. "Here's the good part. Ivy said I have to convince Charity Sparks that you're *not* some delinquent, that you're a good girl. And Ivy had just the method for that!"

"Ma?"

A tiny blob of sweet and sour sauce beaded on The Momster's lip. She beamed. "You're going to volunteer at Bayou Care Center and show them how *terrific you are!*"

My one chopstick dropped. A subpar idea if ever there was one. "What, like, after school? I was going to start *swimming* again. And there's homework."

My mother had actually thought this through. "Weekends. Amber, just tell me you'll *try.* Things aren't easy at work. My stupid pantyhose snag constantly. I keep losing points for *impeccable comportment.* Charity Sparks' grudge-fire against me, us, burns strong. If you could prove yourself at the Care Center, it would really help me. Amber?"

A groan wrenched from deep within me, but I couldn't stop it. If only The Mom-ster *hadn't* had the nicest lunch with Ivy Huckster. I wasn't sure volunteering *would* help. For starters, how many points would my nose ring lose for *impeccable com-portment?* Maybe the point system didn't apply to volunteers.

But then I looked across the island at my mother, with her hopeful good eye and her pleading wonky eye and the bead of sweet and sour sauce on her lip. Somehow, that rogue dab of sauce did it. Swung me. I told her I'd try. The volunteer thing.

She raised her glass of wine in a toast. I raised my green-tea smoothie, less elevated than her glass. For the first time my mother noticed the yarn at the island's far end. "Amber! You bought more yarn. And, blue, that's something new for you. *A colour!* This day has flipped right around. It just hums with possibility, now!"

It was almost *over*, too, the day. But I didn't say that. Life, like I'd learned, was mostly like letter writing, more about what you left out. I *did* inform The Mom-ster about the stranded blob of sweet and sour sauce. She blushed, then wiped it away with her napkin. And said, "What would I do without you, Amber? Just *what?*"

The next weekend I pinned the dorky badge to the baggy powder-blue top they issued me. The badge said *Amber Crouch, Angel in Residence.* Wait until I told Ike I was an *angel*, how he'd laugh. My mother sent me off with a dramatic flourish. *"Do not botch this volunteer gig, Amber."* She told me Charity Sparks was skeptical about signing me as a volunteer, given my 'record'. *Record?* F-bomb me! Luckily Charity, the fake-blonde witch, didn't work weekends, so we wouldn't overlap. But they *watched*, my mother warned. Oh, they watched. The Director, Mickey Chandler, just had these cameras installed – by the meds vault and other places – he called them *slick little eyes on high.* Someone had been filching meds. The cameras were long overdue in any case, for accountability, he'd announced at a staff meeting, my mother said.

Spectacular. King Creep-o watching me through one of his slick little eyes on high, while I wheeled the heavy book cart through the corridors. My arms ached from pushing the cart loaded with bibles, books, and magazines. The Care Center's residents didn't usually want either testament. They mostly asked for those tacky magazines about movie stars gaining weight, losing weight, or being jilted. How that stuff cheered anyone baffled me down to my Doc Martens. Someone threw a bible at me, making a blue bruise on my forehead. At least it would match my infinity scarf. I stuck to the *Angel in Residence* script, pushing my book cart through the halls. I dipped into each room: "Book? Bible? Magazine?" The beautiful old French lady, Mrs. Lafleur, was sad because there were no French magazines. I knew a little French from high school in Toronto. Mrs. Lafleur liked talking with me.

"Why won't my son come visit me?" she asked me in French.

"Je ne sais pas." I squeezed her hand. I'd buy her a French magazine.

Once some poor soul crooked her finger at me. "*Pssst,* little girl – over here." Could I bring her a painkiller?

I told her sorry, I couldn't do that.

My mother's friend, Lucky Mason, worked some weekends. He was cool. I knew this from The Mom-ster's reports. He had her back, and she had his, at work. Lucky and I took smoke breaks behind the Care Center by the loading dock. I told him about the lady's request for a painkiller. "Would've been easy, before the surveillance cameras," he said. "They were lax, that meds vault wasn't even locked half the time."

Lucky was the largest boy-man I'd ever met, like a giant teddy bear. He liked telling stories. He flipped from tale to tale, though, too fast, like a fish swimming away from a predator, which sometimes made him hard to follow. "Wanna know one drug that's in that vault, Amber?"

He piqued my interest.

"Death serum," he said, the knowledge of this puffing his chest until I worried his buttons would burst. "Hydromorphone. *Right there* on the shelf. Used for injections on death row."

I wanted to ask why they'd keep such a thing at the Care Center, but Lucky roller-coastered ahead. "Wanna know something *else*, Amber?"

Before I could answer, he was on it. "There's a rumour floating around this place that I live in my car. It's true. They don't give me enough hours. That's why I work extra weekends when someone's off sick."

Before I could say that must be really tough, he eyed his plastic watch. "Oh, we gotta *go*, Amber. We gotta go *back inside the walls*. You won't tell anyone where I live, will ya?"

"Lucky, my lips are sealed. And you won't tell my mom I smoke, will you?"

"Amber, wild horses wouldn't – we gotta go back in."

We went back in.

Breaks with Lucky out by the loading dock were the best. Bayou Care Center creeped me out. This freaky, old, hypnotic music burbled in the lounge all the time. I asked one of the nurses what it was. She said "Lawrence Welk." After answering me, she'd clipped away, but not before giving my nose ring a quick, hard, disapproving glance. Lucky Mason had told me, too, that someone was always trying to bolt, bust free. I could see why, maybe the inmates knew there was death serum in the cupboard. We were supposed to call them *patrons* or *residents* but to me, they seemed more like prisoners. On my last shift, I got close enough to an inmate, who looked like Alice Cooper, to place a book in her hands, and she tugged my nose ring!

Some of the other inmates asked why I wore army boots. Was the war still on? I guess they'd never seen Doc Martens. Or they thought I was someone else, their granddaughter, and when I told them I wasn't, they cried. I wondered if I should let them keep their stories. Maybe fibbing for comfort was okay. Medicinal fibs. The inmates who tried to speak but couldn't, struck me as saddest. They were forever gagged.

"Book? Bible? Magazine?" Gradually, the residents of Bayou Care Center became my heroes and heroines. They'd made it through another day of Lawrence Welk. I learned to watch for airborne bibles. After a couple of *Angel in Residence* shifts, I asked my mother if Charity Sparks now considered me a delinquent, *a reckless little punk-ass northerner.*

My mother seemed distracted. "What? Oh that. *You.* The jury's still out. Don't you see, Amber? It's in Charity's interests to *keep* the jury out for as long as possible. That way we stay her puppets."

I badly longed to say, Mom, you can't keep going this way. And those freaking white pantyhose! This whole thing might be harming your mental health. But I didn't want to upset her. Instead I finished the infinity scarf. I liked its rich tones, the colour of a deep lake in Canada, a wise greenish-blue eye.

It was June, and, like, so hot. The central air conditioning at Bayou Care Center had broken down. The place was a sauna, the small electric fans they'd placed in the rooms and the lounge a useless ploy. No wonder an inmate had escaped. Remy Despereaux, aged eighty-one. Posters plastered the staffroom as I changed into my ugly baggy powder-blue volunteer uniform top. They reminded me of 'wanted' bandit posters in a western movie. The white-haired 'missing' gentleman in the photograph looked distinguished in his cravat. My mother had told me about this, how everyone was summoned to an emergency staff meeting. How Mickey Chandler had blathered about the bad optics and how the *old geezer's* escape better not find its way onto social media because potential residents' families read reviews of care facilities. How, thankfully, at least the only medication the *geezer* was on was Metamucil. Chandler had no idea how the *geezer* got away despite the new cameras he'd installed. But he'd reviewed the footage and discovered nothing. The *geezer* had vanished, insubstantial as icing sugar on a beignet.

My mother found it appalling that her boss kept saying *geezer*. *F-bomb* me, she was right. So much for *patron* or *resident*. I was cheering for Remy Desperaux. I hoped he was safe, and far, far away from Bayou Care Center. If I had to live in that place I'd turn into the guy in that painting, *The Scream*. Maybe that's what was happening to my mother, the place was doing her harm. As I rolled the book cart through the muggy corridors, my uniform top dampened with sweat. I gave Mrs. Lafleur the French magazine I'd bought; she thanked me, but the heat made her too listless to even open it.

I braked my cart in front of a closed door, unsure what to do. The inmates' doors were almost always open. They lived with so little privacy.

Just knock, Amber, I thought. *That'd be the sensible thing.* But maybe knocks would scare them.

I opened the door and rolled my book cart inside. The door slid silently closed behind me. Bayou doors had those silencer pads so they didn't slam and cause heart attacks. I should have called out, in a pleasant voice, my usual greeting, "*Angel in Residence* – Book? Bible? Magazine?" But something stopped me. The dimness. The curtains drawn, lights off. Maybe because of the heat? Those harsh lights made it worse. A small electric fan whirred and creaked uselessly by the window. My eyes began to adjust to the dimness. The room smelled like cough syrup and dry, flaked skin.

I saw a large, lumpy shadow on the bed. My vision improved; what I noticed then was, *two* old ones snugged in each other's arms, the man in pajamas, the lady in her nightgown. Were they dead?

I tiptoed closer to them. The man's lips, curled into a smile, buzzed with light snores. The lady's spine had this soft lilt, lifted, then floated down like a large magnolia petal loosed from its branch. Her face pure peace. America was so much yammer and noise, it made me jumpy. I clamped my headphones over my ears a lot of the time to block it out. But that moment, even with the weird creaking the fan sent out, was the first time I'd witnessed serenity, like, this *total, whole feeling* I hadn't felt since leaving Toronto. Those warm Sundays when my mother sank down beside me in the grass at Christie Pits Park. She told me a buried stream rippled right under us, but no one would ever drown in it because it was buried forever. It couldn't hurt us, or anyone. And in those rare moments, we were like one person, she and I. Like the two sleepers in front of me.

Angels in Residence were told to report anything out of the ordinary. Two people in one bed was not ordinary at Bayou Care Center. I gazed a long minute at the beautiful sleepers. Then I quietly left a *True Romance* magazine on the night table and tiptoed out of the room, letting the door seal, with a whisper, behind me.

After The Mom-ster hatched her project to find me a friend (Sienna, and look how *that* turned out), she told me I should look for something to do besides school, knitting, and listening to that gloomy, thudding music. (She meant Nirvana.) I should have found a public swimming pool long ago, but I started writing in a journal instead. It felt safer to stay home, I could use the Internet as much as I wanted, too, when The Mom-ster was at work. My journal didn't advance very far, thankfully. Writing in it bummed me out even worse. After yesterday's volunteer gig, I read what I'd written only two months earlier, though it felt more like two years:

Sadness is an alligator. Thrives in brackish locales. Breathes like a gator, too, in one direction (my on-line research) into the dark hole of itself. It can lunge scary-fast, too, gobble an antelope or a girl in one bite. I'm so homesick for Toronto my teeth ache. The air makes sense there. Also from my short-lived journal: *A speculative suicide note: To You Who Discover These Words Pinned to the Suicide Oak in the park: I can't stay in this creepy crawly place anymore. The kids in my school treat me like a space alien. My old buds from high school in Toronto have forgotten me even though they promised to email. My brief friend, Sienna Sparks, got me into a hornet's nest of trouble. And that night uncovered a bit, and I mean bit, of my mother's past I can't ask about or it'll bring more trouble for snooping in her closet. No one can write a prescription for loneliness, no cure except the long sleep. I'd like a white upholstered coffin like Andy Warhol's; this will be pricey so as the last request of Amber Crouch, Desperate Teen, I hereby authorize you who finds this note to withdraw the entire balance from Account #48990 at Whitney Bank (Tulane Campus Branch) as proceeds for my funeral. My mother isn't flush. She has debts. Flowered furniture bought on her credit card. Clothes. My dad may send funds. Find him at warrencrouch@hotmail.com.*

What a lame suicide note. Who'd pin their bank account number to an oak tree in a park? I'm glad I abandoned my journal. It made me twisty, gator-like, breathing into the dark hole of myself. Better to write my History assignment: *meditate on an artifact, a historical object, with which you are familiar.* I decided on my mother's car. I wrote: *My mother parked her car permanently in our garage. She just one day refused to drive. I peek inside the garage sometimes, shove open the wooden door on its rusty hinges. The car looks less like a car as the days grind past, more like some toppled tombstone. There are pieces of us, my mother and I, in that car, our history. It's the same car she drove to my swimming classes, to take herself to College on the Bluffs, a nursing course. It's the car that brought us to New Orleans. That Kelly Clarkson song is probably still in the tape deck. I don't go right inside the garage though. It's this creepy shed with dim pleats of light through cracks between the boards. The south oozes with gross creepers ready to ambush an unsuspecting Canadian. All those spiders, they catch on shards of light. That garage is spider city which is why I don't go all the way inside; being eaten by spiders would be too horrible. I meditate on the artifact of my mother's car, the living world inside the garage, from a safe distance. Spiders out of some horror flick – jumpers and spitters and funnel weavers and wolf spiders, trapdoor spiders. (I looked them up on-line.) Tarantulas, I suspect, though they leave that out of the Mardi Gras hype. Last time I creaked open the heavy garage door, I found a horror scene: my mother's car crinolined with webs, doilies spun from spider slime spewed across the windshield.*

The teacher called my meditation *solid but unfinished. A minus.* Minus eh? Easy for her to say. Writing wasn't a steady, solid thing, like knitting an infinity scarf. Writing felt more like fighting through a spider-web jungle without being eaten, like my *life.* As for the short-lived journal, after rereading my twisted alligator angst, I tore those pages into pieces, took them onto the balcony and flamed them with my cigarette lighter, a tiny bonfire right there. No one noticed. My pages charred into flaked ashes quickly enough. The slightest breeze would blow them away. What mattered was, those manic words were gone. My mother needed me. I had to stick around to make sure some homicidal stranger didn't drag her into a swamp. Maybe in a tiny way the residents at Bayou Care Center needed me, too, every weekend, with my book cart. Mrs. Lafleur needed me to speak a few words of French.

After torching my journal, I stepped back inside the apartment. I stubbed my toe on the big stupid flowered sofa, startling Ponty. He mewled so pathetically and I realized: his life was lonely. He was a victim of neglect, my mother's, and mine. I spooned some food into his bowl. That cat, with his chewed ear, was lonelier, even, than me – which, *Damned Skippy* – was saying a lot, and which hatched a sudden, dazzling concept in my mind.

SUCCOR

The small things that end the world: a cold shoulder in a sweltering gymnasium;
coming home to no Amber; a white sundress missing-in-action; patch of black ice;
the wrong song from last century; a god-awful velvet painting; small talk *so* small,
a microscope can barely detect it, an ear horn barely hear it.

Even on a scorching night, a cold shoulder is still a cold shoulder.
But Gads, I would have thought at our daughters' graduation –
Sienna Sparks' and my Amber's – there might be a truce, a show
of civility. But not with Charity Sparks. Bless Ivy Huckster for
going with me to Magnolia Arts Academy, all decked out in
bunting and rose petals and balloons. Americans adored balloons. Ivy looked sweet in her pink, sixties-style suit and matching pink gloves in that heat. They'd cranked the air conditioning
to the max in the auditorium as each boy in his Hugo Boss suit
bounded across the stage to receive his diploma, each big-haired
girl, in her skimpy, or balloon-y, dress, alarmingly high heels,
tight-rope-walked across it, but the auditorium remained very
warm. Then my Amber loped across the stage in her Doc
Marten boots, her long black hair (newly dyed), in the dress I'd
bought for her. She'd pushed back when I brought it home.
"Aw, not *flowers*, Ma!" But she wore it, for me. Besides, her
father emailed her and made her promise to send graduation

photos. Warren never left Alberta, so there was no danger of him showing up in New Orleans. His parents, retired in Costa Rica, requested photos too. They'd hoped to fly in for Amber's graduation, she'd told me – we hadn't seen them in years – but one of them had fallen ill. Amber begged me to excuse her from attending graduation, but all the pressure for photographs – pressure from me, too – cornered her.

We struck a bargain: she attended her graduation and in return she could go to summer swim camp in Iowa. It was a sweet deal, I thought: one ceremonial night at the Arts Academy versus six aquatic weeks in her beloved element. A graduation gift from me.

Sienna Sparks teetered across the stage in heels thin as darning needles, a tiny dress sewn from sequins and perfect beachy-waved hair. After the ceremony, beside a punch bowl almost as big as a swimming pool, Charity Sparks slid past me, ice-queen-eyed, saying only, "I'm surprised your Amber made it through. *Bravo for her, bravo for you!*" Her tone bent the words into their opposite meaning; Ivy heard them, too. Principal Dyan Chandler's husband, Mickey, wasn't there; maybe they kept their work separate, maybe he was on the road. Ivy told me he travelled often, developing his Care Center empire. He'd planned to open other facilities across the state. Or maybe, because Remy Despereaux was still missing from Bayou Care Center and the press had begun to milk the story, Mickey Chandler kept his head low whenever possible.

While graduation brought its own unique brand of excruciation, sitting for hours in the heat to watch your daughter cross the stage in ten seconds – and Amber ditched her flowered dress as soon as we arrived back at our apartment, photos snapped – that night was still my high point for weeks. Work had been brutal. Hurricane Cindy wiped out the power at Bayou Care

Center. I'd done back-to-back shifts, helping keep everyone afloat. That poor French lady, Mrs. Lafleur, had been so distraught, calling out for her son. *Hector! Hector, please come take me out of here!* Mickey Chandler's mood was vile – he'd returned from wherever he'd been. ("The Care Emperor is back," Ivy had whispered, frowningly, to me.) Chandler called impromptu staff meetings for updates, new protocols, policies. Remy Despereaux's family had taken legal action against Bayou Care Center. There were other complaints. Several residents were dispensed wrong medication. Some meat went foul when the refrigeration malfunctioned, sickening the residents. A *serious image correction* was needed at Bayou Care Center, our boss told us at his most recent summons. "Simply put, people," he'd extorted, pacing, "what we're looking at is a *ramped-up comfort zone* around here." I'd gotten a whiff of his aftershave. If hired by the aftershave manufacturer to name it, I'd call it *Raw Ambition*. His hair was trained back into a severe, oiled ponytail, tied with a tiny leather cord, which seemed at odds with the rest of his corporate suit and tie. In that stuffy staff room, I struggled to focus on the Care Emperor's speech: "What we're going to dispense, people, from now on, is *succor*." His policy: *shift hugs, effective immediately*. I'd pointed out that not all the residents liked physical contact; even a bedroll made them wince. Some dreaded it. Lucky Mason, wiping some icing sugar from a Krispy Kreme donut flaking his lip, chimed in, "Nope, they don't – Faith is right!" Chandler's eyes grated us like we were nutmeg. He asked how badly we wanted our jobs. Silence from me, to signal message received, no challenging him. From Lucky, "Yep, pretty bad. Want it bad."

"All right, *Fat Boy* – then be quiet," the Care Emperor said. "And clean yourself up. You look like you live in your car."

I bit my lip so hard, to keep from calling Chandler out on

his cruelty to Lucky, I tasted my own blood.

Since Remy Desperaux's escape and Hurricane Cindy, and the bad meat incident, Charity Sparks had been a royal grumpus, worse than before. The crevices on her facial makeup had reached alarming proportions, they'd soon become an actual geological *thing*. My white pantyhose would *not* remain run-free, even after I'd tried a more expensive brand. Charity continued to take relish in deducting comportment points from me. "*Some* people won't ever make *Caregiver of the Month*, that's a sad fact," she said the other day as she shoved my shift assignment sheet into my hand. "And see to that *hangnail*, too, Faith."

For days after Hurricane Cindy, the Care Center groundskeepers collected fallen branches. The heritage garden had taken a beating. Cindy frayed my nerves mightily; Ivy shared her anti-anxiety pills with me, they helped me get through it. Ivy said that in the scheme of things, Cindy was 'small potatoes'. Mrs. Celestine downstairs called Cindy a whisper compared to Betsy back in '65. Despite their perspectives, which I knew they meant as helpful, I'd begun to have nightmares, with no one to shake me awake.

I wilted on the crowded bus on my way home from work. My lip sore where I'd bitten it at the staff meeting. I'd been having hot flashes again, and had hoped those were over. I hoped the heat was less fierce in Iowa, at Amber's swim camp; of course, she could cool off by dipping into a pool whenever she liked. She'd been emailing me as she promised, to touch base. She seemed happy there in her watery element. To take my mind off missing her, off the heat, off work stress, I reached for a newspaper on a nearby seat. One of those cheap tabloids but I didn't care. I scanned it. *Control Your Lover With Voodoo. Severed Leg Hops To Hospital*. A tacky ad, swashbuckling photo, a brawny, bare-chested man sporting sprayed-on swim trunks, standing, bulky legs planted apart, in water, a muscled arm hoisted, forming a bicep-bulge like a bodybuilder. His other arm raised, clenched around some hideous, giant lizard. The man's upper body gashed and scarred. I blinked hard. Alligator. CLARK KENT. The man I'd dated at the roadhouse, who'd nipped my neck and left a mark. Who'd said he *had a mean junkyard dog of a job*, and wouldn't talk work beyond that. He wasn't kidding. Even with its tail curved in struggle and writhing, the gator approached the man's height. CLARK's hand clamped shut the ugly reptilian mouth. The ad, in bossy boldface, trumpeted an Alligator Wrestling Extravaganza. The caption under the photograph said: *Hector Lafleur, Champion Alligator Wrestler, takes to the water again with his nemesis Brutus. Don't miss this nasty showdown!* I'd thought that sort of thing, as a sport, was illegal, but what did I know?

I'd made it home on that blistering day. No matter how much possibility I pressed myself to dwell in, I couldn't adjust to the apartment without Amber, with her headphones on, knitting or bent over her homework or making one of those strange green drinks in the blender. She called them lithium shakes, named after a song by the band Nirvana, she'd told me. They were loaded with kale or hemp or something. She was only away at swim camp. What would I do when she left *forever* to have her own life? At work Ivy said, "Oh, Faith, they never *really* leave; she'll be back living with you before you know it." She was trying to cheer me. But as the days wore on, not even the flowered sofa lifted my spirits. I called the cat. "Ponty! Come, let's play with your strand of string." We'd never played, I was too tired after work, but there was always a first time. The cat must have been outside, hunting. I was completely alone. At one time, I would have talked to Malibu Barbie, but I wasn't feeling it anymore.

Suddenly I wondered if Sadie Wilder had felt this lost and alone after I'd left. What was it like for her to come in from the chicken barn day after day, year after year, and dine alone on fried potatoes and eggs or macaroni, our usual suppers, then rise in the morning and do it all over again? Lately my own suppers had shrunk to cheese and crackers. I thought about taking up macramé again but had no appetite for it. For awhile I watched a new television show, *Grey's Anatomy*, but couldn't stand hearing *time of death*. Sadie had hovered in my mind since the Sunday drive incident. Was there *nothing* I could do that wasn't knotted to her, that wasn't, somehow, *haunted*? Maybe the reboots I'd done of my life *weren't* these sparkling adventures like I spun them to Amber, and to myself. Maybe they were just more running away.

I sank onto the flowers and thought about the alligator wrestler with the same last name as the French lady, Mrs. Lafleur, at Bayou Care Center; she often called out for "Hector" to come take her home. Could he be *her* Hector? Hector hardly seemed like a common name beyond the Roman or Greek worlds.

Suddenly I wanted to know what it was *like*, fighting the nemesis Brutus. Was Hector fighting for his life like when I struggled against the Marl Harrower, or against Vinnie Corio? Or was it all just a show? I wanted to know what *someone else's* life was like. I needed some company. Some succor. I hadn't been out in weeks. All work and no play made Faith dull and morose. I shifted over to the computer desk and clattered a quick email to CLARK KENT.

He was surprised to hear from me. He said we probably shouldn't meet, but *what the hay, Cherie*. He sent me the address of The Matador Bar. He'd be there by eight.

That meant he had no nasty showdown with a reptile that

night. I searched through my closet for my white sundress, but it was nowhere to be found. Malibu Barbie stared gloomily down at me from her spot on the shelf, while I searched. How could a dress simply vanish? That white sundress would have been perfect for drinks with the alligator wrestler on a sultry night. I settled for jeans and a tank top. I put my energy into my hair.

The Matador Bar's name seemed to derive solely from a large velvet painting that listed badly above the jukebox: a matador, his cloth extended, baiting a seething bull. Beyond that, no evidence of a bullfighting theme; it was a regular bar with a neon Schlitz beer sign and stagey photographs of celebrities who'd drank there. Mardi Gras bric-a-brac strung about. Sherry Rummage had taken me to a few such watering holes when I first arrived in New Orleans.

The first Abita Amber beer for me and first bourbon for CLARK brought only awkwardness. We kept our dating-site monikers in play. Somehow, the masks insisted on staying in place. CLARK wore the same jeans as last time, along with cowboy boots and a t-shirt with a faded sports-team logo. His arms were muscled, like the alligator wrestler in the tabloid, pocked with nicks and scars. Brutus' teeth marks. If the right moment arose, I aimed to find out why someone would willingly face such ugliness, such malice. As for *Macramé Maggie*, she seemed far away, a distant cousin I no longer knew.

CLARK KENT told me he liked my hair, all stacked like a turbine like that. I thanked him. The night still floundered heavy as a swamp.

After our third round, CLARK drew a small package from his jeans' pocket. He removed a few brown lumpy bits from it and popped them in his mouth. He washed them down with bourbon. I asked him what he'd just eaten.

"Magic, Pretty Lady. Mushrooms. But they don't taste so good, wash 'em down with bourbon or whatever. Want a couple?"

I should have asked a few pharmaceutical questions but that was Care Affiliate Faith's job. She was burnt out. Who knew, maybe CLARK's magic would ease my hot flashes. I took a tiny shard, and raised my beer bottle in a toast. Swallowed.

"Hey, wait a minute, CLARK," I said. "Isn't it illegal to do what we're doing in here with this fungus?"

He laughed, then shrugged. The bartender sent him a thumbs-up through the murky light. There was my answer. It didn't seem like much *was* illegal in The Big Easy. Mushrooms pinged me back to the previous century. Vera Moxon. Her fungal therapy seemed to help move her from one day to the next. I thought of morels, and Sadie Wilder's face streaming across my windshield out on the service road.

"Hey – earth calling – you here, Cherie?"

CLARK KENT was talking to me. I glanced at the velvet painting. The bull worried me. I doubted it would end well for him. Magic drinks appeared on our table while I pondered CLARK's question. I nodded a slow, earthbound nod.

"We need some music," I decreed, and trundled over to the jukebox under the matador's flapping, taunting cloth. I chose tunes from the last century, the kind cover bands now played. The situation called for something familiar. I returned to our table in the twilight zone, hopeful, music often helped. CLARK and I exchanged small talk, mostly about weather. The small talk withered, and would soon vanish altogether. I said, "CLARK do you want to see a Canadian dollar?" And he said, "Why not?" I dug a loonie from my purse and flicked it onto the table and remarked that's a dollar. And CLARK said *bullshit!* And I said "No, *it really is.* It's our dollar coin." And he said, "*What* they got no paper up there at the end of the blacktop, no trees?" He'd thought it was *all trees*, and snow.

Then the jukebox launched into the third song I'd chosen, "Delta Dawn."

CLARK almost choked on his bourbon. "I wish you hadn't chosen *that* one, Cherie."

Much of his mask withered away, I could tell. He'd jolted into a twitchy distress that was real. How did an old hit bring that about?

"What's with the song?" I asked.

"That was my little girl's name. Delta Dawn. Misty Delta Dawn. The song brings her back. I was a long-haul trucker for a moving company. An eighteen-wheeler. My last run, 1979. It was only October. Should've been no problem."

He took a sad, serious drink. "There was a cold snap. Black ice. My truck jackknifed. I had Misty with me."

A bluer intimacy had sabotaged our strangers' play date.

"Tell me about her."

"Sweet as a praline," he said. "Angel's voice. Knew the words to every Eagles song by the time she was five. Her mother would dress her up in a frilly skirt and blouse and Misty would sing for us, put on a little show. Prettiest child ever. Here, look." He gently removed a small photograph from his billfold, the kind taken at school that kids traded with friends. The photograph's faded sheen didn't diminish the girl's sweet smile, trusting eyes. After a minute, he slid the photograph gently back into his billfold.

"A beautiful child, CLARK."

"I shouldn't have taken Misty on that run to Cleveland, but I didn't have much choice. Her mother and I were having problems. These moods would hit and she'd just up and leave and I wouldn't know where or for how long. That's what she done that day in October. Misty was some broke up about it. I told her she could come with me in the truck. I spun it like a treat instead of what it was – my only fix for a babysitting jam. So, I hoisted my girl, thrilled to smithereens, way up inside the cab of my truck. A few hours on the road and we hit black ice. They said she wouldn't 'a suffered but how can they really know? I quit long-haul trucking after that."

The song ended. No succor to be had for him, I knew that. "I'm sorry, CLARK. Sorry – such a useless word, eh?"

He twisted his face. "It's all we got. It's so damned *impossible*, ain't it, to keep them safe? And all the magic mushrooms in the world don't make it better. I figured you'd understand. You got a kid, too. Living, I mean."

Despite the date's sluggish start, I'd begun to feel good. Like a giant candle, but his mention of Amber snuffed me flat out. I'd worked to keep my worlds separate. Keep Amber safe, secret. Had this man been stalking me? Stalking my daughter? I asked CLARK how he knew. Clicked my mood ring in rapid, anxious taps against the table, waiting for his response.

"She wrote me. Must 'a gotten my email address from that dating site. Must 'a hacked your account, kids are smart like that these days. You should change your password soon as you get home. She told me to stay away from you. We shouldn't be here tonight, Cherie. She finds out, you'll hear about it. Hell, *I'll* hear about it."

"You *won't*. You won't ever hear from her again, CLARK." I snatched my purse, made to leave. He grabbed my moving hand softly, patted it, a calming gesture. I pulled my hand away.

He bristled. "Don't get all huffed, Cherie. I never asked for her snippy telegram. I'm no Ted Bundy. I'm just a guy who likes ordinary things, taking my boat out on the Pearl River. Relaxing in my cabin on Honey Island. And I ain't no internet jiggler, neither."

Took me a second to fathom he meant *gigolo.*

I sensed eyes from other tables penetrating the shadows, to our table.

Up in velvet world, the situation had grown full-blown hopeless for the bull.

"*Please.* Just sit, Cherie. Let me buy you one last drink – for the road."

The mushrooms and beer gave me a headache. I felt unsteady. I sat. "Just water," I said. The bartender brought it over. I drank some. I couldn't believe what Amber had done. How had she figured out my password?

CLARK KENT somehow gleaned my thoughts while I drank water. "Don't be mad at your girl, Cherie. She was just looking out for you, get it?"

Suddenly, I understood. "Oh, I *get* it, all right! I see *why you do it* – Hector Lafleur, *Champion Alligator Wrestler* – you're letting that ugly gator chew you up, bit by bit, to punish yourself for what happened to your little girl!"

It was his turn to sit there, stunned.

"I read the newspaper," I said. "I planned to ask why you fight gators. But I don't need to ask. Now I *know.*"

He didn't contradict me. Outside the bar, in the roaring cicada night, I waited for a taxi. Hector waited with me. "Almost forgot," he said. "I got something for you." He reached into his truck and retrieved a clear plastic bag he held gingerly by its bottom. A single, tall stalk, its top a cluster of soft purple blooms. There was a tangle of wet roots bunched like a bird's nest inside a plastic bag, with water in the bottom. The bag had been tied tightly so the water couldn't leak out.

He placed the bagged plant in my hands. Its flowers were luxuriant. "Water hyacinth, Cherie. Keep the roots wet, in fresh water. It'll bloom for ages."

Just before I lowered myself, with the watery plant, into the taxi, Hector Lafleur said, "That girl of yours, take care of her – you dunno how much time you got – and let her take care of *you*, like I said."

A tear rappelled down my face as he closed the taxi door and I rolled away, the purple bloom tall in my watery hands. I held it with care so the water didn't spill out of its improvised pond. More tears escaped from my eyes. Catches of pained sounds in my throat. The cabbie asked if I was okay.

"A lady with a pretty flower shouldn't be sad," he informed my soaked cheekbones.

ⓖ————ⓖ

Bayou Care Center
August 1, 2005

URGENT ALERT TO ALL STAFF –
INFORMATION NEEDED IMMEDIATELY

An unauthorized feline presence has been brought to our attention. Apparently, this cat has wandered throughout the institution for some days and no one bothered to come forward to report it to either Head Nurse Sparks or myself. One of our orderlies, Lucky Mason, has been feeding said cat and aiding and abetting its presence at Bayou Care Center. The animal has apparently also been sleeping on the beds of some residents; what vermin it might carry we do not know. Additionally, some residents have allergies. While Mr. Mason seems to have meant well, claiming that the residents enjoy the animal – 'real affectionate' – and even (brashly) that said cat is part of our 'ramped-up comfort zone,' he nevertheless acted beyond the scope of his position and will be disciplined. What form that will take we have not yet decided. The feline intruder has, for the moment, eluded us. If anyone sees it, report immediately! The cat is black with a gouged ear (old wound presumably), Mr. Mason informed us. Rest assured this matter will be settled only after said cat is impounded and dealt with. Finally, merit points will be awarded to any staff member who can answer this question: How did that blasted animal get in here in the first place?

– Mickey Chandler, Director & Charity Sparks, Head Nurse

TOM PETTY WAS RIGHT –
WAITING REALLY IS THE HARDEST

The small things that end the world: B minus; missing my previous life when I was somebody's granddaughter; waiting through my days.

The swim coach said I did one mean butterfly stroke, and she was right. I'd grown strong, being back in my element. Water. It felt so awesome to *excel* at something again! *Damned Skippy*, nothing beat that feeling! And such a relief to leave that city, that sweltering bowl. It felt right taking Ponty to Bayou Care Center, too. Mrs. Lafleur loved him at first sight. How she'd laughed and clapped her hands together when I lifted him onto her lap. *"Chat! Chat!"* That cat brought her joy, brought others joy. Lucky Mason promised to make sure Ponty was fed. I left Lucky some of my allowance money for cat food. Ponty would bring comfort to the world instead of moping, neglected. He wasn't happy in our apartment, that was pretty obvious.

While I swam, the past weeks beat back through my mind. I didn't have to *think* about my strokes, that was the golden part. Muscle memory. My body in complete harmony with the water. With each pool crossing it became more okay that Ike dumped me just before I left for swim camp. It *hadn't* been okay at the time, though. I'd blown over to his house. I liked going over there – it was a shotgun house. Very cool. The cooking smelled great, peppers and garlic and shellfish. I helped Ike with his homework, the final essay of the year. "Sumbitch jam I'm in Amber, you got to help." So I did. After we finished working on the essay, he lit two cigarettes, one for me, one for him, and went all sullen, slumped there on his bed under a Pamela Anderson poster. Her ginormous cleavage annoyed me. I'd helped him, now he couldn't even talk to me? Music pulled me out onto the porch, his dad and friends were having a jam. They were a trio: claw-hammer banjo, scrub board, accordion. They played a wicked cover of "In the Pines," then rocked it out with swamp tunes. They didn't seem to mind that I listened, leaning with my cigarette against the porch railing, tapping my toes. They jammed in this happy cluster and then – how had I missed him? – I saw a fourth person in a rocking chair, behind the players, half hidden by a large palm plant. An elegant elderly man in a suit and one of those cravat ties and a pork pie hat. He had a striking face. And just sitting there, taking it all in. I'd seen him somewhere before. I took hard, thinking drags on my cigarette. *Damned Skippy!* I remembered him from my *Angel in Residence* rounds. The face on the poster. With each ripple of the accordion I felt surer he was the guy who'd been missing from Bayou Care Center. Right there, foot-tapping to the swamp tunes, not looking worse for wear at all. He seemed to notice me for the first time, too, and popped a broad grin and a wink across the porch. I sent a smile, and my best wink – I'm not a winker – across to him. If anyone snitched on Mr. Despereaux's whereabouts it wouldn't be *me*. He looked so content there on that porch with the music.

When I arrived back at our apartment, I checked my email. There was one message from Ike – he wasn't 'feeling it' anymore, and seeing as I'd be away most of the summer, it seemed like time to deep-six things. *F-bomb* him, he'd only wanted help with homework. It wasn't like I was a top student myself, especially in American History, but my composition skills were sure better than his. I'd coached him through previous essays. He didn't need me now. He could go take his baggy rapper pants with the chains and rattle those chains someplace else. *Ah, Beavertails*, it hurt, though.

Swim camp offered the water cure. I swam and swam, my body tacking past the hurt. The corn roasts and sing-alongs at swim camp were hokey, but harmless. There were no divas like Sienna Sparks. Iowa was a diva-free state! And I'd made it through Magnolia Arts Academy. Weirdly, our final composition made me dwell in possibility. *Write about a ghost in your family.* Typical flakey Academy stuff, I first thought. But then got into the spirit of it. The Mom-ster refused to talk about her own mother whenever I'd asked. We'd fought about it just before moving to New Orleans. "Why won't you talk about her? Is she, like, so *awful?* Just tell me, Ma – is she dead or alive?" My mother had given the strangest answer: "Yes and no, Amber. Over and out."

I thought about how even The Mom-ster's jewellery had baggage. "Then what about that locket you always wear, Ma. Is her tiny picture inside?" (I'd never seen inside.) "Lord, no, Amber – it's me and my brother. He died."

"How?" I asked. "When?"

"Drowned. When he was little, about six, I think. Which is why it's so good my *Honey Stone* is such a strong swimmer."

She knew that *yuck-o* pet name would quiet me. It worked.

My mother, the talker, talked when it suited *her*. I was so done with her head games. "That's no damned answer at all, Ma!" I hadn't learned a thing; she'd only chewed me out for swearing. So, when it came time to write the assignment, which I needed, to graduate from Arts Academy hell, I chose a new approach. I emailed my dad in Alberta. He told me The Mom-ster bore some longstanding grudge against her mother. (Newsflash, Dad.) They'd lived on a farm. Chickens, he thought. "Can you just give me a *name*, at least, Dad?" I waited a few days, which stressed me out – the assignment was due soon. My father had never been a speedy responder. Finally, when I'd chomped my nails almost to the quick, he answered: "Sadie. Her name. Wilder. Your mother had hers changed. She didn't even want the same name. I drove her to Edmonton, she did the paperwork. It was a long time ago. Good luck. Love, Dad."

That's all I needed. I dashed to a computer terminal in the library in my spare period. My fingers went gonzo on the keyboard. I googled. *Sadie Wilder. Chickens. Farm.* It took some tries and different search terms, but finally, I found a badly typed posting on a poultry website, about cruelty to (spelled "too") chickens. It was about overcrowded pens. An appeal to other poultry growers to support her cause (spelled "caws"). The posting was signed, Sadie Wilder, Poultry Farmer, Tipping Creek County, Ontario. And it concluded with – *Damned Skippy!* – her email address.

I'd found my ghost. I typed in her address. What would I say? Dear Family Ghost? That wouldn't do. Too zany, it might scare her. Dear Grandmother? But I didn't know for sure – what if I had the wrong lady? Then, typing fireball-fast, I wrote the most basic thing: "Dear Sadie Wilder. My name is Amber Crouch. I think you're my grandmother?" I told her I'd found her while doing a school assignment, with a little help from my father. I told her I was almost eighteen, finishing high school. I'd no idea what I was going to do next. Just couldn't seem to nail down a plan. I'd struggled with school. I was pretty sure I wasn't *that* dumb, it was the school, the toxic students. And that wasn't me, shifting blame, either. My boyfriend dumped me. I had to take care of my mother the best I could and that was, like, a full-time job. Did a place ever send out a bad feeling right from the first moment? Living in New Orleans rattled me every single day.

How bizarre-o, telling all this to a lady I'd never met. But once I started typing I couldn't stop. I hadn't really had anyone to talk with, to listen, in ages. I told Sadie Wilder I rocked at knitting and swimming. I told her my mother, Faith (her daughter) was a nurse practitioner, and before that, a waitress, and seems she had *other* jobs besides those. I told her my mother had an exotropic condition more often known as a walleye. Her identifying jewellery, if someone found her dead beside the road, was a super-retro mood ring and an old gold locket she always wore. I mentioned Malibu Barbie with her duct-taped neck. I told Sadie my mother talked a good line about dwelling in possibility and having dreams and moving forward, but the truth was, she had bad nerves and had given up driving, which turned our car into a spider planet. I told Sadie Wilder I hoped I had the *right Sadie Wilder*; I hoped it was okay I'd written. I hoped her chicken pen situation had improved because she seemed like a very distinguished chicken expert. I told her it would mean everything to me if she wrote me back.

[Send]

Please, please be the right lady, I prayed to the goddess of water I'd invented on the spot – because there *must* be one, right?

I waited. Knitted. Finished school. I volunteered at the Care Center on weekends. *Ah, Beavertails*, why was so much of life dead-air time, waiting? I ended up basing my family ghost paper on my quest to find Sadie Wilder: what it felt like each day to log onto the computer, hoping she might have written to me, and being crushed every day there was no reply. *A ghost in my family floats out there in feathered cyberspace; I await her mes-*

sage and picture her in a blizzard of chickens. That's how I ended my piece. The teacher called it *poignant, though inconclusive.*

Time passed – and I passed – and wore that awful flowered graduation dress but still received no word from Sadie Wilder. Maybe she really *was* a ghost. Maybe she'd died. I found no obituary on the Internet. Was no news really good news? Yes and no. I received an email from mother's friend Ivy Huckster who told me my cat Ponty caused quite the dust-up at Bayou Care Center. Chandler would have had him *put down,* Ivy wrote. *That man has a gaping hole where his heart should be.* Ivy adopted Ponty, her grandchildren enjoyed dangling a string he chased happily. Bless Ivy, she'd saved my cat's life. I wrote her with fervent thanks. The Mom-ster sent tedious messages – someone had hacked her computer – what a *pit of privacy-invaders* the world had become. Maybe *I* knew *something about it?* Her white sundress had vanished, too. It couldn't have just swished out of the apartment by itself. Maybe *I* had some information *about that?* Then she'd say how badly she missed her *little Amber Honey Stone.*

Ah, Beavertails, she was one wearying woman.

In Iowa, I swam and swam. I quit smoking, bad for aquatics. In the water, I was a machine. Sliced through the water so precise, so intense, Coach Daphne suggested, teasingly, in a previous life I must have been a shark. "No, Coach," I said. "In a previous life, I was somebody's granddaughter."

That Sadie Wilder didn't write I found puzzling, disturbing. I'd sent her a brief follow-up email, still no reply. Something must've happened to her. This worry over someone I didn't even know gripped me, day after day. Was she okay? Lots of days I felt like everything was ending, and only stroking through water lessened my sense of doom.

I was no shark. I was somebody's granddaughter.

TIPPING POINT

The small things that end the world: fatal error; mites; a tea towel turned surgical mask; a sparrow striking a pane; numbered days; a credit card with no credit.

A garden has a tipping point every summer. Maybe this day, maybe that day, usually around mid-August, and after that point, it will never reach the same glory. I knew this would happen soon, marking the aching slide into autumn.

A pox on that buzzing box of history! That wretched computer. Why, oh why did it have to go bust on Garden-Glory Day? The scent of summer roses had been wafting in through the farmhouse window. My blue delphiniums soared on their stakes, the scarlet runner beans were so many happy little orange-red pops. Universe, what lousy timing. The computer flat-out died, it did, just when I'd come to depend on it. I obeyed the bossy little chiclets. That day of garden paradise, the computer declared *fatal error* – after that, darkness. No reviving it. *Fatal error?* No *Farewell, Sadie*. No *Parting is such sweet sorrow, Sadie*. I've had the worst luck with computers over the past decade. They've died untimely deaths, leaving me disconnected for stretches of time and the latest buzzing box was no exception. My old typewriter put them all to shame, it did.

That year's garden was so lush, not only the flowers, the

vegetables, too. Sadly, the garden was the *only* thriving thing on my farm. Nearby, the scruffy lawn ran amuck. The house needed a new furnace, old beast wouldn't crank through another winter. Desperate for a fresh coat of paint were my shabby walls. Especially the mud room. A section of the barn roof had ripped away in a windstorm, rain leaked through it, making the straw mouldy and rank. I sure wasn't climbing up there to patch the roof. The ancient windmill once had a quaint air; now it listed badly. It could topple and kill me in a windstorm and needed to come down. The tractor barely huffed to life. The Dodge Dart, too. Everything was giving up on me. I'd been wearing clothes Cullen Quick left behind years ago, his trousers, shirt, ball cap. No money for new clothes. One mercy was Della-Mae wasn't alive to see how far things had fallen. Ivan Price promised to help with some repairs, but he had his own challenges.

Broken computer, broken-down farm. Everything was coming apart. I had to face it: the farm was sinking. A dying song. My egg quotas weren't exactly soaring, either. The pens were too crowded; I felt sure that was a factor. Crowding sickened the hens. Plus, there was my tremor. The drugs I took for it sent me off-kilter. The doctor said it's either medication, or the alternative. So, I lived off-kilter. (She never *did* tell me the alternative, chop off my hands?) And then that bossy box had to croak. I tried to 'reboot'. As a last resort, I gave the monitor a hearty smack. "Don't give up the ghost on me *now!*" No dice. Bob at Bob's Computer World said, "You can't take it personal, Sadie," after I'd driven the lifeless machine into Tipping Creek. Worst thing was, the computer's malfunction – something about the motherboard – wasn't covered on the warranty. How could that be? Bunch of lingo, but in the end, I understood they didn't intend to replace it or refund my money. My hands quaked so hard, hearing that, that Bob went all flustered, and asked if I wanted a chair, some water. "*No!* I want a *damned working computer!*" A nervous hush fell over the store. Tipping Creek people didn't throw tantrums. Lady farmers didn't throw tantrums.

With the poultry company, I was in a bind. I had to wait for the next egg cheque before I could buy a new computer. My line of credit at the bank was maxed, my credit card ranneth over. Della-Mae would have conniptions if she knew I lived in the deep end of debt. She'd left me the farm; that was supposed to sustain me. The poultry bosses hadn't been impressed with me for quite some time. They sent me a letter, saying they were aware of my postings on the poultry website that painted them in an unfairly bad light. And they'd gone ahead and double-populated my pens anyway *for greater efficiency*. What a nonsense burger. I phoned the regional poultry manager about my latest dead computer. I wouldn't be able to submit my egg reports on-line until I could buy a new one. That would take some time. She ballyhooed about what a generous grace period they'd allow, letting me submit my egg reports in hard copy until I rectified *my communications issues*. They were only granting this grace period because I was one of their 'original' growers. Why didn't she just say it – *oldest?*

No one knew, except the chickens, that some days my tremor went seismic. Even when I took extra medication. The air, heavy with feathers and mites, choked me. I wore a surgical mask rigged from a tea towel, over my nose and mouth or I couldn't breathe as I slogged through the pens, my boots plowing a slow path through gnarled, dirty chicken feet. Their feet are the ugliest part of chickens, but they can't help it. A misery for any living thing to be that crowded. Like permanent steerage. "Hens," I called out over their sour-violin squawks. "*None of us* is getting out of this alive!"

My old television fried. Another fatal error. Maybe just as well – news and weather broadcasts worsened the tremor. So many gruesome storms, tsunamis and earthquakes. Melting ice. A tragic polar bear flailing when the white surface he thought solid turned liquid. Those news clips of trees bent sideways, smashed over houses, half-submerged cars, people stranded on roofs, brought back that night in 1954. The hurricane's treacherous eye on us, its demon-laughter inside the battering gusts. It wanted to grind our bones into the raging riverbed. It had taken so much. All over again I saw the little boy churning away through the curdling floodwaters. And again, Faith, wailing, swept out of the small boat, her mouth clogged with mud, we'd almost lost her. My mother. Bobby's goldfish died, pre-emptive-like, though who ever knew, maybe that tiny fish would have been the last surviving creature in the house; maybe it could have swum through the flood and somehow, miraculously, survived.

The casino of waiting called life. Waiting for egg cheques. For morel season. Garden season. I filled the time by reading books from Tipping Creek Public Library – that's how I learned about miseries like steerage – and typing, an extreme hand-workout, with my tremor, but I got the story down at last, of that night. Hurricane Hazel. And even with typos plastered everywhere on my pages, they'd be easier to read than my handwriting – *if* anyone ever read it. I thought about how the worker in the computer warehouse grabbed the box containing the computer with the faulty motherboard and how I ended up with it; maybe the worker meant to grab a different box, one with a stronger motherboard, but was distracted; maybe a fly buzzed, maybe a ball of fluff blew in the window, who knew, and the flawed-motherboard machine ended up on *my* dining room table. If the mumps virus had landed in someone *else's* throat all those years ago, not Wanda Keeler's, and it had been *her* babysitting the Bannister kids the night of the hurricane, who could say where I'd be today? Chances were, not alone in chicken-feather hell.

Days and days later, a new computer hulked on my dining room table. The same boy got it ticking for me, wishing me better luck with this model. While he fiddled with cables and programs and such, a sparrow made a fatal error and crashed against the window. The sickening thud startled us both. Soon enough the boy beetled back to town, likely relieved to leave a lady farmer with shaking hands and a dead sparrow.

It had been weeks since I'd checked my electronic mail. Everyone wanted to sell me something. Dreary mass-mailings – disease alerts – from the poultry company. Suddenly, my hands heated. Tremored badly as I read a message from an Amber Crouch. She was a teenager, and seemed to think I was her *grandmother*. The girl had a lot to say, she did. I knew how to scroll down the screen, her words tumbled forth like a waterfall. I scrolled and read and pinched myself, and knew it had to be true – it all fit. The walleye. The Barbie doll with the duct-taped neck. The only thing that didn't fit was Faith being a *nurse*. Universe, make me laugh, why don't you? Faith didn't have a caring bone in her body, or she'd have written, called, sent me a Christmas card, over the years, at least told me I had a granddaughter. Was this Faith's cracked idea of an eye for an eye? A walleye for a walleye? A withholding for a withholding? I hadn't told her about her family so she wasn't going to tell me about my granddaughter? Piling up that much spite couldn't be good for a person's health. I'd scanned the self-help books in Tipping Creek Public Library, read a few, even, though I couldn't find *Guide for Grudge-holders*. So, Nurse Faith *cared for people*. Had she ever cared what it was like for me after she left?

My face liquefied. I thought back to that terrible day at the cairn. Faith had been so cruel. She'd demolished me with her angry words, she had, leaving me there on that rock. I'd planned to tell her everything when the time was right. She was always such a skittish colt, still playing with dolls, and almost twenty. She wasn't ready to be told. But she'd discovered it anyway. She'd pre-empted me. She'd *erased* me. But this Amber brought my edges back; how I longed to pick every flower in my cutting garden and fashion a flower crown for that girl I'd never even met.

I wiped my eyes with the little cloth the boy left for me to clean the computer screen. Faith had taken her own child to live where so many of the tropical storms struck. How *could* she? And with all her nightmares about drowning, how could she live there so close to sea level? Would she *never* see the light? Her daughter was unhappy there, the place spooked her, the girl told me in her email. I checked its date; she'd written right when the computer before last, another lemon, had crashed. Then the wait for the new computer to be delivered to the boondocks. There was a second, brief email from my granddaughter asking, had I received her first message? Was I okay?

Their city had been hit by a hurricane, Cindy, I saw on the last news I'd watched before the television died. Good grief, I hoped they were all right. What must the girl, my granddaughter, think of me? That I don't wish to know her? My hands were so convulsed it was murder using the keyboard. I couldn't shift the thing out of upper case but that would get the girl's attention, at least. I told Amber her message had sent me into a divine tizzy. By all accounts I had to be her grandmother, the facts squared. My #@&%! computers kept croaking, which was why I hadn't written sooner. Was she – and her mother – safe after Hurricane Cindy? I asked her to please write, tell me they were fine; to forgive my long silence. It was only because of the machine's fatal error. I told her where I lived, that her *mother* would know the place. I was still on the farm in Tipping Creek County. *Concession 3 by the old elm tree.* And finally, I'd been a poultry farmer for many years but hardly what anyone would call a distinguished chicken expert, or an expert in anything. Though my cutting garden was lovely, how I wished she could see it. (After this I'd tried to type a symbol meant to signify a smile but it came out more like some *help* symbol from a space alien.)

[Send]

I made a royal mess, many typing mistakes, but as long as Amber could grasp the essence. As long as I heard from her again. She'd thrown me a rope, maybe the long scarf she knitted. I had to catch it if I didn't do anything else in my life. I gazed out the dining room window, into the day's falling light. I grasped my hands, ordered them to be still and give me some peace for a moment. Of course, they didn't listen. They ached, and I knew why; they ached to hold the hands of Amber. The swimmer. The granddaughter. Amber.

Some people you just love right away.

GREAT SPANGLED FRITILLARY

The small things that end the world: seeing a pretty butterfly and all you can think about is your child, miles away; *meow*, and now, at work, they hate you more than ever, their little tongue-clicks let you know.

One day, changing a resident's comfort cloth – *never* call them diapers, we were instructed – a quick, black shadow skittered out from under the bed, startling me. *For the love of* – a *cat* – with a ragged ear and raspy mewl I recognized. *Our* cat. This had to be Amber's doing, who knew what possessed teenagers sometimes? I needed to believe it was done out of kindness, and I wouldn't throw my girl under the bus so the Care Emperor and his faded-beauty-queen sidekick could drive over her. I asked Lucky Mason about the cat. He told me Ponty had been living in the Care Center for a good chunk of time. How had I not noticed him? "He musta' kept dodging you, Faith. There's lots of places to hide, here. Guess he don't want to go back home. How'd you keep not seeing him? Same, like, how did Remy Despereaux just waltz out of here and nobody saw? How come Ivy, working the front desk, never saw?"

"Maybe Mr. Despereaux left through the back door, by the loading dock, Lucky. You know, where you have your smoke breaks."

The other theory I harboured was, Ivy had been taking extra

Xanax with her iced tea – she'd had problems with her son, at home – and Remy *had*, in fact, waltzed right out the front door, past her desk. The last person to investigate *that* theory was me. Funny how I'd retreated from the truth-probing heroine of my early days, Betty Kennedy. Of course, she remained a heroine of my youth, but truth was different in real life than on a game show. In real life, loyalty got tangled into it. Loyalty to Ivy. To Amber. And weighing who *deserved* to know and how they'd *use* the knowledge. I'd deserved to know the truth about my parents, and when I learned it, all I'd done was leave a lifetime of unfinished business. Was that why Sadie Wilder's face floated before me that day the world liquefied, when I'd only meant to take a Sunday drive?

I wouldn't throw Ivy under the bus any more than I'd toss Amber into the alligator pit of management at Bayou Care Center.

Lucky had been fired over the cat. I'd filed an appeal, stating the cat wasn't his fault. It was *mine*. I took the feline fall. I mentioned this article on animal therapy in geriatric care facilities – how animals interacting with residents raised morale. I'd just wanted to help, now more than ever, with the new ramped-up comfort zone policy. The cat was meant as *succor*, that's all. Lucky was hired back – they were short-staffed – but after that both Mickey Chandler and Charity Sparks had it in for me, their faces warning signs on sticks. The signs said what made me think someone with temporary work papers had the right to challenge Human Resource decisions? The signs said "Faith, your days are numbered."

The truth was, I was near the end of my macramé string, overloaded with their endless ledgers and points, and succor-enforcement, and my white pantyhose that snagged and stifled me, and all the other women workers, in the heat. We'd been talking. In corridors, the cracks of time. The security cameras beamed down on us, but weren't programmed to pick up what we said to each other. Bad enough they filmed our every move.

With Amber away at swim camp, the days felt heavy, lost. Hector Lafleur had emailed, calling me one *wang-dang-doodle of a lady*, but thought it fitting to tell me he'd met a gal up Honey Island way so he'd signed off *The Big Easy for Singles*.

My white sundress never resurfaced.

Ivy Huckster was concerned about me. We had lunch in the heritage garden. It was steamy outside, but took us beyond the reach of the security cameras. She said I looked tired. Asked if I was angry with Amber for taking the cat to Bayou Care Center, how the fracas over it made the Care Center even more of a pressure cooker for me.

A worthwhile question. My cucumber sandwich was minty and cool on my tongue. I chewed thoughtfully. "You know, Ivy, I *should* be mad at her. I mean, I walk on even *more* eggshells now, as if work wasn't already stressful enough. But I'm not."

The prettiest butterfly skimmed past us.

"What kind is it? The butterfly?" I asked Ivy.

"Great Spangled Fritillary," my friend answered, not missing a beat.

My eyes followed its rapid flitting, receding. "You don't say? I'm going to rename it – Great Spangled Amber," I said. "Reminds me of her, that flickering of dark and light. And the longer I ponder your question, Ivy, the more I realize I'm *proud* of Amber for taking the initiative. For trying to make this institution better."

In tandem we glanced at our watches, then rose from the bench.

"One thing's for sure, Faith – that girl of yours is *nobody's puppet*."

I laughed. "No, she's not. But she's also one unpredictable little – toggle."

My friend laughed, too, a release wispy as butterfly wings. "They all are, Faith. A bunch of toggles."

"Lord, Ivy, what's wrong with me? I didn't even thank you for taking the cat into your home."

My friend squeezed my arm, in the comforting way of an aunt. "Don't mention it, Faith. You've got a lot on your mind, and you're missing your girl. The cat's real nice to have around, he calms my son."

What Ivy *didn't* know was, after Amber left for swim camp, my nightmares returned. They were like my old nightmares, on the farm, but layered over with torrents of water, like the spell, or whatever it was I'd had, while driving my car, that Sunday. My foot thrashing against the bedsheets was like pumping the brakes. I knew there was a medical term for this, *restless leg syndrome*. But my foot's syndrome was more than that, it kicked back through time. Images from my distant and recent past wavered before me: Sadie Wilder's head with its flowing white hair, a child's rubber boot, a velvet matador with bared teeth, then G-strings, pasties, a tall flower on a purple stalk. The feeling of something choking me – ropes of hanging moss or Vinnie Corio returned to finish me off. Then I'd awake, my rogue foot still brake-pumping, my throat severely constricted, yet there'd be nothing around my neck, no water in my bed. I'd hear a siren outside the window and remember I was in New Orleans. Time to go to work. If the nightmares didn't keep me awake, the hot flashes did. They'd returned, too.

The work week ended at last. I was tired. Common sense ordered me to bed but my restless streak ordered me over to the computer. It had been so long since I'd logged onto the dating site, *The Big Easy for Singles*. FUNTRAIN's profile remained, but still no photograph. Maybe he had one of those red blotchy birthmarks over half his face. Wouldn't have been his fault, just the hand life dealt him. To find out what he looked like, what was to be lost besides a couple of hours? My typing fingers remounted the cyber-horse:

FUNTRAIN, it's *Macramé Maggie*. U still there?

[Send]

His reply was so speedy it was like he was right down the hall. We agreed to meet tomorrow, Saturday, for a drink and lunch beside the courtyard fountain at O'Brien's. Odd choice of place, I thought. O'Brien's was an overpriced tourist bar with hundreds of beer steins hooked from the ceiling beams, a stilted joint few self-respecting locals patronized. Amber and I had ordered inedible alligator nuggets there when we first arrived in New Orleans.

I said sure. O'Brien's.

I rifled through my closet. The white sundress would have been ideal. I settled for a black tank top, its hem barely grazed my naval – my tattoo would display when I turned to excuse myself to freshen up in the little girls' room – pencil skirt with back-pocket bling, and my gold platform sandals. I patted concealer under my eyes to hide the dark circles. They reminded me, eerily, of the blue rings around Sadie Wilder's eyes when she'd floated across my windshield, writing on her seaweed scroll. I knew the heat would sweat away the concealer but at least it would conceal – initially. I pinned my hair high in the messy way Hector Lafleur had liked. As I finished dressing, I tried to forget the alligator wrestler's rebuff; it was bad enough seeing him at the Care Center. He'd begun visiting his mother. Good for her, bad for me.

O'Brien's was as tacky as I recalled. I chose a small table

snugged under a palm tree near the fountain's gaudy plume. Nervous, I ordered a Singapore Sling – it gave my hands something to reach for.

The courtyard was surprisingly empty for a lunch hour and the under-tasked waitresses nattered away in a cluster. My sling drained in no time, I summoned another.

Suddenly my boss approached the table. Mickey Chandler, the Care Emperor himself. Last person I wanted to see. Why wasn't he in his office watching security camera footage, or on some golf course? His tanned face burnished with embarrassment, and not far behind that, annoyance. I was the last person *he* wanted to see, too. His hair wasn't oiled and pulled back into that ponytail; instead it flowed down, fringing his shoulders. He wasn't wearing his power suit, either, but a linen shirt with the top two buttons undone. Swinger attire.

He stood awkwardly, befuddled. "Hello, Faith."

The waitress deked around him, delivering my sling.

I was perplexed, too. I craned my neck to see past him. Perhaps FUNTRAIN would arrive any second and mistakenly think I was with this swinger dude. "Hello, Mr. Chandler." I forced a polite tone; he was still my boss, even on Saturday.

"Are you meeting someone, Faith?"

"Kind of. I think. You?"

Even his golf-tan couldn't cover his blush. "Yes. But not sure who I'm looking for. I'm a bit late."

Wait. No way. The ultimate hot flash of revelation firestormed me. It *couldn't* be. What were the odds? Yet surely it *was*. His swinger getup gave him away, his on-edge demeanour. I was floored and abashed and radiantly joyous all at once. I smelled his panic, read his thoughts as they sprinted along the same stadium track as mine. He knew my daughter had been a Magnolia student; he'd helped set it up with his wife, the Principal, when he'd hired me at the Care Center. All I had to do was drop a casual remark about meeting Mickey in this – situation – to someone connected to Magnolia Arts Academy, and everyone would know.

For almost six months I'd sweated in god-awful pantyhose and that tight white dress, trying to live up to his *impeccable* Florence Nightingale brand, to satisfy the points ledger Charity Sparks maintained for him. This was tricky for Mickey. Risky. I wasn't married. I didn't oversee an expanding care empire. I guessed his wife Dyan had no clue she was wedded to the FUN-TRAIN. No one at Bayou knew they worked for the FUN-TRAIN – except me. A warm gust rattled the palm tree above us. How I'd wanted to go on a real date, meet someone interesting. But this moment trumped any other possibility.

I smiled at him gorgeously. "FUNTRAIN?"

My boss sunk slowly, with an audible groan, into the chair across from mine. The chipper waitress hopped over to him. He looked fretful, likely worrying the waitress was one of his wife's piano students.

He ordered a double shot of bourbon. His face a caught-red-handed hue.

I extended my own hand – my mood ring a velvety claret – across the table, careful to not topple my cocktail. "Macramé Maggie," I said.

His bourbon arrived.

My boss shook my hand weakly. He wasn't wearing his wedding ring. He took a long, hard swallow of his bourbon. "I'd have thought you'd be out collecting flea-bitten, *unauthorized animals* to sneak into the Care Center," he sniped. But it was a spineless snipe. I held the smoking gun and Mickey knew it.

I ignored the animal remark. *He* was the only flea at this table.

Kilowatts of moxie surged through my brick house. The

house FUNTRAIN couldn't help gawking at. An old rush, like the one I felt the night I gospel-ized The Beaver Club, galloped across my lower back. Until the juicer, the goon, tried to *drown* me in Lake Superior. I had no plans to let anyone push me under again. Lunchers flooded into the courtyard. The empty restaurant suddenly packed. I remembered these extremes from my waitress days. FUNTRAIN grew twitchier, likely nervous someone he knew would spot us. Maybe that's why he chose a tacky tourist bar, to lower the odds of running into someone he knew. Slinging back my sling, I gazed across the table, enjoying the duress on my boss' face.

"You like slings, do you, Faith?" he asked inanely.

I shrugged coyly. "Old world comfort. Succor. Your hair looks different, Mickey. Not the usual ponytail, I mean."

"Faith. I don't usually do this."

For months, his profile had been on *The Big Easy for Singles*. A stiffer breeze riffled the palm tree as I tried to decide which way to go on this. I could say we all have our lapses; this meeting could be our little secret and someday we'd laugh about it. Except I knew we wouldn't. I thought, too, of all the dollars I'd burnt up on pantyhose. How he subjected us to Lawrence Welk all day. I thought about how he'd humiliated Lucky Mason in front of everyone. How his security cameras watched our every move. How he'd planned to have Ponty euthanized. *Cat killer!* There'd be no mercy for him.

I climbed aboard the fun train. "Waitress!" I volleyed across the courtyard, loudly, so diners' heads pivoted our way. "Another round. Bourbon for my date, Singapore Sling *pour moi!*"

My boss looked fully miserable. Shipwrecked in a courtyard. He tucked back into his bourbon. "Faith, I am *not* your 'date'."

My mood soared. "*No?* That's not what you said on the *dat-*

ing site. Maybe you took a wrong turn on the information highway? Hell's bells, then, if this *isn't* a date, we could convene a
staff meeting right here. The bourbon will provide some *succor*
for you."

Years stampeded onto his face in seconds, a paling, like his
suntan just slid off, a lamentable landslide. "I – don't know
what to say," he stammered. "Things haven't been good at
home for a long time. I hardly know what to call it."

I bobbled the cherry in my drink, hang me if I'd send prompt
succor across the table. "I call it ironic. I mean, here we are,
the Care Center's Image Squad and *look* at us – how *flawed* we
are – how *profoundly, momentously flawed.*"

Another round arrived. Mickey Chandler grimaced. "And
you feel good about that, Faith?" Not letting me answer, he
spat more words my way. "You Canadians, so sanctimonious,
mounted on your high Mountie horses!"

I laughed, snorting haws. Silliest opinion I'd heard in ages.
Across the courtyard, a familiar voice beckoned me with a waving hand – Ivy Huckster in a geometry-patterned dress and
swoopy sunglasses with wings. She was flanked by an overgrown teenaged boy. Within seconds she and the gangly youth
stood beside our table. I greeted her. Mickey scrounged the
weakest nod.

"Heavens, look at *you two*! Here, in *this place*, on a Saturday!" Ivy chirruped. Removing her sunglasses, she explained
that the boy with her was her nephew, Ethan, who was visiting
from Canada. She was playing tour guide, they weren't eating
here, she was just showing him the place, and just look who–

"*Canada!* Isn't that a coincidence," I said. "Mickey, here, was
just speaking about Canadians not a minute ago, isn't it ironic?"

"It was an accident, this – us." Mickey Chandler said. To
Ivy. To me. He spoke through clenched teeth.

Ivy glanced at the empty bourbon and sling glasses on our table.

I laid on my best southern belle voice. "Oh, *fiddle-dee-dee!* Mickey, here, is just downplaying things. It *wasn't* an accident, Ivy. It was planned. I can't wait to tell you all about it at work on Monday."

Ivy chose to drop the thread. "Faith," she said, "I'm cooking jambalaya tonight, why don't you come over?"

The boy shifted his weight from one giant sneaker to the other.

I told Ivy that sounded dreamy, my straight eye gave her an exaggerated, vaudeville wink. The Care Emperor had to have noted it.

"All *righty*, then," Ivy said. "Ethan here, is getting restless. We're off to visit the cathedral now. See you tonight, Faith. You two enjoy your – outing."

Just before Ivy remounted her sunglasses on her nose, she shot me the most quizzical, 'dying to know' look. Then she breezed out of the courtyard, her nephew at her heels.

Mickey Chandler cast glum eyes on me. It was like an invisible trapdoor under his chair was about to open and suck him down into the void. He had *two* incriminating witnesses, now.

Riding the FUNTRAIN had brought a thrill, but it now sputtered to a halt. I told my boss I had some errands to run. I gathered my purse and shawl.

"Faith, I'd appreciate if you didn't mention this, our –"

"Must run, Mickey. You know how Saturdays slip away – *poof!*"

I was off the clock. I didn't have to promise anything. Neither did Ivy.

I signaled to the waitress that the tab would be settled by FUNTRAIN.

Just before I left, I zippered my boss inside my gaze. "Since this isn't a date, as you said, I've designed a new work policy right here in this courtyard: *no more white pantyhose* at Bayou Care Center! I'm pretty confident I'll have the support of female staff."

I turned; he must have have seen my *I Dwell in Possibility* tattoo. I cantered, in my gold platform sandals, away from the table, past the sculpted water spray out into the mean streets of America.

GREAT SPANGLED AMBER

The small things that begin the world: a ball of fluff.

Could knowledge lodge itself inside a ball of fluff? *Damned Skippy,* apparently it could. Whenever I wrangled with the thorns life threw under my bare feet, when I couldn't crack some dilemma at school, or wherever, The Mom-ster always said, "Amber, one day you'll wake up and you'll know what to do, you'll just *know.*" To me, that smacked of flakey, too simple. I mean, that might be how it worked for *her*, but it was, like, risky to assume it worked the same way for me. But one day it *did*.

Beside the pool, I was towelling off after my morning laps, still dripping, when a fluff ball fell off my towel onto the tiles. Who knew why a person would bother to retrieve such a tiny, useless thing, but I did, and in that moment of bending, and pinching the fallen towel-fluff between my fingers, the answer zinged into my brain's core: *go see your grandmother, Amber. Right after camp.* I knew where she lived. I just needed the cash to travel to Canada.

Not many days of swim camp remained. No time to lose now that I had a plan. Thanks to the rogue lint. Right after morning laps I logged onto the camp computer. I knew better than tell The Mom-ster about my plan. She'd forbid me from seeing Sadie Wilder, I felt that to my glutes. She'd freak. She al-ways treated the topic of my grandmother as off-limits which wasn't fair. I'd turn eighteen in a few days. I had a right to know Sadie (who still hadn't emailed me). The vibe that something was wrong in her world stuck, like Krazy Glue, to my heart. Maybe she'd fallen dead on her kitchen floor, and no one knew. Maybe she was sick. I couldn't understand why she hadn't writ-ten me back. I'd find out in person, *that's* what I knew when I nabbed that fluff of lint off the tiles.

I emailed my dad in Alberta. *Ah, Beavertails,* let him respond faster than usual. I said *my bad* for dropping this on him, like, out of nowhere, but I needed money, quite a bit, it was urgent but no, not *that* kind of trouble. He could chill on that score. There must be a fast way to wire it, or deposit it into my ac-count. I sent him the number. Maybe it could be my eighteenth birthday present. I promised to tell him (someday) what I did with the money, if he could just send it as soon as possible.

The Mom-ster would be furious. My plan had been to travel south, back to New Orleans, right after swim camp. She'd bought my ticket. She couldn't know my new plan, or she'd squelch it. I aimed to head in the *opposite* direction, north. To Grandma Sadie's farm. What I was about to do could send me into the doghouse forever. But sometimes a person just had to break rank and face the fallout. Meeting my grandmother, I felt, would somehow help me figure out the future, know what to *do*, now that high school was over.

While I waited to start my journey, I knitted. An infinity scarf, gift for Sadie Wilder. That same light green-bluey color, swim-ming pool colour. I'd bought tons of yarn. I was fast with the needles. I tucked the finished soft circle away in my backpack.

My mother phoned to wish me happy birthday. She asked how I was doing. "Spectacular, Ma, no, *really!*" Then she talked. This butterfly she'd seen, a great spangled something, reminded her of me. "That's sweet, Ma." She had a newsflash: She no longer had to wear white pantyhose to work! She'd started a revolution, couldn't wait to tell me about it. Couldn't wait to see me; she'd been counting down the hours! When I returned home we'd celebrate my birthday. She'd treat me to dinner at Antoine's. Lobster. (She forgot seafood made me queasy, those creatures with their dead eyes, staring up at me. I didn't have the heart to remind her, she was so stoked.) We'd have peach melba with candles in mine. *Jingles*, she couldn't believe her *Honey Stone* was all grown up. The longer The Mom-ster talked the worse I felt about what I was about to do, but the wheels of my northern scheme spun faster. I couldn't stop picturing Grandma Sadie sick, or in trouble. Otherwise, why wouldn't she answer an email from her own granddaughter? She needed me. I could only hope my mother would forgive me. After all, I was the only *Honey Stone* in her jewellery box.

Meanwhile, in Alberta, my dad couldn't believe I was eighteen, either. Were all parents such time-deniers? He'd emailed to tell me this; also, he'd made the deposit into my bank account. *Damned Skippy!* I'd soon be on my way to *Concession 3, by the old elm tree*, Tipping Creek County. I had a passport from when my mother and I moved to New Orleans which felt, like, way longer than six months ago. On a North America map in the library, I drew a bright blue line from where I was in Iowa, to my Ontario destination. I googled the route. *F-bomb* me, what a trip! Bus to Des Moines. Then fly to Chicago. Wing it to Toronto. Bus to Guelph, then Tipping Creek. Then a taxi to Grandma Sadie's farm. I'd have to learn how to fly, like in that Kelly Clarkson song The Mom-ster was crackers over. But making sure my grandmother was okay, meeting her, would be worth it. Too bad I couldn't *swim* to Canada; I'd have made it in half the time.

FEATHERS

The small things that end the world: side effects; a church hat, the bubbled kind that now sold in the town's 'vintage' shop; a losing score in the land of credit; carnage, feather by feather; a kiss-off from the poultry company.

My doctor urged me to try a new medication for my essential tremor but when I read its possible side effects on the World Wide Web I said no thanks. I'd take the shakes over *blistering, peeling, or loosening of the skin,* and *confusion about identity, place, and time.* I had to keep my skin *on,* had to stay alert, for where I was going: New Orleans. It would take all my courage to travel there, to sea level. Being near all that water would elevate my blood pressure, too, it would – nerves. But there was no help for it. Letters weren't enough, I needed to see my granddaughter in the flesh, needed secure skin for that, and for my reckoning with Faith, after all these years. What would I say to her? What would she say to me? No, I couldn't afford side effects; I needed to know *who* I was, *where* I was, the *exact hour.* No room for confusion about identity, place, or time. The drugs I already took tilted me, but at least the basic facts of my lonely existence held together.

The moment had arrived. I could stay on my wreck of a farm and die, or I could board an airplane to meet Amber and see how the rest of my life might turn out. The express passport had cost me an arm and two legs. I sat, shaking, in my old Dodge Dart, ready to drive into Tipping Creek for my meeting at the bank. I'd put on my old navy suit and my bubbled church hat. I'd never worn it to church because I'd never gone, because I'd lost faith and just couldn't pretend otherwise. But now I was glad I had the hat, out of date as it was. I wanted to look respectable. The letter I'd received yesterday from the poultry company had already soared my blood pressure; they were *de-listing* me as one of their growers. Their truck would load my chickens and take them away at the end of August. They thanked me for my years of dedication to poultry. They couldn't even say it in plain English, *you're fired, Sadie*. I slumped behind the wheel of my Dodge Dart, the engine still off, and thought how the company could just suddenly remove my livelihood on a whim – *just like that*. And I started to cry. I said aloud, "*Oy vey*, just what am I going to do now, *just what?*" I felt as helpless as I did that night of the hurricane, with those two kids. Again, no one heard me.

The poultry company's letter smoldered the roots of my hair. They'd schedule their truck to load my chickens at the end of August, that was soon – and I'd be *de-listed*. Deleted. The work was wretched and those hens suffered in steerage but it was all I had. If the company was done with *me*, then I was done with *them* – I had a trip to take anyway. A trip more important than poultry. I'd save them the trouble of loading my chickens, I would. I glanced at my watch – time enough, before my appointment at the bank.

I scrummed my way out of the car and back into the house. I grabbed a broom and headed for the chicken barn. Opened the pen's door wide. The miserable birds looked startled – by my bubbled hat, or the open door, or both. I coughed back clotted air. Several hens closest to the light tilted dubious, beaded eyes my way – looking to the light, then back at me. The prisoners needed to be coaxed into their next phase. They were bound for Colonel Sanders in any case. I pushed through the poultry swarming my ankles, raised the broom and shooed the feathery mass towards the door, broom-beating the air with rapid swats.

The broom worked, scared the stunned white wedges towards the natural light. "That's right," I called out. "Fly the coop – *go!*"

They streamed out the door, a snowy, moving river.

I dropped the broom and walked back to my Dodge Dart. My navy suit flecked with white feathers like someone had tried to beat me with a feather pillow. I'd deal with that in town before the bank. The car started, *Heyzoose Marimba!* It didn't always start, that's why I'd allowed extra time, in case I had to call Ivan Price for a ride. I tore up the long dirt laneway, looking back only once in my rearview mirror to witness the weedy green neglect that was my lawn expand with a winter that rippled and twitched under the shock of sunlight.

The bank wouldn't raise my line of credit. I sat in that sterile cubicle, my quaking hands plucking a few last feathers from my navy suit (I'd thought I'd gotten them all), and was told my 'credit score' was too low. The bank lady zipped numbers into her computer while I de-feathered. I'd planned to go right from the bank to the travel agent, to buy a ticket to New Orleans. I told her I needed the money for a trip, family emergency. I felt sure that would clinch it, despite my credit score. Compassionate reason.

"Can't you notch up my score just enough to see my granddaughter?"

"I'm sorry, Sadie. These numbers get sent into regional head-quarters. That would be considered tampering."

I told her I'd been a loyal customer at their bank since the sixties. She looked as dazed as my hens. Easy to see she'd no notion of history. Just kept saying sorry. She'd asked if I might draw on my savings. I'd sunk anything extra into the farm and it had crumbled into ruin anyway. Those computers cost me mightily, they did. The annual morel profit for years went towards my trips to Toronto, searching for Faith.

Savings, what a notion. *Saving* was what I needed, all right.

Divine intervention was called for. I talked to a pastor, once. Asked how, if there *was* a God, that God could let the things happen that happened. The thing was, life's afflictions – missing Faith, the loneliness, the tremor, the failing farm – outweighed life's gifts. God's ledger was out of balance. Wouldn't God be a better banker than that? The pastor said sometimes we must wait for the answer. I told him Christmas was coming, too. That wasn't very civil of me, it wasn't, but I couldn't help it.

I'd always tried not to sink into self-pity. "There's no future there, Sadie-Girl," Della-Mae warned. But after the bank appointment, I climbed inside my Dodge Dart, my personal pity pod. I'd *earned* that pod. How would I ever see Amber? The credit line increase was meant to replace my final egg cheque which I'd never receive after *the act I'd committed*. The poultry company might even slap me with a criminal charge. Poultry homicide. Those hens couldn't survive outdoors; they couldn't run, could barely waddle. They'd be a fox feast quick enough. Who was it that called hope the thing with feathers? *Way* off the mark, that was, in *my* world at least.

Slowly I drove back to the farm, to face the carnage.

LITANY: TAKE TWO, TAKE THREE

The small things that begin the world: cobs of corn; potatoes; crickets; green beans; duct tape.

F-bomb me, an extreme trek! I finally reached Tipping Creek. A town of strapping red brick houses, fussed-over, and lofty gardens. Yet it was, like, the twilight zone. There seemed to be only one taxi. The hills-old driver looked dumbfounded when I asked him to drive me to Sadie Wilder's farm but drop me at the road. I wanted to walk the laneway. A chance to calm my heart, to feel human again. Travel warped a person.

Ah, Beavertails, the calming unraveled. My grandmother's laneway stretched longer than any banner-scarf I'd knitted. The air felt cooler in the north. I started to walk slowly, drawing the most measured breaths I could, and pondered what to tell this lady I'd never met. I'd never known a lady farmer, and for sure not a *grandmother* lady farmer. Her homestead had this bent-over windmill with blades missing and all these little sheds, what were they called? *Outbuildings?* What looked like a pretty garden in front of the house came into view. The house itself looked almost abandoned. A grizzled car parked in front. Other than the garden, everything else was wild, with overgrown grass and weeds. I reached around and felt the infinity scarf rolled inside my backpack. But suddenly my Doc Marten boots kicked dust and I began to run. I'd been trying to stay composed, but an image of my grandmother splayed on her kitchen floor, sick or –

Walking? What was I *thinking?* Something really bad must have befallen Sadie Wilder, which explained the jungled yard, why the outbuildings seemed to have been sobbing for years, and why the house looked like only ghosts hung out there. Except for the garden, this was no place for a grandmother to be by herself. There was no sign of a dog. Didn't farms come with dogs? I'd been right; by the look of the place she obviously needed me. She must be so lonely there in the ruins.

I approached the garden. The late-afternoon sunlight angled down on it in a way that set it on fire. A lady, her apron fashioned into sort of a basket, filled with vegetables I guessed, stepped out of the flames, out from behind a tall, green row. *Damned Skippy!* She was alive! It had to be Sadie. The staked gladiolas formed a bright yellow and orange floral picket fence in front of her.

She noticed me, released her apron corners – her hands shaking badly – and corn cobs spilled onto the earth around her feet. "Oh, you scared *the jeepers out of me!*" – but with each word her eyes, her smile, widened. She knew who I was, she *just knew.* I arched my shoulders to roll my backpack off my back. It thudded onto the ground. She wore a baseball cap, baggy trousers, and an oversized man's shirt that appeared to have once been white, but had turned a shade of damp sand. She ignored the fallen corn. Stepping over a thick row of blue-spiked onions, she took three long strides, to me, and made her arms into an infinity scarf around me. We stood that way for a long time, there in her garden. *Say something, Amber,* I thought at last.

I loosened her arms, gently, from around me. "Let me help

you with that corn, Grandma Sadie."

She lit into laughs, lovely, bird trills.

I laughed, too.

"You must be famished," she said. "You're thin. You like corn?"

"I *love* corn," I said.

As I followed her closely, making our way towards the house, something looked really strange about her yard, besides not having been mown since forever. The tall, twisting wild vines and weeds and grasses, many of them, had this white film over them, white flecks caught in their stem notches, seed pods. Feathers? And the yard smelt weird, too, not pleasant. A *stench*. The garden's fragrant flowers had masked it, at first. There were feathers and – wings – and – I had to avert my eyes. I didn't want to be rude, but something was *decomposing* in those grasses and weeds. *F-bomb* me, how do you tell your grandmother you just met that her yard stinks?

My grandmother saw me see it. "Don't bother with that, Amber." (It was the first time she said my name, sweet riff!) "Come inside, forgive the mess everywhere – outside, inside. Land's sake, I'm so ashamed of the sad way I've been existing. And forgive my clothes. They belonged to an old friend. This shirt used to be white. Criminy, I once believed a white blouse was the ticket to success; where *I've* been, a white blouse couldn't have saved me. Silly old me. Such a foolish thought, wasn't it?"

Not waiting for an answer, she creaked open the screen door, and we stood inside a small, cobwebbed wreck of a room with a freezer. Wall hooks heavy with old coats. Badly peeling paint. Buckets with open slats, for eggs, maybe? She led me into her kitchen, the country kind I'd seen in movies. It was large, with plenty of room for a table and chairs. She had a super-retro fridge and stove, and this really cool old typewriter on the kitchen table. Papers stacked next to it, and a piece of paper in its roller-thing. The windows held a film of dust. On one sill, a geranium fought for tomorrow. Dirty dishes skulked on countertops. Lots of macramé plant hangers roped down from the exposed rafters, the plants cradled in them lifeless and brown. The macramé had a joyless look and reminded me of so many sad mast riggings from a lost ship. My mother told me once she'd grown up in the golden age of crafts. *Macramé Maggie.* Yeah, crafts.

"Let me help wash those dishes," I told Sadie.

My grandmother objected, said I'd taken such a long trip, I should rest, visit with her while she cooked us some corn and eggs. She removed her baseball cap, fluffed her short silver hair, and pinged about her kitchen shoving things out of the way. She filled the teakettle. Her movements had this purposeful rhythm, despite whatever was wrong with her hands.

I didn't heed her. Didn't need rest. I was strong, a swimmer. Soon clean dishes filled the drying rack.

We shucked the corn together. Tried to figure out how, somehow, I'd missed her email to me. She'd written me. How it could have just, like, vaporized. "Things do," my grandmother said. She told me she'd suffered from a string of computers with fatal errors.

While the corn boiled in the pot, she sat with her tea across from me at the table. Her cup was full and she wasn't able to hold it steadily. I worried she'd scald herself.

"What's wrong with your hands, Grandma Sadie?" I asked.

"Essential tremor," she said. "Had it for years. I take pills, they help, but don't cure it. That's why the typing mistakes in my email to you and –" she pointed, jerkily, to the stack by the typewriter, "those papers."

I lowered my teacup. "What's on them? The papers, I

mean?"

My grandmother picked at something on her cheek. A fluff ball?

"The story of your mother and I," she answered. "In case she ever came back. In case she ever wanted to know."

The elephant with the exotropic eye had lumbered into the room. I'd *wondered* when we'd broach The Mom-ster. When I'd first arrived, it wasn't the right time. My grandmother and I were still feeling our way around, getting used to each other. But the elephant was with us now.

My grandmother had been frying eggs; they were *the last of her eggs*, she said, serving them with butter from a cracked dish. "Matter of fact, last of *all* the food, except for the garden, thank glory for *that*. Amber, does your mother know you're here with me?"

I squinted through the window dust at the lowering sun. It resembled a giant blood orange being squashed down onto the fields. A chill had fallen over the kitchen, and it was only August. I was glad I had my hoodie from swim camp, I huddled inside it. "My mother doesn't know," I said. "I was supposed to go back to New Orleans right after swim camp, but I came here instead."

Sadie's fork dropped. *Ah, Beavertails*, if only I hadn't had to break that to her, she looked alarmed, and I'd caused it. Her hands were trying to vault off her wrists. "Oh, *Amber*. Phone her. She'll be in a frenzy that you didn't come home from your camp. She'll have police out, likely. Go, phone her *now*. The phone is in the dining room."

I walked, hangdog, to make the call. 'There's something wrong with your telephone, Grandma Sadie," I called from the dining room. "The line seems, I can't get it to –"

She was beside me in an instant. "It's that *damned com-*

puter. I forgot to log off the World Wide Web connection. It's dial-up, goes through the phone line and no one can call in, or out. It's been connected for hours. I forgot."

She made like some mad pianist, on the keyboard. "There, now you can phone, Amber."

When I returned to the kitchen table to finish my cold eggs, my grandmother sat gloomily, food still on her plate. I settled back into my chair. A tick of tense silence.

My grandmother broke it. "What did she say?"

"Nothing. No answer."

"She's likely out looking for you, Amber. You left a message, at least, did you, to let her know you're okay?"

It was my turn to shake. "We don't have voice mail. We do email check-ins sometimes. What should we do now?"

"We should light a candle," Grandma Sadie said. "Email her. There's no worse feeling in the world than not knowing if the person it's your job to take care of is safe."

I emailed. My grandmother switched on lamps with dim bulbs. It felt more like being in a room lit by coal-oil lanterns. We drank chamomile tea through the evening. Every twenty minutes I called our number in New Orleans, but no answer. I emailed Ivy Huckster. I emailed my mother again. Now *she* was the one missing in action. And me, frantic about her again, like when she went on those dates.

Outside the farmhouse, the night world raved with crickets. My grandmother kept the window open; I guess she was used to the evening's chill. I was grateful for the cricket roar because Sadie was very quiet after supper. Not angry-quiet. Thought-ful-quiet. I didn't know if it made things better or worse, to talk. So, I tried.

"What happened out there in your yard, Grandma Sadie? That decaying *smell*, all those feathers?"

She winced. "Pretty much what it looks and smells like, Amber. Chicken Armageddon."

This only confused me. "Did your chickens all, somehow, *escape*, Grandma Sadie?"

"In a manner of speaking. They took their leave."

"Are you in trouble?" I asked.

She nodded. Sleeved at her eyes.

"That makes *two of us*," I sighed. "Then let's be in trouble *together* – to infinity."

I pulled the scarf out of my backpack, and filled her unsteady hands with yarn. "Wear this, Grandma Sadie. I knitted it for you. You might be in trouble, but at least you won't be cold."

She wound it around her neck. Her tears, lavish. I'd never seen knitting make someone cry. *Ah, Beavertails!* I hadn't meant to mess this up.

"It's called an infinity scarf," I said. "A closed loop. I'm sorry, Grandma Sadie – you don't like it?"

Her fingers tickled the wool. "Amber, it's lovely. It's been so long since I received a gift from *anyone*. This is grand and, even better, you made it yourself. The colour got to me, that's all." She dabbed her eyes drier with the scarf.

"Mint? Aqua? I'm not sure what it's called," I said, glad we were talking again. "I only knew I liked it. I thought *you* might, too."

"It's *seafoam green*," she remarked, with a sad smile, one corner of her mouth tipped higher than the other. "I saw it once, in the prettiest kitchen, before the world ended."

She was speaking in riddles, sad riddles, so I left it. It was enough to see her warmed by the work of my hands.

We took turns calling my mother through the night. My grandmother stayed awake and drank tea and dialed our number in New Orleans every twenty minutes and checked email – I gave her my password – while I dozed on the living room sofa. Then I did a shift so she could rest. If we'd gone to bed upstairs we might not hear the phone in case my mother called. We wouldn't have slept anyway. Sleep wasn't a luxury those in deep trouble could afford. Hunger pulled hard at me, too, and I wondered what my grandmother meant about last night's supper being the last of the food. The lamps coursed through the night. And my mother kept not answering the phone in New Orleans.

At five o'clock – the sky still that milky veil before full daylight, when the world is a grainy old movie – we heard a siren. It was my shift. I was groggy, and halfway conked out. I stumbled to the screen door and saw a police car spray strobing red light over the yard's wreckage, giving it a bloody cast.

"Wake up, Grandma Sadie!" I hollered into the living room.

She appeared beside me so quickly it was like she'd been beamed in, like some instant hologram.

We walked out onto the front porch.

Day's light was rising quickly. The police cruiser's back door punched open and two giant platform sandals hit the dirt. Then the rest of The Mom-ster – in her awful pink track suit, her hair sticking out everywhere – shunted out. She looked at us, and squeezed her face into this mutant shape – at *us*, or the yard's stench, I couldn't tell. She told the police officer he could go.

I heard him ask, "Are you sure, Ma'am?"

She was sure.

The cruiser jounced back over the potholes, down the long dirt laneway towards the road. We three stood in a freeze-frame, like, no one wanted the first word. Grandma Sadie and I on the porch, my mother still pretty much where her platform sandals had hit the dirt when she exited the police car. She made that repulsed face again.

Seconds, each a tremor. Minutes, each a mallet.

"Gads, what's that *smell*, Sadie Wilder, that *stink, like something died* in your yard?" The Mom-ster said at last, her face wild now, scanning the outbuildings, the canting windmill. "This place is a *disaster!*"

My grandmother stepped down the porch steps and walked right up to my mother, who was much taller in her platform sandals. At first I thought *F-bomb* me, Sadie is going to *slap* The Mom-ster! But she didn't. I stayed where I was, higher, on the porch.

"Faith, you've been gone for thirty-three years, and *this* is how you say *hello?* It's not like you were here to help keep up the place. I hardly think you're in a position to judge."

"You need to get *your telephone fixed!*" my mother shouted. "I couldn't get through – I've travelled for hours – piled a fortune, and I mean *thousands*, onto my credit card for airfare. And the airport was chaos, everyone buzzing about some storm on its way."

I wouldn't let The Mom-ster be mean to Grandma Sadie. No way. I stepped down from the porch. "Don't you raise your voice," I told my mother. "Sadie has dial-up internet. It's not *her* fault that's what they've got here in the country. She forgot to log off her computer. You're on *her* turf. You're a guest."

"*Ghost!*" Grandma Sadie squeaked.

"Listen, you two," my mother said. "Can't we go someplace that *reeks less of death?*"

Someone had to take charge. "*Garden!* Both of you! *Now!*" I made a 'follow me' signal. I knew the smell wasn't as bad there, the flowers masked it.

Soon the three of us occupied the bean patch. We planted our feet in a way that formed an edgy, loose triangle. Like some smack-down was about to happen. Riled as we were, we were also starving. At least I was. I snapped a few beans off their vines, and crammed them into my mouth. Didn't bother to remove their tiny green comma-like tails. I'd hardly crammed my mouth with green when my grandmother followed suit.

I held a bean out to my mother. "Bean, Ma?"

"I'd like to *bean you*, Amber Crouch," she brayed. But she took the bean. Bit into it.

"How did you know I was here?" I asked my mother, who was now pillaging the bean patch with the same gusto as my grandmother and I.

"Your school paper," she said. "I searched your bedroom for clues. Amber, when you didn't return from swim camp I thought you'd been abducted. In your bedroom closet I found your 'family ghost' paper, not to mention that heartbreaking diary of yours. Amber, *suicide*? Why didn't you *talk* to me? There are school counsellors, they could have – if anything ever happened to you –"

She choked on her bean, almost.

"Ma, you barged into my *closet*? I don't care *how* worried you were, that's wrong, it's an invasion."

The Mom-ster chomped her bean's tail, sending me one of her best – or worst – mother-glares. "*Wrong*', Amber? Really? Was it an *invasion* or simple *reciprocity*?"

Our 'family ghost' smiled. "Our Little Plum knows some mighty big words, she does!"

"Sadie, please stay out of this, this is between my daughter and I."

"Right. *Litany of grievances*, likely," my grandmother huffed, bending to pick more beans.

My mother had lost me. "Reciprocity? Ma?" She'd always loved it a little too much when she knew something you didn't.

Her good eye slathered me with gloating.

She de-tailed another bean. "You invaded *my* closet, I invaded *yours*. Now we're even. And for the record I didn't steal any of *your* clothes. I'm talking about my white sundress."

"Ma, how did you know about the closet thing?" *F-bomb* me, her mother-smirk was as bad as her mother-glare.

"I kept searching for my white sundress, Amber. And in the course of that, I found a poodle barrette tangled among my things. You'd *never* wear a poodle. That's how I knew the Sparks girl likely lead the charge into my closet, and filched my sundress. Why she would do that, I don't know. Kleptomania? Who knows why teenaged girls do what they do. And I couldn't say anything. A person can't go around calling her boss' daughter a thief."

Grandma Sadie held a fistful of green beans out to us, peace-offering-like. "Are you two *always* this intense?"

"No," my mother said.

"Yes," I said.

Somehow, the beans helped us chill.

"About my diary, Ma. I was *lonely*. I didn't have a Malibu Barbie to talk to like you did – do. And Charity Sparks branded me a juvenile delinquent. And you were always working or – out. And they posted nasty things about me on the school's social media site and *I* couldn't tell anyone, either. It might've gotten tangled up with your job, which was already stress city."

"Not more tangled than I am *now*," my mother said, beaming, and wagging her bean. "While you were away at swim camp, Amber. I spearheaded the petition: *End Mandatory Pantyhose for Female Care Staff.* Everyone signed except, of course, Charity. I started to tell you about this while you were at camp."

Grandma Sadie brushed the garden earth off her hands onto

her baggy trousers. "We're *all* safe here on *homeland soil*. Now stop *haranguing each other* and the world, won't you?"

The sun soared high in the sky. My mother laughed bitterly. "*Homeland?* Sadie, this place is dismal. And look at *you!* Do you always wear men's clothing? And Lord, why are we eating raw beans? Couldn't you maybe rustle up some breakfast, seeing as I've travelled all this way?"

"There's no food," I told my mother. "We ate the last of it last night."

These words sparked my grandmother. She scurried to a nearby little lean-to at the garden's edge and fetched three spades. She doled them out, one to each of us. "Start digging," she said. "Potatoes."

The soil held summer's warmth. Butterflies cha-cha'd around us. Potatoes, such happy little things, down there. We boiled this huge vat of them. Then we fried them in the last of the butter, and heaped them onto our plates. Root vegetables made things better.

"What are those papers stacked on the typewriter?" my mother, her mouth crammed with potatoes, asked Sadie. "You've been typing out *War and Peace* to pass the long winter nights?"

My grandmother flashed hurt eyes.

"It's no joke, Faith. It's your *story*, your life – until you left so *suddenly*. It's what I would have told you if you'd given me a chance."

Then my mother said something that nearly knocked me off my chair.

"Sadie," she said. "I'm sorry."

The Mom-ster had never apologized to anyone for anything, least of all for being *herself*.

I wondered when one of them would raise the topic of what

died in my grandmother's yard, but neither one did. Maybe some gentlemen's agreement, only with lady potato-eaters. After we ate the potato patch, my mother clicked on the old radio. "Just for a lark," she mused. "I haven't heard the radio funeral roll call program in decades. It's about that time."

I had no idea what she meant, but whatever program my mother had tuned into was interrupted by breaking news. A hurricane hurtled towards New Orleans. It had a name. Katrina.

"Oh, Lord," my mother gasped. "Do you have a working television, Sadie?"

My grandmother shook her head. "Just Internet. Get my news through it now. When I can bear news at all."

My mother chunked her platform sandals to the dining room table and logged onto the computer.

"I'll go make up your bed in your old room, Faith," my grandmother said. "Looks like you and Amber will be staying here indefinitely and Land's sake, I could use the company."

She scaled the stairs.

I stood, staring over The Mom-ster's shoulder at the ugly, swirling shape on the screen, the hurricane. It looked like some weird x-ray of a throbbing tumour. My mother always scolded me when I stood over her shoulder while she used the computer, my lurking made her nervous. There was no complaint this time. She googled another news site for New Orleans. There was an exodus of cars. Store shelves emptied of bottled water, food, and batteries. For those who couldn't leave, or wouldn't, it was home or dome.

Her face dropped into her hands. "Oh, Amber, those *poor people*! And at the Care Center, what will happen to them? And Ivy? And –"

"Mrs. Celestine, downstairs," I added. I thought, too, about Remy Despereaux. My fretting extended even to Sienna Sparks, that bottomless pit of princess. And Ike, even though he'd dumped me. And Lucky, living in his car. I thought about my mother's tombstone-car hulking in the spider-garage, that Kelly Clarkson song lodged in the tape deck. Ponty, with his chewed ear. Where did cats weather out hurricanes? I even wondered where the alligators went. I pictured Malibu Barbie, down there alone in the closet, with her duct-taped neck. How long could duct tape hold?

I thought about us, the three of us, how *we* were, like, this family, duct-taped together. And how we'd just begun.

My mother didn't sleep in her old bedroom. She stayed in front of the computer all night, hypnotized by hurricane reports. Her mood ring took on this ominous glow. The monitor's light silvered a few strands of her hair. I hadn't noticed any grey before. Or maybe she'd been dying it, for her dates. Grandma Sadie stayed upstairs though I heard her clunking about so I knew she couldn't sleep either. She had her own disaster: her ruined farm, empty cupboards, and quaking hands. I dozed on the sofa in spurts, but mostly I watched the on-line news, too.

Things had gotten very bad. Ruptured levees, storm surges. Water-hazed internet newsfeeds showed trees slashing sideways, toppling. The giant yellow arch of a McDonald's sign ripped from its anchor. Vicious, sluicing rains. Houses totalled before our eyes.

I'd been shifting my weight from one foot to the other, behind my mother when these strange choking sounds came from her. Coughing? Crying? Between chokes or sobs, I thought I heard, "deliver them some supper."

"You alright, Ma? *Deliver them supper?* What do you mean?"

Through chokes – or whatever – she replied. "*Succor*, Amber. Could you bring me a prompt glass of water, please?

(Hack, cough.) My throat is clogged."

I scooted to the sink. My back to her, I suggested it might be a good idea for her to step away from the computer for a bit.

"Ma, I know you're worried about everyone in New Orleans, but you can't do anything right now. Why not read the story Grandma Sadie typed for you? Bring your water over to the sofa. I'll keep you company. Read it out loud to me if you want."

She tore herself away from the computer. I brought her the stack of papers.

"Are you going to read it?" I asked.

"Later. And not aloud, Amber. I doubt it's a bedtime story. Right now, I'm thinking about our apartment, our flowered sofa, my clothes, the songs on my vinyl records, now drowned or blown away, most likely."

My mother's talking mojo had rebounded.

"Katrina will wake up little Susie, that's for sure," I said, the lack of sleep made me punch-drunk.

She was sleep-starved and punch-drunk, too, I guessed. She began to not talk sense. "I still need to learn what became of the broken-hearted. And who da doo da who wrote that book of love."

Quiet from upstairs. Grandma Sadie must have settled down and slept at last. I was going to tell my mother we *all* did, we *all* wrote the book of love, its pages, duct-taped, each to each, to a single spine. But maybe I just dreamed it, and didn't actually say it. I'm pretty sure I fell asleep instead.

It was some days before we were able to make contact with our friends in New Orleans. Lucky Mason had driven away in his car. No one knew anything about Mr. Despereaux. Ivy Huckster was fine but her son was missing. Bayou Care Center had been hit hard. There were fatalities, she'd send us news when more was known. She was just trying to move forward from one moment to the next, poor Ivy. We were finally able to connect with Mrs. Celestine; she phoned us as soon as she could. That was some fierce voodoo, our neighbour said. She was safe; good thing my mother had left her the key to our apartment, thinking Mrs. C could water our plants; she'd been able to get higher than ground floor, and she'd hung on for dear life to our massive flowered sofa, it had anchored her through the blasts.

No one knew what happened to the cat.

September was this magic island of milkweed fluff on Grandma Sadie's farm. We learned new and different ways to cook pumpkins, squash, too; her garden had a bumper-crop of both. "You like squash, as I recall, Faith," my grandmother quipped. The poultry company didn't sue my grandmother. They chalked it up to mental instability. She let them think what they liked.

My mother and I didn't plan on returning to New Orleans.

"What about all our stuff down there?" I'd asked my mother.

"Amber, it's just *stuff*. For all we know, it might have blown away. Sadie needs our help."

The Mom-ster sure had moved past her accumulation phase. Then my nose ring nearly fell out from the shock when she turned to my grandmother, and said, "You saved *my* life, Sadie, now I'm going to save *yours*. Call it *reciprocity*."

We hired a neighbour, Mr. Price, to help clear the yard and cut the grass. Even after that, we stepped on dead chicken parts for days, totally gross. And feathers would drift from out of nowhere. Poultry ghosts. I asked my grandmother if she thought any chickens escaped the foxes. She doubted it.

Of all things, Ivy Huckster phoned to say my swim coach from Iowa, Daphne Drew, had been trying to contact me. Daphne had done some spadework on my behalf, *a lot*, apparently. I'd been offered a swim scholarship at a Canadian university. I called my swim coach right away. "It's not too late?" The school year was well underway. They'd still take me, she said. Tuition and residence were covered by the scholarship. They'd even give me a little extra time to get myself organized.

When that news came, my mother and Grandma Sadie were cooking pumpkin stew together. I told them about the scholarship. My grandmother beamed. "Swimming, now isn't *that* something! *Heyzoose Marimba!* Our Amber is going to university."

My mother seemed pleased in a nervous way. She asked where. I told her: Lake Superior University. Thunder Bay.

The image of the leopard-print box popped into my mind. "I think *you've been there*, Ma, to Thunder Bay?"

The Mom-ster stopped stirring the stew for a second. "*Briefly,*" she said. "I hope you're not swimming in that lake, that water is *perishing* cold!"

"Ma, they've got a state-of-the-art, Olympic-sized pool on campus. And I'll wear *plenty of clothes* up there to stay warm." I couldn't resist punting her a badass smile. She returned my smile with a pinched, tense face.

Grandma Sadie served pumpkin for dinner – again. She must have sensed some riptide vibe between my mother and I. "After lunch, would anyone care to throw the Frisbee? I can't catch so good with my hands, but I'd love to try, I would."

I said "*Damned Skippy*, what a *spectacular idea*!"

My mother and Grandma Sadie didn't argue after that;

maybe because I was leaving soon, for university. They didn't even spar about where they'd live after the farm was sold. They'd move to Guelph, no major bodies of water. There was a river, but they'd find a place far from it. My grandmother said she might even look up her old friend, Wanda Keeler – even though Wanda hadn't once reached out over the years.

My mother could commute to Toronto with relative ease. She'd set herself up as a Care Consultant. Grandma Sadie laughed, hearing that, a disbelieving kind of chortle, but even that didn't spark bickering. The closest they came was a tiff in Tipping Creek Paints. Grandma Sadie talked the bank into extending her line of credit. She'd tried before, no dice, but now she had *us*, so we went with her. She'd pay the bank back with proceeds from the farm's sale. The extended line was for repairs to the outbuildings and paint for the farmhouse. My mother suggested a nice, neutral paint shade. But Grandma Sadie insisted on that same soft greeny-blue as the infinity scarf I'd knitted. We spent ages in the store, studying paint chips. My mother groused: "Just *settle* on one, would you, Sadie? It's not like you're going to be living there, so what does it matter?"

"It matters because I'll remember; the shade needs to be *right*, it does, Faith."

More looking, my grandmother's fingers jumping among the paint chips. Someone had been busy inventing colours. *Misty Teal, Scuba Green, Menthol Mist, Aqua Spray, Tangled Thicket, Ripple Effect, High Roller, Shore House Green, Celadon Stranger, Capris Seas, Wintergreen, Whirlpool, Total Green Girl, Jewel Weed, Dinner Mint.* Even a shade called *What Happens in Vegas.* No Seafoam.

Rescue Me came closest. We bought five gallons.

After a bout of painting, my grandmother called a break. The paint fumes were strong, and we craved fresh air.

We crossed the fields and helped Grandma Sadie over a rickety, cobbled-together fence.

We followed a path that appeared trampled by cows though we saw none, through bright scarlet leaves. *Damned Skippy*, what *music*, hearing those two able to walk and talk and not snipe. I shadowed their footsteps.

We reached a clearing in the woods, where silver poplars rustled. A stone tower stood there, with wilted flowers poking through the cracks between stones, and more flowers strewn along the base, flowers and dried herbs stuffed in something small, boot-shaped. It was like standing in a hushed, outdoor chapel in the still-warm autumn afternoon.

We didn't say anything for a long time.

My mother spoke first. "Sadie, you once told me, in *this very place*, that *some people you just love right away*. But what about *other* people? Can you answer *that* for me? What about *them*?"

A soft, sudden breeze wafted the scent of wild apples.

"I *can* answer, Faith, I can. Some people you *do* just love right away."

My grandmother beamed at me. Her words warmed my face, right to my cheekbones.

Then she turned to my mother, and spoke – "*Others*, Faith? Others take *much longer* to love – they take a *lifetime*."

The little boy's rubber boot, crumbling in the clearing. Its rim chewed by time. Time will conquer a rubber boot.

NOTES AND ACKNOWLEDGEMENTS

This is a work of fiction, and, like much fiction, its vision bends towards redemption and hope for human resilience. However, this story is also underwritten with awareness of the tragic losses caused by natural disasters.

I have accumulated numerous debts of gratitude during the eight years this novel has been in the making. I wish to thank The Canada Council for the Arts, Artscape Gibraltar Point, Metropolitan Toronto Library, Archives of Ontario, University of Saskatchewan, and Bard Graduate Center, New York City. Thanks to Helen Humphreys and Robyn Read for providing critiques of earlier drafts. Martha Baillie's workshop at St. Peter's College re-sparked the project at a critical point. Special thanks to my editor, Janice Zawerbny, for her wisdom and focussed attention. I am also grateful to University of Saskatchewan colleagues Norma Stewart and David Blackburn. Thanks to those who supported me in various ways during this project: Denise Bukowski, Barbara Langhorst, Iain Reid, Merilyn Simonds, Catherine Graham, Wayne Grady, Leona Theis, Kim Aubrey, Carla Hartsfield, Donna Kane, The Lower Union Street Bug, Ginger Pharand, Elizabeth Greene, Marianne Miller, Tracy Hamon, Andy Stubbs.

My mother's stories of Hurricane Hazel's ferocity felt even a hundred miles northwest of Toronto on our farm formed, for me, a ghostly local legend. Numerous sources proved valuable, most notably: Jim Gifford's *Hurricane Hazel: Canada's Storm of the Century*; Betty Kennedy's *Hurricane Hazel*; Mark

Sinnett's novel, *The Carnivore*; Greg Hollingshead's short story, "The Force of the Wind." *Baby and Child Care* by Benjamin Spock and Michael B. Rothenberg (New York: Pocket Books, 1945; 1985) provided perspectives on childrearing in the mid-twentieth century. The novel's epigraph is from Gwendolyn MacEwen's iconic poem, "Dark Pines Under Water" from *The Shadow-Maker* (Toronto: Macmillan, 1969, page 50). The quote from Act 1, Scene 1 of William Shakespeare's *The Tempest* is taken from *The Oxford Shakespeare*, Ed. Stephen Orgel (Oxford University Press, 1987; 1991, page 100). The quote from Emily Dickinson is taken from *Emily Dickinson's Poems as She Preserved Them*, Ed. Cristanne Miller (Harvard University Press, 2016, page 233).

ABOUT THE AUTHOR

Deb Stagg

JEANETTE LYNES' first novel, *The Factory Voice* (Coteau Books) was long-listed for the Scotiabank Giller Prize and a Re-Lit Award. Her seventh poetry collection, *Bedlam Cowslip: The John Clare Poems* (Wolsak and Wynn/Buckrider Books) received the 2016 Saskatchewan Arts Board Poetry Award. A recent Visiting Fellow at Bard Graduate Center in New York City and the University of Edinburgh's Institute for Advanced Studies in the Humanities, Jeanette directs the MFA in Writing at the University of Saskatchewan. She lives in Saskatoon.

FSC
www.fsc.org

MIX

Paper from
responsible sources

FSC® C016245